Dancing in Small Boats

"At once wrenchingly brutal and infused with hope, this novel is a timely, visceral reminder to take nothing that is dear to us for granted."

KATE WINTER

"A compelling read, gripping in its realism."

GABRIELLE NOBLE

"The suspense had me on edge from the start, absolutely gripping."

PATIENCE DUBE

Dancing in Small Boats

⊱

Oonagh Charleton

Copyright © 2025 by Oonagh Charleton

All rights reserved.

No part of this publication may be reproduced, distributed, or transmitted in any form or by any means, including photocopying, recording, or other electronic or mechanical methods, without the prior written permission.

The story, all names, characters, and incidents portrayed in this production are fictitious. No identification with actual persons (living or deceased), places, buildings, and products is intended or should be inferred.

First edition 2025

ISBN 979 8 31745 638 2

For Alec, Ben, Joshua and Eva

1

She dragged herself out from under the old coats and stepped down into thick mud, her face illuminated by the watery blue light of early morning. The dog shot out ahead of her and circled the jeep, nose down into the earth, searching gleefully for his marked territory. A lone bird singing sweetly close by soon faltered, its song abandoned to the black, still thatch of forest.

She stretched, watchful of the shadows, then without opening the top button, pulled down her jeans and squatted. A long, hot stream of urine hit the ground, splashing off her scuffed designer boots and seeping into the forest floor. The dog, having completed his investigations, bounded over to her and licked her face. He was wagging his tail cheerfully, as he always did. She nearly lost her balance.

'Hey, careful!' she said quietly, pushing him away. Her voice seemed loud and disembodied in the sprawling silence around them.

She gave a little wiggle, then pulled her jeans up over jutting hip bones and shrinking belly, the silver stretchmarks and C-section scar less visible now.

As usual, she had slept fitfully, unable to find a comfortable position in the cramped interior of the jeep. But it was the only shelter they had. For weeks she had been lulling herself to sleep by pretending she was sitting in front of her old stove at home. She would linger over the feel of her reddening cheeks and the simple twist of the handle that opened the cast iron door, then throw in a perfectly cut log of old beech and watch it catch, spitting and crackling, before giving itself over to the joyful furnace. She hoped that if she concentrated on the memory hard enough she might dream of it too, that the heat would penetrate her subconscious. But the dog provided the only warmth now and she was glad of him. Every morning when she woke, it was his face she saw first, hopeful, bright, waiting for her to do something.

She looked out into the tightly stacked trees and listened carefully. Whining softly, Brin sat expectantly in front of her, shifting his weight from one foreleg to the other, his ears twitching. Then he got to his feet again and shook himself, his heavy black-and-tan coat spiralling from head to tail.

She jumped back up into the boot space, suddenly thirsty, but irritated again by her damp underwear that never got the chance to dry out. Her favourite pink silk pants were grey from weeks of being washed in streams and puddles. Every night, rivulets of condensation trickled down the inside panes of the jeep, settling on the upholstery, penetrating the coats she used as blankets and pooling on the floor where she lay. She felt around for her Barbour jacket and pulled it on.

Using an old rag, she wiped the condensation off the nearest window. The forest looked the same as it had the day before... and the day before that. They had been there too long, surviving on fresh rainwater filling the craters left by fallen trees, and foraging – often in vain – for berries and mushrooms; she encouraged Brin to hunt for animals in the undergrowth, something she had trained him out of when he was a pup. Now that the warmer months were over, there was little left to scavenge, and most of the food she had brought with her had run out. When she stroked the dog now, she could feel the jut of his ribs beneath the thick fur.

She twisted the cap off an old plastic water bottle and took a long drink, watching the dog through the window as he raised his leg against the nearest stump, then, nose fervently pressed to the earth, sniffed and wove around the tree trunks and their gnarly roots. She whistled low and long and he flew back to her. Panting and whining, he leapt up into the boot, muddy paws streaking her shirt. A couple of months ago she'd have told him off, but now it didn't matter. No one was going to see her – not if she could help it.

'Breakfast?'

He sat back on the coats, his tongue lolling happily from one side of his mouth. His wagging tail swept backwards and forwards over the rough fabric. He stared at her brightly, his soft brown eyes adoring and trusting.

Daylight continued to inch its way along the forest track towards the jeep. She climbed into the front cab and pulled out what was left of the dog kibble from under the driver's seat. It was the only place she could keep it safe from him. She had been rationing it carefully. They had four days-worth left at most. She took out an empty plastic butter container and counted out twenty pellets. He tried to leap through the gap between the seats in his excitement.

'Sit! You'll knock it over.'

She frowned at him, then opened the door and stepped down into the soft, peaty mud. He leapt out and sat in front of her, tail rigid with excitement, quivering and impatient. She placed the butter container on the ground and held up one finger to remind him to stay.

'Go!'

He bounded forward and scoffed the lot in a second, then sat down and looked up at her expectantly.

'All gone,' she said sadly, showing him the palms of her hands.

Her children's faces suddenly flooded her mind – their pink, sunny, animated little faces. She was kissing them, stroking their cheeks, running her fingers through their hair. Conor and Lila running down a hill, Brin sprinting after them, trying to shepherd them, keep them close. Where were they now? Did they think she had abandoned them?

She closed her eyes and set her jaw tight in an effort to control the rising anxiety. Her old meditation classes had taught her that pushing the thoughts away only made it worse in the long run, so she focused on her breath and tried to allow the panic to move through her. *Here we can learn to pay attention to things from below the waterline,* her mindfulness coach had intoned as wisps of incense drifted around the room. *As they present themselves. We can simply allow them to be.* 'Easier said than done,' she muttered to herself now. The kids needed her back. They were depending on her. A deep inhalation turned into a long sigh.

Hunger burned in the pit of her stomach. She counted out another twenty dog pellets into the plastic butter tub, splashed some water over them and left them to soak on the roof of the jeep, well out of Brin's way. While she waited, she tidied the back of the jeep.

She rolled up the coats and stacked them neatly in the corner, the sleeves carefully tucked in. Folding and pressing the old army blanket into halves, then quarters, she set it down, perfectly square, next to the coats. Next she lifted the stiff rug the dog had been sleeping on and flicked it towards the forest, watching as dander and fuzz hung in the cool morning air. Then she brushed out the boot from the cab to the back door with a small blue hand towel, sweeping grit, fur, dried mud and pine needles onto the ground, before replacing the dog's rug near the boot door. She had started to take a great deal of pride in the cleanliness and order she created in their tiny living space. The sense of control and calm that the routine brought offered her a much-needed respite from her clattering thoughts.

She checked the kibble in the plastic tub with little enthusiasm. It had swollen into a brownish-grey mass of processed animal protein. But she was famished and could bear it no longer; she spooned the slop into her mouth with a finger, trying not to gag. She thought about the rich chocolate mousse cake from the French café near the river back home, their dainty lemon meringue pies, tangy and sweet in the one mouthful, and the freshly ground coffee served with an oven-warm madeleine. The kibble wasn't food to linger over, but at least it took the sharp edge off her hunger.

Afterwards, she and Brin walked through the forest in an arc around the jeep. All she could hear was the suck and squelch of bog as she walked across stretches of saturated ground in between tree trunks and their gnarled roots. She thought of the native woodlands near her childhood home and how noisy with birdsong they had been compared to this silence. Nothing grew in these woods; they were all commercial Sitka spruce farms. She hunted for something to eat – wild mint, nuts, charlock, blackberries, nettles – but there was nothing. After a while she lost sight of the jeep. They had gone too far.

'Come on. This way.'

Brin bounded back towards her, the cold air around him carrying puffs of rapid, panting breath. Together they walked back towards the jeep. She wrapped her arms around herself and tried to feel better. Tried not to feel anything but hope. *You'll never believe what freaking happened*, she'd tell Johnny when she saw him again. *Ditto*, he'd say, and they'd hold each other tight and pull the kids close.

She looked down the long track between the banks of trees, considering her options. There had been neither sight nor sound of the vigilantes she had sped away from a week ago. Anyway, hunger trumped fear, and it was forcing her to move. But going back to the main routes was too risky. They were in a bad state from the endlessly surging floodwater, and there were dozens of gangs roaming the countryside, organised and ruthless, looting and ransacking everywhere they went. They would take her jeep and the dog. And her too. Perhaps she could find a minor road on the other side of the forest, take her chance in the daylight.

She opened the passenger door of the jeep and the dog leapt up and settled himself on the seat. She walked round to the other side and got in behind the wheel.

Before she put the key in the ignition, she used it to mark the new day by scratching another notch on the dashboard. Just over six weeks. She was running out of space. According to her impromptu calendar, today was a Wednesday. Wine Wednesday, she and Johnny used to call it. She snorted. Fat chance, she thought, turning the key in the ignition.

As the engine burst into life, she remembered snippets of her dream from the night before. *It's all blue ocean and warm white sand. Johnny is wearing black shorts and runs into the waves. He swims up to a bridge suspended above the water and climbs onto it. It's a shimmering mirage in a startling blaze of sunlight. Then he's suddenly back, jumping through space and time, arranging flat grey stones into small towers on the sand. She watches him stare across the sparkling blue ocean towards the horizon. Then Johnny is gone, and the beach is empty, the ocean and the bridge gone, leaving no visible horizon. Thousands of razor shells lie on their backs, blades upturned and sharp, a natural* cheval de frise, *blocking her path.*

Her dreams were becoming more lucid, vivid, full of obstacles, as though keeping her in touch with a lost world, but placing it beyond reach.

She put the jeep in gear and, checking she had locked all the doors from the inside, pulled out onto the track. The tyres wrestled briefly with the soft, boggy ground but quickly found traction.

'You're quiet,' she said, as they crawled along, diesel fumes thickening the air behind them.

Brin looked at her, ears forward, head cocked to one side, his tail wagging gently at the sound of her voice. He turned to face the front and yawned.

'Keep an eye out. That's a good boy.'

They drove on slowly, the trees eventually thinning out. The rain had cleared, giving them a temporary respite from the endless downpours, and a beam of sunlight darted out through gaps in the clouds onto their faces. Then the track turned to rough hardcore before meeting a waterlogged road. She stopped, the engine idling. Left or right? Her phone battery had died within hours of leaving the house six weeks earlier, so the GeoMap system was inaccessible. Instead, she'd been relying on memory and a long-redundant instinctive compass. She nudged carefully out onto the narrow road, alert to any sort of movement or activity, and turned left, away from the now-obscured morning sun and the grey outline of the Dublin mountains to the south.

Maybe she could risk stopping at a house to look for food. The last two places she'd visited had been stripped bare. In one bungalow, the bodies of its elderly owners were still in their bedroom beneath mottled, stained sheets. In the other, they'd been sitting in armchairs in front of a long-dead TV. She gagged at the memory. Even the dog had hung back as she'd moved silently through each room. She'd looked for telephone landlines; the older generation preferred them. She desperately needed to speak to Johnny, see where he was, find out if he and the kids were okay, but there hadn't been any dial tone.

The inside of the jeep warmed up quickly with the engine running, and she shrugged off the Barbour, one hand on the steering wheel at a time. The fields on the left were wild and overgrown with no cows or sheep to graze them. Most were badly flooded in the lower sections. She shuddered to think what had happened to the animals. She'd seen some stray cows and sheep living wild, foraging like everyone else, but many more had been killed by gangs looking for meat. Not for the first time she wondered where the Defence Forces were and why they'd failed to protect everyone and curb the lawlessness. Already knowing the answer didn't stop her from resenting their incompetence.

Adrenaline surged through her as she got a flashback to her old life. Only two years ago she would have been shopping in the city for designer dresses and lunching on expensive vegan salads with her friends. How pointless that all seemed now. Such hard work to stay thin and pretty.

Brin, curled up on the seat now, yawned again and put his head back down onto his paws.

'Thank God I've you,' she said, patting his warm fur.

The countryside around her was uncharacteristically beautiful, and the sky, while cloudy, was remarkably clear of rain. She moved through the gears until the jeep built up speed and ploughed comfortably through the flooded sections of road. Brin sat up straight on his seat and stared at the world flashing past outside the window. She was going faster than she normally did and was hyper-aware of the noise of the engine. She drove like that for twenty minutes, the longest she had managed in one burst since she'd got the jeep.

The trees along this part of the road had survived the worst of the weather. Though almost bare, some held clusters of gold and red leaves. She opened the window and, turning her face to the sky, inhaled deeply as she drove. The air was lighter than in the heavy, peaty forest, and smelled sweet and fresh. Yet anxiety rippled through her as she approached each bend, the relief at seeing an empty stretch of road only temporary until the next bend spiked fresh apprehension about what might be on the other side. A deep, muddy ravine carved out by the flow of torrential water yawned across the fields to one side of the road. Enormous sections of land had collapsed, leaving sheer muddy gullies filled with fat offcuts of tarmacked driveway, and bright white gable walls of upended houses and outbuildings.

Around the next bend, the back end of a faded red car poked out of the ditch, its bonnet buried in the hedgerow. She slowed to a crawl and looked in as she passed. Slumped on the back seat were two still, small shapes; blonde hair, identical rainbow-coloured jackets. Children. Long gone. She looked away quickly, her knuckles white on the steering wheel. Brin raised his head to look at her, his soft ears pulled back.

Not far from the abandoned car was a wrought iron gate that opened into a steep, tree-lined driveway. Catching a glimpse of a house at the end of it, she braked and slowly reversed to take a closer look. There were half a dozen apple trees in the garden loaded with green and pink-red fruit.

'We need food,' she said to the dog. 'I can't eat what you eat anymore.'

Still in reverse, she turned in through the gate and drove halfway up the drive. Then leaving the engine idling, she lifted an old sweater and jumped out. The dog leapt out after her. Small green apples hung in the shadows; pink, bird-pecked, over-ripe fruit hung in dense clusters on more exposed branches. She fashioned the sweater into a basket of sorts and concentrated on the lower branches, giving them a shake and catching the apples that fell. As she gathered her harvest, she glanced up at the house. There would be no one there; its insides would have been stripped long ago – at least, that's what she preferred to tell herself in the moment. She felt so exposed. She was taking a massive risk, yet hunger forced her hand.

She rushed back to the jeep through the long, wet grass and tumbled the fruit into the passenger footwell. The apples rolled around and gathered in one corner. Sweat was pouring off her despite the cool autumn air. She would be feasting for days on this haul. Brin too. Then a glint of silver in the grass beneath a beech tree caught her eye. It was a bucket. She ran over to check its contents and after finding nothing but water and sodden leaves in it, something pulled her gaze up into the branches. Above was a clumsily assembled treehouse. A small hand and arm, pink-sleeved, hung out over the edge, the child's thin fingers scrubbed white by the elements. A cloud of starlings whooshed past, blurring the air with their wings. She swallowed down the cry that wanted to escape and fled to the jeep, calling for Brin in a low voice as she ran.

She clambered into the driver's seat and he leapt in after her, climbing across to the passenger side. Then she put her foot on the accelerator and shot down the driveway back to the road. The haul of apples rolled around on the floor. She should go back and search the house, just in case something useful might be there, but the children – it was too much. It was the one thing she could never get used to.

She reached out for Brin with one hand. 'I was scared again. Sorry.'

He pressed his wet nose to her hand and gave it a little lick.

And so they set off again, continuing along the road they had just left. As she drove, she ate four apples, one after the other, and fed the cores to the dog. They were sweet, crunchy and delicious. They would be hard on her stomach, but she needed to eat. Ten minutes later she spotted some signposts and she slowed down to read them.

Just then, a man stepped out from the hedge and stood facing them in the middle of the road.

2

Brin leaned forward on his seat, ears pricked. She dropped back to third gear and floored the accelerator, surging forward through the deep puddles, flicking on the full headlamps to dazzle him. He remained where he was, feet anchored to the tarmac, staring straight at her. What the hell was this – a game of dare?

She gripped the steering wheel, knuckle-white, a peculiar anger rising alongside the terror of an ambush. Who was he to stand in the middle of the road and make her choose. She heard a shrill sound that rose to a yell, her own voice unrecognisable to her as she kept her foot on the accelerator. The noise filled the cab, prompting the dog to burst into a volley of loud barks and lunge towards the windscreen.

The man leapt out of the way just in time.

She was shocked at herself that she hadn't jammed on the brakes. She'd caught a glimpse of his face, his mouth open, eyes wide with surprise. She watched him in the rear-view mirror as he picked himself up and gesticulated at her with wildly flailing arms.

She eased off on the accelerator, her eyes darting back and forth, checking for others. They usually appeared in groups, tribes, gangs. She drove on for three or four minutes. Nothing. Just a rare shaft of sunlight pushing through the clouds on that cold October morning, tipping the yellow hedgerows with gold. A small, silent bungalow set back from the road. A farmer's gate. Black bin bags partially submerged in the waterlogged ditch. Patches of tar appearing between the deep puddles. There were no signs of other people.

She slowed to a stop, her thoughts racing in strange uncertainty. *If he's alone he might be useful… if he's not insane. He could be insane. He'd stood in the middle of the road after all. He hadn't looked like one of those hard men. He'd no dog or weapon. But he was weird-look-*

ing, all beard and hat and layers. Yeah, I did the right thing. It could have been an ambush. I'd have been gang-raped and thrown in a ditch and left for dead. But what if he's one of the good guys – like Johnny? I have the dog. That's two against one if it goes bad.

She kept scouring the road and ditches for movement. Fear was roaring at her to drive on, but behind all the noise was a steady, persistent whisper to go back. Surely it would be better to travel with someone else. And he could protect her. Couldn't he? Maybe some men can't kill. She was certain she could never take someone else's life. Was it fair to expect him to do that for her? No, no, she didn't need anyone. Other people brought complications. She could make her own decisions. But she desperately needed to reach the family lake house and she might need help to get there.

Shouting at herself again, she jammed the gearstick into reverse and crawled backwards for what seemed like an eternity, allowing some unfamiliar instinct to override her fears. Her neck ached from looking over her shoulder, then checking the wing mirrors for signs of movement in the hedgerows. When he appeared in her rear-view mirror again, doubt crept back in. What the hell she was doing and look at all the fuel she'd just wasted.

He was standing in the middle of the road once more. How was he not afraid, out in broad daylight when the world was so unsafe? She reversed up beside him, aligning him with the passenger door. Brin was up on all fours, lips curled back, muzzle quivering over his teeth, snarling and growling. She put the jeep in first gear and kept one foot on the clutch, her other foot hovering over the accelerator.

'Shh. Sit. Quiet.' She had to say it a few times before the dog quietened. Taking hold of his collar, she pulled him back so she could see the man more clearly, remaining alert for movement in the ditches nearby.

She leaned over and rolled down the window a bit. He stared at her through the glass. She waited for him to speak first, the silence between them filled with the soft growling of the dog and the idling engine of the jeep.

'Hey there,' the man said after a minute or so, tilting his head slightly to one side.

Brin barked raucously. 'Shh,' she said, as he whined and pulled on his collar. He was poised and ready to pounce.

'Well, are you going to say anything?' he said more loudly.

'No,' she said, then instantly realised that she'd just said something.

The semblance of a smile passed across his face.

'Oh for God's sake,' she said.

They regarded each other in silence again, tense and vigilant.

'Are you lost?' he asked eventually. 'Or did you come back to finish me off?'

'What?' She could barely hear him above the noise of the engine.

'I said are you lost, or did you come back to finish me off?' he shouted.

'I don't have time for this.'

'Time for what?'

'This – this kind of thing.'

'Then why did you come back?'

She chewed on her lip, deciding not to answer, and tapped the accelerator nervously.

'So where are you going anyway?' he asked, pulling his hat further down on his head.

'Away from Dublin. Not that it's any of your business.'

Beneath the unkempt sandy-blond beard he seemed to be young enough – maybe her age. He held her gaze with eyes that seemed to shift from blue to almost grey. It made her feel uncomfortable. She tapped on the steering wheel, trying to think quickly. 'So why were you standing in the middle of the road?'

'I don't know.'

'I could have run you over.'
He shrugged. 'Ah, but you didn't in the end.'
'Only because you got out of the way.'
'Yeah, there is that.'
'So you aren't suicidal then?' she said, trying to appear indifferent.
'Maybe I was, then changed my mind.'
Was that a flicker of sadness or regret? She couldn't tell with all that hair in the way.
'Where are your family? Are you alone?' she asked. She suddenly became conscious of the fuel she was burning up while they chit-chatted. She needed him to tell the truth and quickly.
'Yeah, I'm alone. You?'
She pressed her lips together and didn't answer.
He looked out over the sodden fields. 'My wife, my son. They're gone,' he said, his voice just about carrying over the noise of the jeep.
She waited for him to say more but he didn't.
'What happened?' she said, feeling resentful that he'd made her ask.
'They're just gone.'
'Gone as in missing or…'
'Gone as in gone… dead gone.' He looked straight at her.
'Oh.' She glanced at the rear-view mirror. 'I'm sorry.'
'It wasn't your fault.'
She scowled at him. 'When did it happen?… if it's okay to ask.'
He shrugged. 'Last winter. I wasn't there.' He swallowed hard and looked away.
She decided to change the subject. 'Have you seen all the lads in the black gear?'
'Yep, I have.'
'When?'

'Good few weeks ago.' He sighed heavily. 'I'm an engineer. Part of a maintenance team. We were on our way to repair servers at a data centre. They stopped me at a roadblock, took the car.'

'They didn't hurt you?'

'Not really. A few digs. I was probably lucky when I think about it.'

'Anyone else you know still alive?'

'No.'

'You don't *know* if they're alive or they're actually not alive?'

'Wow, you really know how to spit out the questions, don't you!' he said, suddenly frowning.

'Sorry. I used to be better at this stuff… before. Anyway, I wasn't even going to come back.' She cleared her throat, suddenly feeling a little ashamed of herself.

'Why did you then?'

'I'm not sure, but I'm leaving now.' She revved the engine a little.

'Last winter, after I got back home, my wife and son were already gone,' he said hurriedly.

'Oh.' She searched for the right words, unable to trust a single thing he said but not wanting to sound altogether heartless. 'Sorry, that's devastating.'

'Yeah, they took everything. And her body… what they did to my wife…' He turned his face to the sky as if seeking solace from above. When he looked back at her, a shadow had fallen across his face.

'How did you… what did you…?'

'I didn't.' He was quiet for a moment and stroked his beard absentmindedly.

'Well, when I heard my brother had died, I spent the whole week drinking,' she said somewhat casually, then realised how stupid that sounded, how juvenile.

'Did that help?'

'No, not really.'

He looked at her more carefully now. 'And how did he die?'

'It's complicated.'

'Sure isn't everything complicated?'

'He killed... he couldn't go on himself after...' There was another silence. 'So when you found them, your wife and son, what did you do?'

'Unfortunately, I had to bury them in the garden,' he said matter-of-factly. 'Like everyone else was doing.'

She could see him trying to steady himself, stay composed. 'Oh.'

'No choice really.'

His voice and body language told her he was telling the truth. Either that or he was an excellent actor.

'I did hear of people having to do that. And then?'

'Then I drove back to the campus where I was working at the time.' He shrugged as though trying to cast off the bad memories. 'There was food there, a canteen. It was easy to secure... well, for a time anyway. Nowhere else to go.' He looked out across the fields with an air of resignation or futility, she couldn't tell which.

'Your work must have been important,' she said.

'What do you mean?'

'Well, to have left them at home with all this going on.' She suddenly realised the implication of what she had just said, but it was too late – the words were out. She watched him closely, alert to any tell-tale flickers of rage.

He stared at her and, lips pressed tightly together, shook his head. 'So what about you?' he asked. 'What are you doing here?'

The field behind him shimmered silver with surface water. The bitter smell of exhaust fumes drifted in through the open window.

'I bought this jeep from a farmer me and my husband knew, and I was supposed to bring it back to the house,' she said finally.

The man tilted his head slightly. 'And the husband didn't go instead? Assuming you have one left, that is.'

'He stayed to protect the kids. No matter what, they come first.'

He shrugged. 'Fair enough.'

'The plan was I get the jeep back to them and we drive to our holiday home by the lake up north,' she continued. 'But the last time I talked to him was… well, weeks ago.' She didn't know why she was telling him all this.

'Now it's my turn to say sorry.'

'What's there for you to be sorry about?' she asked.

'Well, they're all probably… they won't have made it.'

'What do you mean?' She stared at him.

'Ah nothing, forget it.' He pushed his hands into his coat pockets, then quickly took them out again.

'Are you suggesting they're dead? You don't know they're dead. You don't know Johnny.'

He sighed the way a parent might with a child who never listens. 'It's almost certain they'll have got taken or killed. Or sick from the flood water. There's cholera everywhere. Did I ever think I'd hear myself say that? No way!'

She shook her head. 'You're very hard on hope,' she retorted. 'They're already there, waiting for me. I know it. If I can last this long, they can.'

'You just got lucky. Where's the hope in all this anyway?' He looked away.

'Hope is always the last thing to die. Anyway, I still have faith,' she added brightly. Things were getting too heavy between them. 'So where are you off to now?'

'Nowhere really.' He shuffled from one foot to the other, his brow furrowed with renewed concentration. 'I'm staying in a cottage – about half an hour's walk from here.'

'Ah, that's good you've somewhere.'

'Yeah, it's old and a little damp, but there's well water and a bed. You can't tell anyone about it though, okay?' He gave her a little half smile, then looked at her gravely. 'I'm very serious.'

'Sure who'd I tell.' She wrinkled her nose. It was a habit she had sometimes when she talked to people. Johnny said it made her look like a rabbit. She didn't want to look like a rabbit now. She wanted to look in control, as if these kinds of conversations didn't faze her in the slightest. 'So do you have much food?'

'Not a lot. A few bits. Always hungry.' He patted his belly and smiled again.

'So what are you eating?'

'A few hazelnuts, blackberries, dried fruit mostly. With the break in the weather today I thought I'd come out to check a few places.'

'God, you'll need more than that to keep going.'

He looked at her long and hard, then nodded at the dog through the window. 'What about him then? Is he dangerous?'

'If I let him out, it won't end well for you.'

He laughed. It was a warm, melodious laugh, which unnerved her.

'He'll take anyone down and keep them there,' she said crossly. 'I had him trained with an attack word.'

'I see.' This information didn't seem to bother him… or he was skilled at feigning a casual disregard for things that actually unsettled him. 'So what have *you* managed to find?' he went on. 'Any houses along this road with food? I haven't been back that way yet.' He gestured in the direction behind the jeep.

'Just one. A garden full of apples. Some dead kids in a car outside. The decomposing body of a child in a treehouse.'

He flinched, and she allowed herself a moment, somewhat inexplicably, to enjoy the effect this small yet shocking piece of information had on him and how powerful it made her feel. She watched closely as he took off his hat, ran his fingers through his hair, then pulled his hat back down again. Although he looked rough, he seemed clean. And stout – the old navy seafarer coat was tight on him. He was straight-backed, tall, confident, but there was something vulnerable about him too.

'Yeah, I still can't get my head around that… you know the little ones…' His voice trailed away.

She waited to see if he'd say anything else, but he didn't. 'I suppose we're finished here then,' she said loudly. 'I might leave you to it. But just so you know, there might be stuff in the house. I didn't look inside, even with the dog. I don't want to see anymore dead people… especially kids. They could easily be mine, you know?' She was talking fast now, the built-up adrenaline untethering a part of her that needed to ameliorate her previous bluntness.

He said nothing.

She nudged the gearstick into neutral, took her foot off the clutch and toed the brake pedal. Then leaning into the passenger footwell, she picked up a couple of apples and tossed them to him through the gap in the window. He caught them before they hit the ground. Brin followed his every move.

The man ate them in five or six bites, the core and pips too. She tapped the steering wheel as she watched. The breeze had risen slightly, pushing clouds across the sky and wafting the dank smell of the water from the sodden land in through the open window. Sunlight fell hot on her hand as she held it on the gearstick.

'There are loads more,' she said finally. 'Dozens in the garden and in the tree.'

He caught her eye again, seemingly curious and somewhat gratified, she thought. His eyes were the strangest shade of blue-grey.

'Can you show me?' he said. 'I've a bag.' He turned and pulled a tattered khaki green rucksack out of a raised bank of nettles and hawthorn.

She hesitated, trying to tap into her gut, ever conscious of the cloud of diesel fumes belching out of the exhaust.

'Okay, listen,' she called out, as he stepped back from the window. 'I'm burning through fuel. There's a ladder running up the back of the jeep. Hang on to it and I'll bring you back to the house.' The words fell out of her, scraping past fear as they hurried on, faster than her mind was able to wrestle with the risk she was taking. 'There's one condition,' she added, not wanting to seem like a pushover. 'You get more for me while you're there.'

He grinned. 'Sure, can do. Thanks!'

'Just drop them in through the window. I'm not getting out. If anyone shows up, I'm gone. You're on your own.'

He nodded. As he made his way round to the back of the jeep, she acknowledged to herself that so far, she felt safe. No trap, no ambush. Yet. If things went bad, she could just drive away. Anyway, it was worth it. The extra apples he collected would keep her going for another four or five days. It was the wise thing to do, she told herself, in case there was no more food between here and the house by the lake.

When she could see in the mirror that he was hanging on to the ladder, she turned the jeep around and headed back towards the house with the apples. She glanced anxiously down at the fuel gauge. Ten minutes later she spotted the small red car in the ditch that marked the entrance to the house.

She edged the nose of the jeep through the wrought iron gate, drove slowly up the driveway, turned at the top, and crawled back towards the entrance, stopping just inside the gates and leaving the engine running. A bed of burnt red dahlias and pink mallows blazed in the long grass, surprised into bloom by the rare sun. She hadn't noticed them earlier.

He jumped off the back and strode towards the apple trees, glancing back at the house. She inched her window down and watched him. He was alert yet composed and worked deliberately and efficiently to fill the rucksack to the brim with fruit.

'Do you have any bags in there?' he called out in a low voice.

'No. Come on, I don't want to hang around.'

He looked at the house. 'We should check it out. There could be food.'

'Not for me, I don't want to see anymore dead children. Look.' She pointed to the tree above his head.

He glanced up, then closed his eyes in a long blink. 'Come on,' he said, his voice cracking a little. 'We can look out the back. If we find another bag, we can fill it.'

Did she feel safe getting out of the jeep? Her mind raced through the scenarios. He could force her to hand over the keys and take the jeep, even with Brin there. But hunger and curiosity pulled hard at her. She'd love to find some soap and toothpaste, maybe even tampons or pads.

He came over and peered in through the window. 'So how much fuel's left?'

She didn't need to look at the gauge. 'Um, just over half a tank.' He was right up against the glass now, his eyes focused on the dashboard. It was the closest she had been to a man other than Johnny in two years.

He glanced up at her. 'That won't get you far.'

'I've another five litres in the boot.'

'Still. If I found a garden hose, I could siphon any leftover diesel for you from that old car out front.'

'I don't know.' The more time she spent in this man's company with nothing going wrong, the more she thought they could help each other. She had the dog, she reassured herself, but he could have worse. 'Do you have any… you know, weapons?' She immediately felt stupid for asking. He was hardly likely to tell her the truth.

But he didn't hesitate. 'Yeah, a knife.'

'That's all?'

'Yeah, that's it. Not even a slingshot,' he quipped, opening out both sides of his old coat and turning around. He was wearing layer upon layer of flannel shirts. He lifted the back so she could see there was nothing tucked into his loose-fitting jeans. 'And you've seen under my hat.'

'Fair enough.'

He grinned.

She narrowed her eyes at him. 'So what's your name?' she asked.

'Marcus. Yours?'

She reached out for the dog and stroked his head. 'Sara,' she said eventually.

'Okay, Sara, well hurry up and decide. Either go and leave me here or hop out and we'll look in there together.'

She had to resist the urge to put her foot to the floor and leave him there. But if he was able to refuel the jeep and find something useful in the house, it could be worth the risk.

She looked at the dog, silently consulting him about what to do. He whined softly. She turned off the engine and sat there for a moment, the silence rushing in to fill the space. Then she opened the door and jumped down onto the gravel punched with weeds and rough meadow grass. Fragments of broken glass twinkled in the sun. The dog leapt out after her. She grabbed her jacket, putting it on quickly, then locked the jeep and pocketed the key.

'Heel, Brin,' she called out.

The dog pressed his body against her thigh, coiled and stiff, nose pointed towards Marcus, ears forward. She could feel the warm thickness of his fur against her and the heaving of his chest.

Marcus turned out to be tall – maybe six foot one or two – and it took her by surprise. She found herself adjusting her posture, putting her shoulders back, jutting out her chin and raising her head high. She suddenly became self-conscious about her unwashed hair, the dank smell she emitted, the dirt under her fingernails. She caught him sizing her up and stiffened.

'Right, let's go look in the house. You first,' she said, trying to sound decisive and confident.

'I thought you were staying out here.' He looked at her quizzically, but she could sense something beneath it, like he was poking fun somehow.

'There's stuff I need to look for.'

'Okay.'

He set his bag against a tree and walked towards the house without looking back. She followed, the dog staying close by her side.

'I'm taking out my knife,' he called over his shoulder.

'Fine.'

'Now I'm going around the back,' he said.

'You don't have to keep telling me what you're doing.'

'Just keeping you in the loop.'

They walked around the side of the house, which was shadowed by trees. She kept several metres behind him. There was nothing to stop him suddenly turning on her, taking her by the throat, forcing himself onto her. Into her. Nothing but the dog. Or maybe it was a longer game he was playing. She tried to slow her breathing.

He passed a window and glanced inside.

'There's the kitchen,' he said.

'Anyone in there?'

'Yeah, looks like it.'

'Are they dead?'

'Almost certainly, yes.'

He took a grey neck warmer out of his pocket, slipped it over his head and pulled it up to cover his nose and mouth.

'Maybe you shouldn't go in,' he said, turning to look at her.

'It's fine. I've done it before.'

'In a room with the dead?'

'Yeah, just for a bit.' She felt a trickle of sweat run down her side from her armpit.

The back door was ajar and the glass in the centre of the sun-bleached wood was smashed. He stood at the door and waited. The trees in the back garden rustled softly, helpless in the autumn breeze. There was no movement other than that.

'What do you see?' she whispered loudly.

'Nothing much yet.'

He flicked open his knife and used the point to push the door further open. Then he edged sideways through the gap in the door.

'Ah, there they are,' he said, glancing back at her quickly.

'How many?'

'Just the two. Probably the parents.'

'God help them.' She crossed herself instinctively, the long-rejected Catholic rituals still a muscle memory. 'Can you see anything else?'

'Looks like other people have been here.'

She peered in through the door. The kitchen had been ransacked. Smashed crockery and upturned chairs and tables were scattered across what should have been an airy, sunlit room. A large marble-and-oak kitchen island that had probably once hosted cocktail parties with neighbours and fairy-cake baking sessions with children, stood in the centre. Instantly, she was back in her own kitchen. Hand-thrown pottery lamps placed for ambience, light gathering them all together. Large sap-green ferns clustered in tasteful wicker planters, long tendrils drifting and swaying as someone passed by. The woodstove running steady at a low, slow, orange burn. The music, always the classics, swing, even Elvis. The comforting smells of freshly baked scones and still-warm raspberry jam. Johnny dancing with the children, their feet on his. The laughter. 'Look at this pair,' he'd say. 'They've all my moves.'

'They've really done a number on this place,' Marcus said, as he tiptoed between the toys and books sprawling across the floor, covered in a thick layer of dust. He put his head around the door of the utility room.

As she walked through the kitchen, the dog at her heels, the dank sourness of the air filled her nose and mouth. All the cupboards and presses were open, the contents scattered. Anything not broken had been taken. There was no food to be seen.

The bodies were about a metre apart, lying on their backs on the grey glitter-flecked tiles, grinning up at the ceiling, their yellow cheeks dried and paper thin. Someone had gone through their pockets, linings pulled inside out. Brin sniffed at them; she pulled him back by the collar. She wondered about the rainbow children entombed in the car out front, the child in the tree, its small decaying hand reaching for help. Were they all the same family?

'What do you think killed them?' she asked.

'Don't know.'

'Oh, wait, look. Their throats…' He leaned in. 'Yeah, looks like someone got them there all right.'

She shivered and clenched her jaw. She could feel the warm rush of saliva; this was not the time to vomit. She switched her mind to practical matters. Maybe the woman had supplies.

'I'm going upstairs to check the medicine cabinet,' she muttered. 'Don't follow me.'

'Okay.'

'I mean it, don't follow me.'

'I said okay! Why would I follow you?'

'I don't know. I don't know you at all.'

'With the greatest of respect, that's not really my thing!' He wandered off, a palpable current of irritation trailing behind him.

'What isn't your thing?' she called after him, testing the fragile accord between them even further.

'Do what you need to do,' he said loudly. He muttered something else, but by then he was out of earshot.

She knew she was being unpleasant but she couldn't help it. And she didn't care. She walked out to the hallway, her heart pounding. Brin leapt ahead of her up the stairs and waited for her at the top. The landing was strewn with toys and hundreds of pieces of Lego. The dog prowled in and out of the open doors, nose to the ground. There were two bedrooms for children, the pink play castles and expensive dressers the only remaining evidence of their existence; even their duvets and pillows were gone. The press on the landing was stripped of sheets and bedspreads.

She walked slowly into the master bedroom. Sunlight poured in through the window, slicing through the swirling layers of rising dust, casting angular shadows on the walls, and reflecting off an enormous, gilt-framed mirror.

She suddenly caught sight of herself in it and gasped. Two years ago, she would have been standing in her favourite high-heel pumps and fitted black designer dress, her hair twisted up into an elegant French knot. She would have been rehearsing her speech before leaving for yet another awards night. Johnny would have come up behind her and kissed her neck, then pulled her, squealing, backwards onto the bed, whispering half-seriously, 'Go on, a quickie.' She'd have been cross that he'd messed up her hair and make-up, then relent and kiss him back. Then hearing the commotion, the children would have piled in and all of them would have ended up on the bed, wrestling, laughing. She'd have loved the vitality of them all, yet been irritated by them pulling at her, mimicking their father who compulsively demanded possession of her, staking his claim on her groomed and perfumed self before she temporarily left his orbit. Eventually, the pre-paid taxi with its champagne fridge and recliner seats would have arrived and she'd wave at Johnny and the children as they clustered at the window, Johnny standing back a little, detached, expressing his aloof displeasure at her departure. By the time she'd got to the hotel, she'd have taken on a new persona – controlled, sophisticated, with a heightened awareness of her ability to impress. And after her acceptance speech on behalf of the charity, there would have been Sauvignon Blanc and delicate smoked salmon canapés, and she'd have mingled with colleagues and been charmed by the compliments and the attention.

Now a pale, thin person hidden inside an olive-green outdoor jacket looked back at her, dark circles under large doleful eyes. She became unexpectedly conscious of the now tatty silk lingerie beneath her dirty clothes. She desperately wanted to have a good wash and suddenly felt like crying. She went into the ensuite, but the cabinet above the sink was empty. No soap or toiletries. She went back into the bedroom and checked under the bed. A pair of old shoes and a shoebox. She pulled the box out.

'You okay up there?' Marcus shouted from the hallway below.

Startled by the unfamiliar man's voice, the dog broke out in a volley of deep barks and raced out onto the landing.

'Stop,' she commanded Brin. 'Here!'

He ran back in, eyes fixed on her.

'Yeah, fine,' she called back. 'Stay where you are. Nothing left up here. Down in a minute.'

'Suit yourself. I'm going back out to the garden.'

She opened the lid of the box. Wedding photos. Nostalgia. Tat. She stood up and threw the box against the wall, a culmination of rage and frustration. Bright silver coins and ticket stubs fell onto the dirty cream carpet along with old pregnancy tests and ultrasound photographs. Another woman's treasure stared up at her from the filth. A hospital tag, a brown pharmacy bottle. She knelt down and shook the bottle. Tablets. She turned it around to read the label. Diazepam. She unscrewed the lid and tipped the contents into the palm of her hand. Maybe twenty pills. She put them back in the bottle, tightened the lid and put the bottle in her jacket pocket.

She looked around the rest of the room: tangles of wire clothes hangers strewn across the floor; an old pair of slippers. The bedside lockers were turned over, the drawers empty. Women's knickers lay beneath one. She checked them for size. They were miles too big. Useless. She surveyed the wardrobes one by one. There was nothing left of any use to her.

'Come on, Brin.'

The dog turned to her at the sound of his name.

'Let's go.'

She walked past the mirror without giving it a second glance and went down the stairs.

Outside in the garden he had been busy. He had found a length of hose in a shed and had cut a section off it. Two large plastic bags were filled with apples from a second tree near the shed.

'Hey, I found a hatchet,' he said, glancing up at her. 'It's rusty, but it might come in handy.'

She remained at a distance from him, wary and watchful of his every movement. 'Anything else?'

'No... well, a tin of cat food for your dog maybe.'

That was thoughtful of him, she thought. Maybe he was one of the good guys. She felt bad for being so tetchy with him. 'So what about the cottage you're sleeping in?' she asked, trying to sound bright and friendly. 'Is it like this one?'

'No, it's small and very old. But there are no dead people in it.' He straightened himself up and adjusted his hat. 'Right, I'll check the car out front and see if I can siphon any diesel for you.'

He picked up the bags of fruit and walked past her. He was one of those, she thought, feeling suddenly annoyed – goes and does something without seeing if you agree. Huge self-confidence, or the need to control everything. Probably both. Either way, he'd get to do what he wants.

'What about you?' he called out, eyes fixed in front of him, not bothering to keep his voice down. 'Find anything upstairs?'

'Nope. Stripped bare. Just toys,' she said with a sigh, deciding to let the irritation go. She was so tired of being on edge. In a lot of ways, it had been easier in the forest with just her and the dog. No people to be wary of. But she'd felt a different kind of fear there. She turned and followed Marcus, the dog walking just in front.

'There's a house backing onto this one,' Marcus said, looking back to see where she was.

'Oh yeah?'

'Behind the hedge where I found the hatchet. Do you want to check it out?'

'No, I'm done.'

'I think we should look.'

'You can if you want.'

'I guess we have a few things from here.'

She didn't like the way he said 'we'.

'I found a lighter that works,' he added. He took it out and flicked up the flame.

'I have one too,' she said.

When they reached the jeep, Marcus hung back as she unlocked the driver's door. The dog jumped in.

'Your apples are there,' he said, gesturing towards one of the plastic bags.

'Thanks.'

'You're welcome. Now, if you want to follow me out the gate and park up beside the car.'

Was that a question or an order? 'Eh, I don't know.' She frowned.

'I'm not up to anything,' he said. 'I'm just going to check the car for diesel and if it has any, use the hose to siphon it from the car to the jeep.'

'But what if it's dirty? Then I'm finished!'

'Any dirt will have settled at the bottom. It's too good to turn your nose up at. Diesel is a lucky find. Most of the cars around here are electric or hydro.'

She shrugged. The extra fuel could make all the difference in helping her get to the lake house. She had to decide quickly.

He put the rucksack on his back and picked up his bag of apples. The hatchet hung from a strap on the rucksack. She watched him walk out onto the road, confident and reckless. He was working hard to make things amiable between them, but all it did was make her twitchy and afraid of dropping her guard. She took her bag of apples and placed it in the back of the jeep. Then she got into the front cab, started the engine and, fighting her compulsion to accelerate away from him, edged up the driveway and out onto the road. She had to reverse back towards the red car so their fuel caps were on the same side. She cut the engine and opened the window, watching him closely in the side mirror. How could he stand being so close to the children inside the car, their colourful little bodies folded in on themselves? She was suddenly astounded that *she* could stand being so close. She closed her eyes and tried to squeeze out the image burning on to her brain.

He unscrewed the fuel caps of both vehicles and placed one end of the hose into the car.

'All good?' she called to him through the window.

'Yeah. Hey, it's about a quarter full,' he said, looking pleased with himself.

He put the other end of the hose in his mouth and she could see his cheeks hollowing as he sucked. A few seconds later, he snatched the hose out of his mouth and thrust it into the jeep's tank, spitting onto the ground and wiping his mouth with his sleeve.

The only thing she could hear was the dog's panting as he lay on the passenger seat. It was warm in the cab with the extraordinary sun pouring through the windscreen. She hadn't seen it for weeks, not since midsummer when there had been a few days respite between the relentless rainstorms. She checked the clock on the dashboard: 15:38. The light would start to fade in about four hours.

After a couple of minutes, Marcus pulled the hose out of the jeep and gave it a shake. A few drops of diesel spilled onto the road and that was it. He yanked the other end of the hose out of the red car and shoved it into his coat pocket. Then he patted the side of the jeep and screwed on the fuel cap. He's enjoying himself, she thought.

'Start it up,' he called out.

She turned the key in the ignition and the engine kicked into life. The needle on the fuel gauge rose to three-quarters full. She found herself wanting to smile.

'Thanks,' she shouted, trying to sound indifferent, as if acts of kindness like this happened on a daily basis.

He gave her a thumbs up. He looked as if he was about to say something when she interrupted.

'So now I feel like I owe you one.'

He walked up and stood by the driver's window. 'It's all good. You don't owe me anything.'

'Well, good luck with whatever's ahead then,' she said, in her best *see ya later* voice.

'I suppose I could do with a lift though.' He raised the bulging bag of apples. 'The handles on this won't last long.'

She hesitated, feeling suddenly lightheaded. 'Look, I'm sorry, I don't know –'

'Don't you think I'd have done whatever it is you're worried about by now?' he said sharply.

'What's that supposed to mean?'

'I mean you've absolutely nothing to be concerned about with me.'

'You would say that, wouldn't you. No offence.'

'None taken. It's up to you. Either give me a lift or don't. There's no point me trying to convince you I'm not some kind of predator. We're all in the same mess out here.'

There was a long silence between them, filled only by the rumble of the engine. Jesus, she had to stop burning through fuel! Nothing dodgy had happened in the time they'd spent together, nothing big enough to freak her out.

'Oh my God, *fine* then,' she blurted out, the good-girl part of herself wanting to be kind. 'Hang on to the ladder again. I'll drop you back to your place.'

'Brilliant, thanks. Appreciate it.' He sounded like he'd just accepted a lift home from work after missing the train. 'So let's go,' he said, turning towards the back.

'Wait, where is it from the crossroads then?'

'Turn right. It's about five kilometres up. Long driveway. Hard to find. I'll bang on the jeep when we get there.'

'Is anyone else there?' Why did she expect truth from him, she wondered.

'Nope. Just me.'

He walked to the back of the jeep. When she saw him in the mirror hanging on to the ladder with one hand, she drove off.

At the crossroads she turned right, away from the sun. The narrow road was hemmed in further by tall trees along the ditch, their branches arching over and blocking out the light. She had to stop several times so he could clear the road of fallen debris before they were able to continue. Having done this on her own before, she was glad of him and his efficiency now. After a few minutes, he thumped the back of the jeep and pointed to the left where she saw two old farm pillars partially obscured by blackthorn bushes. She passed them slowly, scanning for movement. Nothing.

Before he had time to jump off, she reversed the jeep back between the posts. In the rear-view mirror she could just about see a small, run-down cottage, covered in ivy, set on higher ground at the top of a long, sloping driveway. A stone hay shed with a rusty corrugated tin roof stood near the gable wall. The garden was wildly overgrown. No movement.

Marcus stepped off the ladder and walked up to the passenger window.

'So you want to come in?'

'Eh, no.' She tilted her head like the answer was blindingly obvious.

'Sure?'

'I really don't know you. The answer's still no.'

'I do get that. You need water?'

'I can sort it along the way.'

'There's fresh water here. From a well.'

'I'm not coming in. I'll be fine.'

'I don't bite. Anyway, you have the dog.'

His eyes appeared soft, unthreatening. This conversation could go back and forth for a while if she let it.

'No, I'm just going to head off now,' she said, staring straight ahead out the windscreen.

He put his bags down. 'I hate to tell you this, but you won't get far.'

She sighed. 'Of course you'd say that.'

'But it's true. There's a roadblock further down the road you were on.'

'What kind of roadblock?'

'Cars. Three of them parked sideways across.'

'That's no problem. I can go around them through fields.'

He shrugged. 'They're all waterlogged. Anyway, think about it just for a moment. We could do this together. Two's company.'

'Do what together?'

'Figure out how to get through this.'

She glanced in the mirrors again. 'What do you want, though?' she said, suddenly wearying of the chit-chat and wondering why she didn't just accelerate off.

'I could do with you and your dog. Call it self-interest if you like. But it's better for both of us if we stick together. Like-minded people should stick together. It's how we survive.'

'So we're like-minded now. That's a bit presumptuous.'

'Not really,' he said confidently. 'I know women like you. You're survivors. You get what you need.'

'You know nothing about me,' she said, emphasising each word for greater effect. 'Just like I know nothing about you.'

'That's easy to fix. I'm a family man – a man who used to have a family, at any rate. I'm no different to anyone you knew before all this kicked off and I'm stuck in the same shitshow as you.'

'Yeah, but I've only got your word for that.' She became conscious again of the idling engine. She didn't have time for this. 'Anyway, I'm doing okay,' she said eventually. 'I've got this far on my own... And it's a problem for me that I don't know what you want.'

'That makes two of us,' he said, sighing. 'All I know is that I don't want to be alone.'

'Well, I'm not good company.'

'I'm tempted to agree with you,' he said wryly. He prodded the tyre of the jeep with the toe of his boot and looked up at her. 'Okay, think about this – if we work together, we can get more stuff. Tag team, you know? I can search the houses along the way and you can keep watch with the dog. It'll make it easier to find food.'

'Nope, I'm leaving right now.'

'Listen, there are people who'll stop you and take your jeep. Take you, kill your dog. You need someone like me.' He sounded frustrated now.

'And how do I know *you* aren't one of those people?'

'You don't, but I'm not.'

'But stand in my shoes for a minute.'

'Yeah, I get it. A woman alone. I *have* been seeing things from your perspective. But do you want to know what I'm thinking?'

'No, enlighten me.'

He scratched his nose. 'I'm wondering how long it's taken you to get out of the city… how many weeks have you been hiding out. You look starving. Your dog is skin and bone.'

She bristled with indignation while resenting the truth behind his observations.

'Look,' he said, exhaling slowly as though he were talking to a recalcitrant child, 'just park up at the side of the house and rest for a few hours. Eat some apples. I have a few other things left. I'm happy to share. Have a wash in the bathroom. Use the toilet. I'll leave you completely alone. Just take a breather from hiding out and being afraid all the time.'

'Ha!' she said. She didn't know why she said it. It just popped out.

'You won't get far without help,' he went on. 'And I can help you. A second pair of eyes. Just take a few hours to eat and do what you need to do. The house is clean and I have a fire. You can get warmed up. You're obviously exhausted.'

The desire to wash at a sink and use a proper toilet, instead of holes dug with sticks in the forest, suddenly overwhelmed her. She looked out onto the road. The dog panted heavily on the seat beside her.

'A few days ago men passed by here,' he said, encouraged by her silence. 'They weren't good people. Don't you get it? You're better off not being on your own.'

'I'm not on my own,' she said, caressing Brin's ears.

'You need to be with people. I need to be with people. You're the first person I've spoken to in months.'

She said nothing.

'When I first arrived here, there was an old man living in the cottage,' he continued. 'He was already sick. Cancer, he said. There wasn't much food, but we shared it. He was in his bed all the time. I think he was glad to see me. He wasn't at all afraid.'

'So he's still here?'

'No, he's gone now. He was in pain, a lot of pain. He cried a lot of the time. I thought about legging it but I couldn't leave him to die alone. Eventually I helped him.' He stroked his beard slowly and stared at the ground.

His words broke over her like strange weather. 'How exactly did you help him?' she asked, not sure she wanted to know.

'A pillow. I'd have wanted the same myself in that situation.'

'Jesus.'

'Yeah.' He looked away.

The dog yawned beside her and rearranged himself on the seat. His eyes never left Marcus.

'So then what did you do?'

'I buried him over there.' He pointed to the far corner of the garden.

She reversed slowly back up the long driveway so she could see the grave, see evidence of his story. He picked up his bags again and followed, keeping pace with the driver's window. Wiry grasses grew along the middle of the lane, brushing off the bottom of the jeep. The garden on each side was wild with swamp reeds, rough meadow grass and hogweed. An overgrown dog rose, laden with plump red hips, grew over a low wall. Remnants of an old hand plough, orange with rust, languished on its side at the front. She looked out the passenger window, over the head of the panting dog, and stopped when she saw a mound of fresh earth with a small stone at one end near a hawthorn hedge.

'What was his name?' she asked.

'Jim.'

'And everything he had in the house was untouched?'

'Yep. The house is hard to see. There was one other night that people passed by. Young lads – maybe four or five of them.'

'They never came in?'

'No. Too dark. I went out the back and listened to them.' He jerked his head towards a deep ditch between the garden and a field. 'They were loaded up with bags. They never came back.'

'They could still be close by somewhere.'

'Maybe.' He shrugged.

'What did you hear them say? What were they talking about?'

'You don't want to know.'

Was he dodging her question because he was making it up, or did he genuinely want to protect her?

'What else do you have in there?' she asked, nodding towards the house.

'Not a lot. There wasn't much to begin with. His bed and sheets. I cleaned them after… I sleep there now. A few basic tools in a shed out the back, plates and cups, pots. There was a cat. It came and went, but I haven't seen it for a while now. Good water. It's fresh. I light the fire, but only at night or when there's wind.'

She had lit a fire once after finding shelter in the forest. But the thick, white smoke rose up through the trees in the twilight. She might as well have had a finger pointing down at her.

'So how long are you planning on staying here?' she asked.

'I've no plans really. I'm just going from day to day.'

Something imperceptible shifted in her. The way he spoke was disarming, reassuring. He seemed so normal. She couldn't stop thinking about washing herself and feeling clean. Was it worth the risk? There were still so many sides to him she didn't know.

'Why did you stand in the middle of the road when you heard me coming?' she asked, more softly now. 'I could have been anyone.'

'I can't answer that,' he said. 'Some days I just don't care. Today was one of those days.'

His story sounded plausible in the context of the horror stories she'd read online and heard from neighbours and friends. Who'd admit to euthanasia? And Marcus's indifference to life, if it was to be believed, was somewhat understandable too. She shrugged and looked away for a moment before meeting his eye.

'Okay, I'll stay for a few minutes,' she said brusquely. 'But just to get water and use your bathroom. And on my terms. You understand that? He'll see to it.' She looked at the dog and then back at Marcus.

He nodded, and she caught the hint of a smile before he suppressed it.

She squinted into the side mirror. 'I'll go up round the side of the house. I can hide the jeep there – cover it with branches or something.'

He walked off towards the side of the house and immediately set to work with his hatchet, slicing through branches from the yew and willow trees that lined the driveway. She watched as he hacked and pulled at the trees. She would be no match for him if he turned on her. Brin would be the only deterrent against any darker impulses he might have.

She reversed the jeep around the side of the cottage where a rusting, red-painted gate, tied with rope to the hedge, separated the front and rear gardens. She cut the engine and watched Marcus drag the wide green branches towards her and lob them over the bonnet of the jeep.

She opened the driver's door slowly. Brin leapt out over her lap and ran towards him.

'Wait,' she called sharply.

Brin stopped and turned to look at her.

'Come here.'

The dog reluctantly turned back, then relieved himself before bounding to her, pawing at her to get out.

She jumped down and went round to the boot to fetch her handbag, her body on haptic alert to Marcus's whereabouts. Her bag was crammed with remnants of her old life – tumbled crystals for abundance and joy, organic essential oil for stress, cherry-red lipstick. A front pouch held oval grey stones and white shells from three summers ago. A Star Wars Lego man that belonged to Conor was at the bottom among the loose change. Her wedding rings were zipped into a pocket; they kept slipping off her too-thin fingers. The bag was a repository of artefacts from a previous existence. Her need to stay alive, to stay dry, to remain in the shadows quietly watchful of change hadn't altered her desire to hold on to these small tokens of her past life.

A handful of apples had fallen from the plastic holdall, and she stuffed them into her handbag along with the bottle of tranquilisers she had found earlier, then locked up the jeep. She stood in the driveway in front of the house, watching as Marcus finished covering up the jeep. He'd done a good job – she could hardly see it herself and she knew where to look.

The sun had disappeared and a bank of low grey clouds had moved in over the countryside. A chilly breeze picked up. She shivered. Was it the start of a new wave of storms? Her instinct was still to look it up online, but she hadn't had an internet connection for months now. Were they even providing forecasts?

The cottage was rambling and untended. Large cracks and fissures had broken through the external plaster cladding, evidence of decades of subsidence and neglect. On closer inspection, the two front windows were dirty and cobwebbed on the inside. Greyish net curtains mottled with black spot and mould obscured the view into the front rooms. A small white statue of the Virgin Mary stood between the glass and netting.

'I've been using the back door,' he said cheerily. 'This way.'

She followed him around the side of the house and down a cement path. Grab rails had been installed the length of the path, which ended with a ramp leading up the back door. Marcus put his shoulder to the door and disappeared inside.

Brin pressed himself against her leg, ears pricked and pointed forwards.

'Come on, stay with me now,' she whispered.

He was alert and attentive, every noise and smell pulling his head from left to right. He went in ahead of her and she followed.

'I'm bringing the dog in,' she said, her throat suddenly feeling tight and closed.

'No problem.'

She stood at the door and looked around, her eyes adjusting to the semi-darkness. They were standing in an old kitchen.

'When was the last time you were with people other than the old man?' she asked, for something to say.

'When my car was taken.'

'And when was that again?'

'Good few months back. Why?'

'No reason. It's a long time to be on your own.'

'Yeah, no more than yourself,' he said.

She looked at him more steadily from across the room. 'My dog needs water. Can I get him a drink?'

'Sure. And what about you?'

'Yeah, please. Why not.'

She watched him carefully for signs of erratic movement or strange behaviour, especially now he was indoors and on his own turf. He walked over to the sink, rinsed out a mug that sat on the draining board and filled it up with water. Then he pulled out an old stainless-steel saucepan from under the counter and filled that too. He placed the saucepan on the ground but the dog didn't move.

'Go,' she said, touching Brin gently on the side of his neck.

He leapt forward and drank and drank, his tail quivering with excitement.

Marcus placed the mug on the countertop nearest to her. She reached for it and took a huge gulp. The water was cold and deliciously fresh. She could feel it running down her insides, spreading its chill through her, enlivening her. He watched her drink, then wiped the counter with his sleeve.

'Thanks,' she said. 'That's lovely water.'

'It is. Safe too, and hard to find.'

She stood there, uncertain, like a guest needing direction as to where she might sit. Despite the circumstances, it was hard to shake off the ingrained good manners, the polite conventions that came with being in other people's homes. There was a long uninterrupted silence between them while the dog, more at ease now, padded around the room snuffling and sniffing, returning to her briefly every so often.

Now that her eyes had adjusted to the poor light she took in the rest of the room. It was a time capsule from decades ago, a relic of an Ireland still in possession of its rural simplicity and the decorative symbolic artefacts of Catholicism. The linoleum on the floor had curled up around the edges, reminding her of dry fronds of seaweed. A wide cut-stone fireplace containing the remnants of a fire filled one wall. In the centre of the mantelpiece was a large erratically ticking clock, the battery on its last legs. To one side of the clock was a purple Child of Prague statue and a selection of partially used pillar candles; on the other side was a small, faded photo in a gaudy pewter frame of a woman at the seaside. Christmas robins on plastic holly-berry yule logs gathered dust at either end.

Placed close to the fireplace was a single bed covered with layers of old wool blankets neatly folded back over pale yellow daisy-floral sheets and a small yellow pillow at one end.

An old cream-coloured range cooker stood to the left of the fireplace, its temperature gauge locked at zero. A stainless-steel teapot sat lifeless on the hot plate. It made her ache for tea – warm breakfast tea; Earl Grey, maybe, with a thin slice of lemon. Beside the range was an old dresser stacked with delph collectables, good crockery used for visitors, Waterford Crystal sugar bowls filled with dust. In the corner was a pile of women's shoes – an array of heels and slip-ons, buckles and straps, shiny patent brown leather flats. A dressing gown belt and a pink mohair hat hung from a hook on the wall above.

Involuntarily she squeezed her thighs together. She really needed to pee.

'Um, where's the bathroom?' she asked.

He nodded towards a door on the far side of the fireplace. 'There's a bedroom through there. Bathrooms behind it. Can't miss it.'

She went to the door and walked into the room, calling the dog after her. There was no bed in it – it was probably the one set up in front of the fire – but there were clothes everywhere –dresses, blouses, hosiery, scarves – spilling out of an old closet and onto the floor.

Running into the bathroom, she pulled the dog in beside her and bolted the door. The room was furnished with an ugly avocado-coloured suite with dirty pink pedestal mats at the foot of the sink and the toilet. She wrestled with her jacket, pulled it off and tossed it over the side of the bath. Then she yanked down her jeans, sat on the cold toilet seat and let go, trying desperately not to notice the smell. The relief was palpable, even to the dog. He sat in front of her and licked her knee as the stream eventually reduced to a trickle. There was no toilet paper, but someone had cut small squares of flannel and set them on the corner of the bath. An old kitchen bin sat next to the toilet. She used one of the squares, marvelling at the luxury of it – for weeks it had been damp moss and leaves – and deposited it in the bin.

She examined the bath as she pulled up her jeans. It was very clean. He must have been using it. A half-full bottle of washing-up liquid sat beside the taps. She could wash her underwear and jeans in there, wear one of the woman's dresses while she waited for her own clothes to dry. She could hang them off the rails of the jeep or a place in the back garden that caught the sun. She found herself imagining lying in a bath of hot water, washing away the layers of dirt from her arms, her shoulders, her legs and thighs, the back of her neck; shampooing her hair and rinsing it out by ducking her head under the water. And afterwards, towelling herself dry and putting on fresh clothes, combing her hair, a quick spritz of perfume behind the ears. The fantasy overwhelmed her for a moment and almost made her cry.

A small mirror with de silvered edges and mottled spots hung above the sink to the left of an old glass-fronted cabinet. She washed her hands and stared at her pale reflection. Her pink, healthy cheeks had vanished, sucked inwards, and her once sparkling violet-grey eyes were dull and listless. Her long lashes, that she used to accentuate carefully with mascara, were still striking and her naturally full lips and white, even teeth should have given her some comfort, but all she could see was how terrible she looked. She had never fully appreciated her appearance before, the ever-present inner critic always dissatisfied with some feature or another, but now she seemed to have aged ten years in as many weeks and she longed to see that younger, more familiar face, imperfections and all.

She was suddenly awake to her body and how Marcus might see it, and in the same moment hated that the thought had even crossed her mind. His presence had brought up in her a desire to be seen as she had once been – elegant, wholesome, primped and preened, in control. But there was safety in the filth and stench, she thought, in downplaying her female attributes; they were extra defences against unwanted advances. Then she caught herself on. She was curbing her own desires to be clean and second-guessing his wild impulses in order to survive. No, she would do what she needed to do for herself. She had the dog, after all.

She opened the bathroom door and walked back into the bedroom, Brin following close behind. Now that her bladder wasn't nagging her, she had a closer look at the clothes in the closet. A long grey wool coat, shapeless with wide black buttons, hung on the far right. To the left was a selection of pleated navy and green skirts, but they were too wide at the hips. For a moment it made her think of her of her grandmother's closet. As a child she used to play dress-up for hours, jamming her feet into peep-toe sandals to keep them on as she flounced around, weighted down by costume jewellery. A long mustard-coloured wool cardigan with fat brown buttons caught her eye. It would be perfect as an extra layer, especially at night. At the end of the rail, a black crepe blouson dress with side pockets and a string belt was paired with a pink neck scarf. *My God,* she thought, *it must be from the 1970s.* She took it out and held it up against her. It would do with the cardigan to keep her warm. She tucked a pair of skin-coloured tights into one of the pockets of the dress.

She set the clothes aside and returned to the kitchen. As she walked past the front window, she peered outside at the overcast achromatic sky. The rain was never far away. In her absence, Marcus had lit one of the candles on the mantelpiece and had set a small fire in the grate.

'It's raining again,' she said, then felt silly for stating the obvious.

"Tis.'

'Are you sure you want to do that?'

'Do what?'

'Light candles and a fire.'

'It's fine. It's the only way to heat up water… that's if you want it –'

'But will it not attract attention? It's not dark enough outside yet to hide the chimney smoke.'

He smiled at her. 'Honestly, it's not a problem. The wind's picked up. Anyway, no one'll come out with the rain starting up again.'

'But someone might be looking for shelter.'

'Unlikely.'

She suddenly felt irritated. He was going to do what he wanted to do regardless of what she thought. Yep, he was used to having his own way without taking direction from others.

The dog had wandered up to him and was sniffing around his feet. Marcus patted Brin's head and stroked his neck, then hunkered down so his face was close to the dog's.

'Come here,' she said sharply.

Brin immediately trotted back to her. She didn't want the dog to trust him, to start to like him or to get used to his company.

The rain was falling heavily now, bouncing off the old slate roof and pouring noisily out of a side gutter. It wasn't the walls of water that had fallen from the sky for months on end, but it was still raining. Several weeks had passed since the last band of rainstorms had pulled sections of the city from its foundations and swept entire housing estates and motorways into yawning caverns and freshly carved river valleys.

In the last two years, torrential rain had changed Europe utterly, bringing months of ceaseless flooding and unprecedented power cuts. Disease had spread and political disarray was the new order. Wars in the north-east that had been rumbling on for years intensified as instability offered the perfect breeding ground for opportunists and organised gangs. Mercenaries had yet to appear as far west as Ireland, hampered by a collective European military response that maintained a high-functioning aerial defence. Instead, the Irish had to contend with local gangs and a highly organised far-right militia. Their country, no longer forty shades of green, was now just as washed out as the rest of Europe, environmentally, economically and politically.

The lies they had been told for decades about the warming planet, the gaslighting by big corporations and the denial of climate change had been relentless and pervasive. The post-truth world had struggled to respond and adapt. No one trusted anything now unless it was happening in front of their eyes. All it had brought was loss of life and a dangerous new world with no time to repair the damage.

The fire had started to hiss and crackle, and strong flames were working their way up through a tidy pyramid of kindling and sticks. A stack of freshly chopped wood was drying out beside the hearth.

Marcus filled a large cast iron pot with water at the sink and heaved it back to the fireplace, hooking it to the blackened wrought iron chimney crane that swung above the fire.

'I think this place used to be an old farm,' he said casually. 'There are some old stone outbuildings in the field beyond the back garden.'

She said nothing.

'If you want, I could pour the hot water in the bath for you,' he continued breezily. 'The cold tap in there works.'

His suggestion startled and enticed her all at once, but primal instinct kicked in. 'Yeah, I'm not staying, thanks.'

'You might've little choice. Look at the rain.'

'Could you cover the windows?' she said, feeling suddenly tired from weeks of little sleep and the new weight of having to make small talk. 'It's just that the light from the candle and the fire will stand out from the road.'

'Yeah, of course. I've a few sections of ply over there by the alcove. I've been using those the odd time to cover the glass.'

'So any chance you can put them up now?'

A flicker of impatience crossed his face. 'Sure thing.'

'And actually, I could do with that hot water,' she said. She felt dizzy and a little nauseous.

He pulled a low-set armchair across to the fireplace and set it close to the heat.

'Sit there for a minute and warm yourself up while the water boils.'

She walked over and sat down, placing her handbag on the floor by the chair. It felt faintly ridiculous to carry it around with her, this relic from long ago. She made a mental note to take out her rings and put them on a string around her neck to keep them safe. The dog sat heavily at her feet, resting his head on his front paws and watching the man.

Marcus slid out a drawer on the dresser and took out a bottle of whiskey.

'Drink?' he asked, wiggling the bottle in mid-air.

He took two old teacups down from their hooks on the dresser and gave them a wipe with the corner of his shirt. Then he set them down on the hearth and measured two loose capfuls into each cup. She watched the deft turn of his wrist as he filled and poured. Taking his own, he sat back on the makeshift bed.

'Cheers,' he said, holding up his cup.

She picked up her drink and sat back in the chair. 'Cheers,' she said, looking straight at him.

Her thoughts swung wildly between the desire to stay put and the impulse to run. He caught her eye, then glanced away and knocked his drink back. She sipped it slowly, waiting for the burn to move down her throat and into her stomach.

'It's good,' she said, finally breaking the silence.

'Green Spot. Was a treat to find it. Want some more?'

'Maybe later.'

'Plenty for now and later. There are two more bottles under the dresser.'

'No wonder you're happy to stay here.'

He laughed. 'Yeah, but it's not a good habit to have. You go into yourself.'

'It's like a bad trip, isn't it,' she said, as if talking to herself.

'What is, now?'

'This whole mess,' she said more loudly. 'The country – Europe. The absolute state it's in. Nothing makes sense anymore. It's horrifying.'

'That's one way of describing it.' He poked at the fire and placed another log on the flames. 'How long have you been on the road again?'

'Five, maybe six weeks?' She sighed and took another sip of the whiskey. Her feet had warmed up a bit with Brin sitting by them.

'And where did you start out from?' he asked.

'Just outside Dublin. We live in a small estate in the suburbs.'

'Long time to be on the road. You haven't made much progress.'

'I've spent most of the time hiding,' she said defensively. 'All the wannabe soldiers stopping cars, stripping them, pulling people out, doing unspeakable things… It was too dangerous to move, especially at night, with half the roads swept away and it too dark to see without headlights.'

'So where did you stay?'

'Well, up until today in wooded areas mostly – forests, smallholdings off the motorway. Sometimes for a couple of weeks at a time. I heard people pass through, but I managed to stay out of sight, keep the jeep hidden.'

He nodded, appearing somewhat impressed. 'Smart woman.'

She narrowed her eyes at him.

'And how have you survived the last few years?' he asked.

'We managed to stay in our house until… well, until we decided we'd no choice but to leave. That's when I went to get the jeep.'

'You were lucky to last that long – at home, I mean.'

'There were lots like us. All the neighbours, our friends. We all helped each other.'

'So when did you decide to go?'

She stared in his direction, remembering the faces of her children, no longer able to play outdoors, the diseases in the water, the rats trying to get into the houses. Johnny. The familiar rush of panic surged up in her chest and she drained her cup of whiskey.

He unscrewed the bottle, not taking his eyes off her, and refilled her cup just short of the brim.

'All right?' he asked.

She nodded.

'We should have left much earlier,' she said after a long silence. 'We were caring for a neighbour. She wasn't coping – you know, psychologically. Then we saw on social media what was happening in the city.'

'A lot of those videos were fake.'

'Yeah, of course. But it's tiring always having to discern the truth from the fiction. It's easier to decide it's all fake and proceed from there.'

He half laughed.

'So when did *you* know things were really bad?' she asked.

'When the power finally went. When that goes, everything goes with it.'

'Yes, that and the army. All hell broke loose when the army gave up. We knew it would only be a matter of time before the gangs made it onto our estate, and now that there was nothing to stop them, no one was safe. Johnny and a few of the neighbours had a rota to patrol the housing estate, sometimes in their holiday kayaks, but it wasn't enough. We had to think of the children. We heard of some terrible things happening to children… in front of their parents.' Her voice cracked. 'Never in a million years did I think people in this country were capable of doing some of the things I've heard about.'

'Yeah,' he said softly, leaning back in his chair and stretching out his legs. 'They've been organising online and waiting for the opportunity for years, radicalised by anarchists and glorifying a new order.'

She liked the way he assessed things; it seemed measured, objective, well-informed. *He's just trying to impress you*, Johnny would have said drily. *He's figured you out. Wants to appear like a thinking woman's man. Your kind of man.* 'And how do you make that out?' she'd have asked him, snorting at his jibe. *Because that's what I did.* And he'd have been right.

'I think everyone knew that,' she said, resolving again not to let her guard down. 'But very few took it seriously. Everyone thought it was alarmist. Conspiracy theories. Everyone assumed the government wouldn't let it happen. And not just here – across Europe too.'

He tilted his head slightly and opened his mouth as if to speak, then closed it again. 'It's better sharing whiskey,' he said eventually with a smile. 'So what did you use to do... for work, I mean?'

She took another sip of whiskey and felt the burn of it in her throat. 'Charity.'

'Charity? What kind?'

'Environmental. I created awareness projects, climate action ironically.'

'Did you like it?'

'Yes, at the beginning. Thought I was fighting the good fight. But then I got cynical about it. We were fighting a losing battle. People were only interested in buying more stuff and taking refuge in their online "reality", forgetting there was a real world out there.'

'Spoken like a true cynic,' he said, giving her a lopsided smile, 'but I actually agree with you.'

She shrugged. 'Anyway, I'm one to talk. I've bought lots of stuff I didn't need or really want.'

He nodded soberly in what felt like a shared understanding. 'I see.'

She could feel herself starting to relax. He was a good conversationalist. 'I used to get really angry about all the denial – you know, the big fossil fuel companies with the research organisations in their pockets. But if you hang around in that world long enough you end up not knowing what's true or who to believe.'

'Wow, if that's how you felt, can you blame ordinary people for being confused?'

'True. Anyway, I think it's in my nature to be a bit cynical.'

'And what is your nature?'

She felt herself tense as the conversation shifted towards something more personal. But the whiskey had loosened the knots of tension that had held her together for the past few weeks.

'I'm not sure anymore,' she said, smiling wryly. 'I've been seeing a different side to myself lately.'

'Different how?'

'Oh, I don't know. Maybe in another life I was one of those prepper types waiting in the woods for the apocalypse.'

He laughed. It was deep and warm.

Their silence was filled by the sound of the rain hammering with ferocious intensity off the roof while the dog snored gently on his side, his long legs sticking straight out across the flagstones towards the fire.

'It's still too close to the city here,' she said eventually. 'It's only a matter of time before desperate people push further and further out.'

'Yeah, I know. And there are locals here too.'

'Have you seen them?'

'A few. Just shadows at windows really. But who knows what they're capable of. We need to avoid them.'

She noticed the 'we' again, as though they were now a unit of some sort. 'I don't trust anything or anyone,' she said stiffly.

'Not even me?' He looked at her, his eyes twinkling in the firelight.

'No, not even you.' She smiled thinly at him. She had made the choice to be here for the moment, but Marcus – if that was his real name – could still be a calculating sociopath, charming and manipulative. Best to appear affable for the time being. 'So tell me about your family,' she said. 'What was he like, your son?'

He stared into his drink. 'He was only three. Too young to know what was going on, but old enough to be afraid.'

There was another silence and she decided to not press him any further.

'Do you still have your phone with you?' he asked suddenly.

'Yeah, but it's been dead since the day I left the house.'

'Oh. Is that why you don't know where your family are? Don't you have a charger so you can check your messages?'

'No, but sure there's no power to charge anything anyway. The grid's been down for weeks.'

'Yeah, but you could use an old car charger if your phone's compatible. Run it off the jeep.'

A bolt of hope ran through her. She hadn't thought to look for one of those. 'Do you have one?'

'No. It was in my car when they took it.'

'But didn't you find any others in the houses you were in? There must be cars around that haven't been stripped. Christ, I never thought to look.'

Now she was kicking herself. She had passed several on the road and accelerated past them because of the bodies slumped inside. There had to be others.

'I'll help you look,' he said. 'The phone networks are probably down too, but it's worth checking, just in case.'

He got up, refilled his cup with whiskey and topped hers up before she had a chance to protest.

'So what are you going to do next?' she asked.

'Next?'

'After I leave. What's your plan?'

'I don't know. Maybe I can convince you to let me tag along.'

She bristled. 'I think it's better if you have your own plan, one that doesn't involve me.'

He looked at her and back at the fire. 'I used to have lots of plans.'

'Like what?'

'Same as everyone, really. Family plans. More travel abroad, maybe another college degree, go for promotion, move to a bigger house. No point in planning now.'

'I only have one plan – get to the lake house. Johnny and the kids will be there.' She felt guilty saying it, knowing it was a luxury he didn't have, but she couldn't help it.

'I told you before, it's unlikely they've made it and that they're alive,' he said quietly.

'You don't know that. You don't know him.'

'Well, I didn't make it five minutes without having my car taken and everything in it. It was pure luck I wasn't shot or killed.'

'*I've* made it this far.'

'True. How you've managed that, what with all the roadblocks, is an absolute miracle.'

'I can't just decide to stop having hope. And I refuse to consider the possibility they're dead.'

'It's a possibility you may have to accept.'

'Jesus no! Never.' Her voice caught in her throat.

He sat back and regarded her somewhat patiently. 'Sure. Whatever you want to believe yourself. But I think you'd be better managing your expectations.'

'I *know* my children are alive.'

'How do you know?'

'I'd sense it if they weren't.'

'You would sense it! Yeah, right. Okay.'

An image flashed through her mind of Lila in her purple hat being pulled from a car with her small teddies, and Conor standing there not yet ready to protect his sister or defend himself. She blinked hard to picture them playing safely in the garden of the house by the lake.

'You're blunt, that's for sure,' she said tightly.

He shrugged. 'I'm a realist.'

'What would you do?' she asked, forcing herself to sound calmer, more together.

He leaned forward in his chair, rubbing his hands together gently. 'What I'd do isn't important.'

'Ah now, that's a cop-out. You can't pass judgement on me and then refuse to say what you'd do differently.'

'Fair enough. So if I were you, I'd continue heading north to the lake house or whatever you call it. There's no going back to the city, and it should be safer up there, provided no one has occupied it. There might even be people there who can help you, who've found a way to work together.'

'But that's already my plan,' she said, feeling suddenly irritated. And why was he now suddenly talking as though she'd be travelling alone? What happened to all the 'we' talk, the stuff about working together as a team?

'Yeah, but I wouldn't count on finding your family in one piece,' Marcus went on. 'Unless you can contact them and find out where they are, if they're even alive. The circumstances aren't in their favour.'

'Okay, okay, you've said your bit. That's enough,' she said sharply. A subdued anger burned away beneath the surface. 'So what are you going to do next?' she asked.

He sat up straight in the chair and without missing a beat said, 'I need to find something worth living for.'

She was momentarily taken aback. 'Sure you have yourself.'

'Sometimes I wonder if that's enough.'

'That's the drink talking.'
'No, it's what I've been reduced to essentially.'
'But only if you choose to see it like that.'
'Mmm.' He smiled wryly. 'Anyway, it's easier for you because you have hope.'
'I suppose,' she said, and sighed heavily.

The dog looked up at her briefly, then closed his eyes again. The fire was burning brightly now, crackling and popping, creating an atmosphere of cosy geniality and casting dancing shadows on the walls. A pungent odour wafted from beneath her clothes as she warmed up. For a moment she felt deeply embarrassed.

She could see steam working its way through a gap under the lid of the heavy pot of water dangling over the fire. She ached to have a good wash. Could she trust him enough so she could do that? He seemed respectful of her presence; he wasn't wary of the dog; he had nothing left to lose. But maybe the whiskey had dulled her fear of him. That, and sheer exhaustion. And the need to not feel quite so alone.

Marcus selected three dry logs from the pile and put them on the fire. A long time passed when nothing was said; they just stared at the flickering flames.

'What do you fear most,' she asked abruptly, vaguely aware she was testing him.

He looked up, startled by the sound of her voice. 'Fear? Since I found my wife and son dead I haven't felt any fear. For the last few weeks, I haven't cared whether I was alive or not.'

'Is it different now?'

'I'm not alone now. Perhaps I should worry more.'

'Why?'

'Because it's not just about me. I wouldn't want anything to happen to you... now that you're here.'

'Oh for God's sake don't be ridiculous!' She blushed, suddenly mortified.

He smiled sheepishly. 'I didn't even know I felt like that until I said it out loud. Sorry if it comes across as creepy. We've only just met. I don't know you.' He took another drink.

'You certainly don't, and you aren't responsible for me,' she said angrily.

He turned his face towards the fire.

'I'll give you the benefit of the doubt and assume that's definitely the drink talking!' She drained her cup and put it on the floor beside her chair. 'I might have that quick wash now before I go. Is there enough water in the pot to fill the sink... or maybe even have a shallow bath?' The words were out of her mouth before she could catch them.

'Of course,' he said, standing up quickly. Brin jumped up, ears back, eyes fixed on him, watching his every move. Marcus ignored him and lifted the lid of the pot. 'Sounds like the drink's talking in you too. A bath!'

'More like desperation,' she muttered.

'I'll block off the window before you go in. You can take in one of the big candles,' he said pointing to the mantelpiece.

⊱

She stood naked in the flickering candlelight, her filthy clothes kicked into the corner of the bathroom. The outfit she had picked out earlier lay folded on the freezing tiles. The dog, in the bathroom with her, was on strict orders to stay next to the locked door. He watched her constantly, on high alert in this cold dark room. Now that she was on her own she became acutely aware of the position she had put herself in with this strange yet affable man. But the whiskey had smoothed the sharper edges of her fear and heightened her desire for a little self-indulgence.

Swaying gently in the half-light, she looked down at her body. Her hip bones jutted out and her knees looked like huge knots in her skinny legs. Her breasts had shrunk and hung flattened on her chest. She had lost all her soft gentle curves, the very things Johnny had loved most about her. 'Paradise City,' he used to murmur as he watched her change for bed, prompting her to snort with mock outrage at his objectification of her while relishing his adulation. Running her hands over her body, she became aware of the parts that would usually have been smooth and waxed. The old man must have had a razor of some kind.She slid back the mirror door on the cabinet above the sink and found an old tub of petroleum jelly, a plastic bottle of talcum powder, a glass pot of face cream with a rusting tin lid, a powder puff, a small bottle of crimson nail varnish and a used lipstick in coral pink. On the bottom shelf was a small cut-glass bottle of perfume – French cologne – and an old pink toothbrush, its bristles almost flattened. All this women's stuff.

Like a slap on the face, she suddenly realised – there was nothing here belonging to an old man. Even in the bedroom next door. Her mind started to race. He had lied to her. *Think!* The main room with the fire – what was in there that might have belonged to a man? She scanned the room in her mind's eye, concentrating hard and slowing down her breathing. Nope, nothing. Was it a woman he'd found here then? Why would he want to hide that from her?

He lied to me. I'm totally naked and he's only on the other side of that door. Jesus, what should I do? But I'm about to get into a bath! Oh, how I long to be clean… He's not giving off rapist or murderer vibes… Yeah, but would I know what that felt like? I don't think I've ever met a rapist or murderer before, not that I know of. But why did he lie to me? Maybe there's a perfectly reasonable explanation.

She checked the lock on the door one more time.

'Good boy, Brin,' she said, stroking the dog's sleek head, then she stepped into the shallow bath. She could take her time about this without raising his suspicions. It would give her time to think. She was trembling as much from the anxiety that crawled across her skin as from the chill air in the room. She slid down into the bath, trying to immerse as much of her body as she could in the tepid water. For a moment she was overwhelmed with such gratitude that it brought tears to her eyes.

First she washed her hair, working a few drops of washing-up liquid into a good lather. Then she lifted a piece of cut flannel and used it to soap her body, giving her armpits and groin extra attention. By the time she reached her feet, her mind had stopped racing and a plan had started to form.

The detergent was astringent but it worked. The water had become murky and small bits of moss and pine needles were floating on the surface. Kneeling forward, she rinsed her hair under the water from the cold tap and splashed the rest of her body. She stepped out onto the freezing tiles, shivering violently, and patted her body with another clean flannel square. Without waiting until she was completely dry, she put on the black blouson dress and the mustard cardigan. The tights were a good fit but were uncomfortable without underwear.

Then she picked her dirty jeans, shirt, socks and panties off the floor and dropped them into the bath, swirling them around to get the worst of the dirt out of them. The water turned an even darker shade of brown and the bitter smell of perspiration and urea formed a noxious odour above the bath. She got to work with the washing-up liquid, scrubbing the clothes until her hands were raw. This is how they used to wash their clothes before washing machines were invented, she thought. We've taken so much for granted. She rinsed them under the cold tap until the water ran clear, then wrung them out and hung them over the back of a chair.

The familiar ritual of washing had helped to calm her down but mostly she was relieved to have clothes on again. She looked over at the dog. He raised his head slightly and cocked it, one ear up, one ear down.

Her fingernails might still be ragged but they were clean. Her hair, now well below her shoulders, hung damp against her back. She ran her fingers through it, working out some of the knots and tangles. She hadn't been able to find a comb or brush. She could feel herself warming up under the layers of soft satin and wool. The dress was too big but had a vintage feel to it that she liked despite everything. When she glanced at herself in the mirrored door of the cabinet, she saw that her cheeks were red and her face was glowing. She took her old perfume out of her handbag and out of habit lightly spritzed her neck and wrist. It smelt divine but she immediately felt silly. He would notice and think she had done it for him.

She pulled the plug out of the bath and hung the chain around a tap, then rinsed away the dirt and wiped off the tidemark with the flannel. She put her boots back on over the tights. They were cold and uncomfortable, but she needed to keep them on in case she needed to leave in a hurry.

She had decided that she'd manage this like she had managed everything so far – stay casual, breezy, nonchalant, charming. She'd calmly find out why he lied, leave quickly if she had to. Brin was her trump card.

She gathered up her wet clothes, nudged the dog out of the way with her foot and opened the door. Immediately she could feel the heat from the kitchen and hear the rain pouring down outside; it sounded even heavier than before. She stood in the bathroom doorway for a moment, practising one of the pranayama breathing techniques she had learned long ago in yoga class, then went back to the kitchen.

Marcus looked up as she came into the room. He had taken off his hat and roughly chopped sandy-coloured hair fell over his eyes. He had clearly tried to cut it himself at some point. He was sitting at a small table positioned close to the fire. It had been set with two empty plates and two mugs of water with a selection of apples in a wicker basket in the centre. A saucer was piled with raisins and a small breakfast bowl had been filled with tinned grapefruit chunks.

'Dinner,' he said, smiling. 'It's not much. I was saving the raisins and grapefruit, but now's as good a time as any.'

'Thank you. You're very kind to share,' she heard herself say in saccharine tones.

'Well, you found us the apples.'

'I need to dry my clothes. Can I hang them on the back of those?' She gestured towards the dining chairs lined up against the back wall.

He nodded. He was relaxed yet had the attentive energy of someone eager to please.

She pulled a couple of chairs nearer to the fire and hung her jeans and shirt over the backs. She could feel herself blushing as she spread her pants and socks out on the seats. She shook her hair out; it had started to curl as it dried.

She walked over to the table with her handbag and sat down. Brin curled up next to the hearth.

'This looks lovely,' she said, giving him the hint of a smile. 'You make a good host.'

They avoided each other's eyes. She nibbled politely on a few raisins and sipped the water. The grapefruit had been sweetened by the syrup in the tin and was delicious. Had she been alone, the food would have been gobbled down within seconds. She wondered if he noticed the change in her scent, then pushed the thought quickly out of her head. The whole situation was utterly bizarre. Only hours before she had been hiding in a murky wood. To be here now, freshly washed, in front of a blazing fire, drinking whiskey and eating fruit with a stranger, and a man to boot, was a surreal and somewhat terrifying turn of events.

She reached into a side pocket of her handbag and pulled out a small pocketknife. It had been a gift from Johnny when they went on a fishing trip years before they had the children. He'd had the blade engraved: *Amor vincit omnia* – 'Love conquers all'. She watched Marcus watching her as she opened the lock and flicked out the thin blade. They were both playing at trust, faking civility amidst deep uncertainty.

She used the knife to cut slices from an apple and chewed each piece slowly. The dog's food was still in the jeep, so she tossed the core to the dog who jumped up and wolfed it down. It would stave off his hunger until she braved the weather to go out and get some.

'Come here,' she said to Brin. He trotted over and stood by her, watching first her, then Marcus.

'I'm curious,' she said, her hand on the dog's collar as she pretended to stroke his neck. 'You say a man lived here?'

Marcus looked directly at her, cocking his head slightly. He didn't stop chewing.

'It's just that this house is full of women's things,' she went on, trying to sound unperturbed and calm.

'And?'

'Well, I don't see anything belonging to a man.'

He kept on chewing and didn't take his eyes off her face.

'No shoes, shirts, books – nothing in the bathroom. Have I missed something?' She frowned, hoping it appeared more bemused than angry. Brin waited patiently beside her.

Marcus broke eye contact, sat up straight in his chair and stroked his beard. 'You're right.' Looking straight at her again.

For a moment she forgot to breathe. 'So, what really happened?' she asked, still trying to keep things casual.

'Her name was Helen,' he said, and his shoulders relaxed. She was old – very old – and on her own. She had some kind of cancer that had spread to her bones. She was in terrible pain when I found her. Her carer hadn't come in months and the morphine had run out.' He stared over at the fire.

'Poor thing,' she said matter-of-factly. 'So why tell me it was a man that lived here?'

'Because I thought it necessary at that exact moment.'

She continued to stroke Brin close to his collar. 'I see... Why?'

'Well, I thought that if you knew I'd helped a woman to die, it would make you even more wary of me than you already were. It just seemed easier to say it was a man. It was a split-second decision, taken in the moment.'

She didn't move. She didn't know what to make of it.

'Look, it made sense at the time,' he said. 'You weren't for hanging around.'

She studied him and saw nothing in his expression or body language that made her doubt the truth of what he said.

'Okay, yeah, you're right,' she said eventually. 'It would have made a difference if you'd told me you'd buried a woman and shown me her grave.'

'Sorry about that. We were at the gate and you were about to drive off. It was only natural you were nervous and I didn't want you to leave.'

'Well, for future reference, if I can't trust people, I walk away.'

He nodded. 'Fair enough.'

'Without trust, you've got nothing to work with.'

'Yep. I agree.' He smiled and relaxed back into his chair. 'So what else should I know?'

'Look, if we're going to help each other, I need to be able to believe you. It's that simple.' She was suddenly conscious of trying to bridge something between them, of meeting him halfway. 'So what should I know about you then? Again, for "future reference".' She let go of Brin's collar and patted him. He circled for a moment before resuming his position on the warming flagstones. He regarded them, one after the other, from under his eyebrows.

Marcus put his elbows on the table and leaned his chin on his clasped hands. 'I used to value loyalty and courage,' he said finally. 'But now I'm not so sure. Loyalty can come with a lot of ego.'

She nodded. 'True. What about courage?'

He got up and went to the kitchen counter where he had left the whiskey.

'I think it's essential,' he said, filling two cups to the brim. 'Without it, everything that is good will eventually die. If we don't step up, we lose hard-fought-for things. Like women's rights.' He gestured towards her. 'It only took ten years to unwind fifty years of progress there, didn't it? Cowardly political leadership manipulated by religious extremism everywhere you look. The media only interested in clickbait profiteering. Newspapers beholden to lobbyists and shareholders.' He leaned back against the counter facing her, a cup in each hand.

'Mmm, but why do I sense a "but" coming?' she said, trying hard to appear unimpressed by his articulate argument.

'No real buts,' he said. 'I just think people misrepresent courage. They think it's all about big actions – David standing up to Goliath, the little man against big business or government. I mean, yeah, it's all those things, but for me it's more than that. Little things, subtle things can be courageous too.' He sat back down at the table and put a cup of whiskey in front of her.

'Thank you.' She took a sip. 'What, like helping someone to die?' she said, not taking her eyes off his face.

He met her eyes. 'Yeah, although I guess that's not so subtle. But it does take courage.'

She nodded. 'My parents lived longer than they should have, thanks to medicine and private hospital care. But they struggled so much at the end. It was difficult to justify their suffering.'

'What you have is courage,' he said quietly.

'What do you mean? I haven't killed anyone.'

'No, but you tell the truth – your truth. You're not afraid to take risks so you can see your family again. Even being here with me – I appreciate why that may feel risky for you.'

She half laughed. 'That's very magnanimous of you. But for me that's just survival. I guess courage may be part of it, but I'm driven by something deeper.'

'Like what?'

'Love. Lila and Conor are my life. Nothing else matters.'

'Nothing?'

'Nothing. I need to find them. I need to know they're okay.'

'And your husband?' he asked, rubbing the side of his cup with his thumb.

'And my husband, of course.' Why had she left him out of her roll call, she wondered.

Marcus watched her carefully, then took another drink.

'Anyway, sorry,' she said, suddenly feeling self-conscious. 'I know you lost your wife and son. I should be more sensitive.'

'No need to apologise,' he said quietly. 'Look, you're in your world and I'm in mine. You've no idea where your kids are or if they're even alive. We're both in our own versions of hell.'

They sat in silence, sipping whiskey, listening to the rain pelting down outside, lost in their own thoughts. After a while he got up and poked the embers of the dying fire, stirring up the heat.

'That's a good fire,' she said, suddenly feeling very sleepy.

He turned and smiled at her. 'Yeah, when you have a fire, you're never quite alone.'

3

The next morning, she awoke with a start to the sound of him removing the sections of plywood from the windows. A milky blue light filtered into the room and across the floor. She was curled up tight in the armchair by the hearth, an old coat thrown over her. She was thirsty. She thought back to the night before and the last thing she could remember was the distant sound of logs sparking and settling in the fire. Brin was over by the window standing beside Marcus. He turned and looked at her, as though he sensed her wakening up and, trotting over, lay his head on her lap.

'Morning,' she said. She unwound her stiff legs and stretched up her arms to the ceiling.

'Oh hey, good morning. You fell asleep in here in the end!' He smiled.

'Sorry. I meant to go out to the jeep.'

'It wasn't a problem,' he said. 'Anyway, it's still raining hard. You'd have had a bad night out there.'

She sat up straight and looked around, the events of the day before flooding back all at once. Her head was muzzy from the drink and she was thirsty. 'I'd better hit the road,' she said, reaching down for her handbag. 'I want to look for a charger.'

'Wait. Sure there's no panic. I'm making tea and we can finish the bag of raisins.'

'What kind of tea?'

'Mint. From the garden. There's some warm water left in the pot.'

'Sure, okay. Thank you.'

She went over to the sink, stretching some more as she walked, and filled a mug with water from the tap. She drank the lot, barely stopping to swallow. Her stomach growled with hunger; raisins wouldn't do much to alleviate that.

'I'm just going to use the bathroom,' she said, flexing her right foot, trying to get the feeling back into it.

'Sure thing.'

She noted that her acute wariness of Marcus had eased somewhat – maybe it was the hangover or the good night's sleep – and she chastised herself for letting her guard down. She called Brin and he dutifully followed her. He would need to go out too; she hadn't let him out the previous evening.

She used the toilet, shivering with the change in room temperature, then washed her hands and face in freezing water at the sink. It helped to clear her head and she quickly took stock of the situation in the cold light of morning. She needed to leave. It had been a welcome break in routine, but now it was time to go. All her old fears about Marcus rushed back, sending a surge of adrenaline through her body. She tried to temper them with practical thinking. Could she use him? See him as a temporary resource?

She went back to the kitchen, where he handed her a mug of hot water with chopped mint leaves floating on the surface. He had brought the fire back to a blaze and the room was cosy.

'It's actually good,' he said.

'Oh, lovely. Thanks.'

She went to the back door, unlocked it and slid the bolt across. The dog shot out through the open door and into the torrential rain. She watched him weaving between the trees and bushes, his long amber and black tail moving like a wagging periscope through the overgrown grass. She stepped out onto the path, well aware she had no shelter, but she wanted to be alone to think, away from Marcus, and didn't care about getting wet. The back garden had become waterlogged overnight, and she watched Brin splash through the deep puddles and pee against a dying ash tree as she warmed her hands on the mug of tea. He wasn't in any rush. Within seconds, the rain had soaked through her cardigan and dress, and her hair hung like a heavy curtain around her face.

'Hey, you're getting drenched out there,' Marcus called from the kitchen. 'Come back in.'

She turned her head slightly so he could hear her. 'I'm fine.'

He came out and stood beside her. 'Here,' he said, laughing and thrusting his hat into her hands. 'Put it on.' He went back in and returned with her jacket.

'Thanks,' she said, stepping back into the doorway.

She stood there, leaning against the doorframe, with the jacket around her shoulders and his hat pulled down to her eyebrows. The dog eventually raced back inside and shook himself all over the kitchen, spraying water everywhere. She found herself apologising. Marcus shrugged and opened a tin of cat food. Brin barely gave him time to scrape it into a bowl on the floor before wolfing it down in seconds.

'Okay, so I have an idea,' she said, exhaling. 'And questions.' She went to the fireplace and stood with her back to the fire.

'Shoot.' He sat down on the chair he'd sat in the night before and sipped his tea.

'So how far have you walked and in what directions?'

'I've walked maybe ten, fifteen kilometres in most directions. The road you were on was the last route I tried.'

'And what about the other roads?'

'Well, some were blocked so I went across fields.'

'I see.'

'I've only gone as far as I'd be able to walk back with a full bag if I found things worth taking.'

'Have you checked all the houses around here then?' she asked.

'Some. The abandoned ones anyway.'

'What do you mean the *abandoned ones*?'

'Well, some people are still hiding out, but you can tell which houses are empty if you watch them for a while.'

'And what did you find in the empty houses?'

'Bits and pieces – a little food.'

'So which road is the best one for me to take to go north?'

He ran his fingers through his hair. It was a soft reddish blond that seemed bright even in the gloom of the cottage and looked surprisingly clean to her.

'Mmm, well, I think it would be best if you went left when you leave here,' he said.

'And then?'

'Then there's a T-junction onto another road. I walked it before. It's about an hour on foot between here and the T-junction when you factor in the flooded sections.'

'How many houses along that stretch – like roughly?'

'Oh, maybe ten, fifteen, all mostly stripped. Then there's another junction with a cul-de-sac, well off the beaten track. I turned back at that point because it got dark.'

'So you don't know what's beyond that?'

'There might be more houses at the end. It's the only place I haven't got to yet.'

'You never found a working car?'

'Nope. None with keys and most of them were electric. Batteries all dead. The Volkswagen yesterday was the first diesel I've come across with fuel still in it.'

'You were so close to it really when you think about it.'

'Yeah, I probably would have got to it eventually, but then I wouldn't have been able to get in… you know, what with the kids.' He looked away and frowned. 'Anyway, if it had been working where would I have gone in it?'

She finished her tea and set the empty mug down on the table. 'Well, thanks anyway,' she said.

'What for?'

'A place to stay, warm water. Half your raisins.' She smiled.

'Ha! That's no problem.' He got up and stretched. 'So, what's your idea? You said you had questions and an idea.'

She hesitated, then looked straight at him. 'Okay, well, it's something I think may be of benefit to both of us. We could set off in the jeep together. I can take you further than you've walked before.'

He raised his eyebrows.

'I saw that,' she said.

'Saw what?'

'That surprised look.'

'Well, yeah. Why are you surprised that I'm surprised? Yesterday you were dead set against us doing anything together.'

'Well, now I think we can help each other out. Just this one time. I have the jeep and a dog obviously.'

'And what do you think I bring?'

'An extra pair of hands?'

'Is that all?' He grinned.

'Yep, pretty much.' She smiled again, despite herself. *Oh, for Christ's sake*, Johnny would have said. *He's flirting with you. Can't you see that?* But she squeezed his voice out of her head. 'So, we find a house that's you know, still untouched…'

'You're definitely feeling braver this morning.'

'… and we fill the jeep with food, supplies, whatever we can find. Bring it back here.'

'What do you want in return?' he asked.

'Not much. A share of whatever we get… and your help in finding a charger that'll run off the engine – that's all I need. With the two of us and him,' she nodded towards the dog, 'it'll be safer. We'll have each other's backs.'

'And after that?'

'I check my phone, figure out where my family are and go and find them.'

He nodded. 'Okay, I'm fine with that.'

She went to the fireplace and felt the clothes she had washed the night before. They were still damp in the folds and the jeans weren't yet dry around the waist.

'I'm going to change back into these,' she said. 'We can go when you're ready.'

The thought flashed through her mind that he hadn't mentioned the dress or how she'd looked after her bath last night and she felt suddenly irritated with herself.

She took off her wet jacket and draped it over the back of a chair closest to the fire. Then she gathered up her washed clothes and returned to the bathroom. It was only when she was inside and naked that she realised the dog was in the kitchen with him and the keys to the jeep were in her bag beside the fireplace. Everything that kept her safe was in another room. She dressed quickly, throwing the wool cardigan on over her shirt and fastening up the buttons, then pulled her hair back into a loose ponytail with an elastic band she had in her jeans pocket.

When she walked back into the kitchen, all was as she had left it. The dog was walking around sniffing in the corners for food; Marcus was at the sink, rinsing the plates and cups. He set them on the counter to dry and put on his coat and hat, still soaked through. The hatchet was on the table beside him; the empty rucksack was on the floor at his feet.

He turned to face her, looking more serious now. 'You ready?'

'Yep,' she said, trying to appear breezy.

She took her coat off the back of the chair, pulled it on quickly and reached for her bag. The keys were still in the zipped pocket, thank God! Relief coursing through her, she called the dog.

'Okay,' she said. 'I'll go and start the jeep.'

'I'll be there in a minute.'

She stepped into the torrential rain again and Brin bounded out in front of her. She would keep the dog nuts for another time. After all, he'd just had a full tin of cat food. She was glad not to have to eat them herself today. Hunger still tore at her, but the fruit the night before had taken the edge off, and she was revitalised by this new mission. She hopped around the huge puddles and dodged the rivulets that ran down the path from the overflowing ditches as she made her way round to the jeep, but the water seeped into her boots anyway. She heard him close the door behind them and knew he was on his way.

She looked around the waterlogged landscape. Leaden clouds were emptying themselves over the fields and roadways, the curtain of water drumming all colour into the drowning earth. At any other time, she would have found beauty in it, the perfect ensemble of random harmonics. A song of sorts, she thought, an awful, beautiful rain song.

Marcus came up behind her and started pulling the branches off the jeep. She jumped in and started the engine. She reached across the front seats and opened the passenger door. Brin leapt in and sat in the passenger seat as usual.

'Sorry, you'll have to go on the floor today,' she said to him, tugging on his collar to show him what she meant. Without any fuss, the dog got down onto the floor, but he looked forlorn, she thought.

She drove the jeep forward and Marcus hesitated outside, the rain pouring down on him.

'Jump in,' she shouted, beckoning him with her hand.

He stepped up and sat down heavily in the seat, gently nudging the dog to one side to make room for his legs. He propped the hatchet against the side of the footwell and stuffed his empty rucksack down between his feet. Water was coursing down his face and for the first time, she had a sense of what he smelled like – musky, smoky, sweet. It wasn't unpleasant. It was the closest she had been to another human being since she'd last seen the kids and Johnny. Brin flattened his ears and kept his eyes on her as Marcus leaned down and cautiously rubbed his head.

She drove down the rutted lane from the cottage, the windscreen wipers working hard, and turned left, just as he'd suggested. The road was badly flooded; where the day before she'd been able to see the tarmacked surface, now it had a skin of water reflecting the sky.

'You were really lucky to get this jeep when you did,' he said. 'And keep it hidden for so long.'

'Well, I've been hiding for a long time. Fear is a terrible thing.'

'Yeah, but you reach a point where you're forced to face it or you stop caring.'

They continued along the narrow road until they reached a T-junction. The ditches all around them were brimming with water. The fields were already flooded, wide lakes covering most of the pastureland. The houses on higher ground looked dark and empty, their black windows like vacant eye sockets, their gardens untended. Late gladioli bent double over cobbled driveways and brambles reclaimed the once-manicured hedges.

'This way,' he said, pointing straight ahead. 'There's another junction further up and then the sign for the cul-de-sac.'

He scanned the fields to left and right, alert and watchful. 'This is as far as I got,' he said, squinting through the windscreen. 'Up that side road to the left. See it? I think there are houses up there, but I didn't go up.'

She nodded and edged the jeep up the track, keeping pace with a swollen stream that had rerouted itself alongside them. Sheets of rain swept across the countryside and the weather showed little sign of easing up. It was awful to be out in, but it meant they were less likely to encounter other people hunting for resources.

'Look,' he said. 'Two houses at the end. No more road.'

She could make out a small house with a pebble-dashed façade and driveway that led around to the rear. She reversed up the drive slowly and cut the engine.

He turned to look at her, his eyes suddenly a darker blue. There was no twinkle now. 'Ready?' he said.

'Yeah. Let's do it.'

He opened the door and jumped down, then pulled the rucksack over his shoulders and grabbed the hatchet from the side of the footwell. The dog was about to follow him when she called him back.

Brin stopped and watched her, muscles tense. She jumped down on her side and whistled. He scrambled across the seats and leapt out but stayed close.

She followed Marcus around the side of the house. All was quiet save for the noise of the overspilling gutters. An old silver BMW was parked at the rear. Marcus tried the door handles, but it was locked. He eventually prised open the fuel cap, but the tank was empty.

She peered in through a window of the house, her heart thumping in her chest. A bedroom, tidy and undisturbed. Not far away, she found the back door slightly ajar. She pushed it open with her foot and craned forward, squinting in the dim, murky light to see what she could make out. The dog whined and nudged past her; she followed. Her hand flew to her mouth as the smell hit.

Around a table in the centre of the room were four chairs. Rows of glass jam jars filled with some kind of claret-coloured fruit stood on the counter. An open cupboard door revealed what looked like tins of fruit and veg, maybe even tuna. A wicker basket containing onions and cooking apples sat on the shelf underneath. Boxes of baby food – she recognised the labels – were stacked neatly near the door and a kilo bag of rice and packets of spaghetti lay unopened next to the cupboard. A half-finished pale blue baby hat and ball of wool, crochet hook still holding a stitch, had been left neatly on a rocking chair. The cold tap was running in the sink, crystal clear water swirling down the plug hole. A fine crimson-brown spray formed an elegant arc across the magnolia wall opposite the door. A woman, shrunken within her clothes, legs bent at awkward angles, lay on the floor, her eyes staring at the man slumped forward in his chair, a big hole blasted through the top of his head. A rifle was on the floor at his feet.

She took a step into the room, her hand still over her mouth but now it was to stop herself from screaming. On the other side of the door a tiny baby, carefully tucked up with a handmade knitted blanket of bright marigold and marmalade squares, lay in a Moses basket on a stand.

She felt a hand on her shoulder and without giving it any thought, she turned and pressed her forehead against his chest. He held her tight without speaking.

After a few minutes he pulled her back and walked her towards the door, one arm around her shoulders.

'Get some air,' he said quietly. 'I'll clear the cupboards out and leave everything on the path outside. You put them in the boot. then we go.'

She looked up at him, her eyes wide with horror. 'Are we all just animals?'

He looked away, avoiding her eye. 'I'm afraid we are, when it comes down to it.'

'Seriously?' She shook her head and swallowed the bitter saliva that had filled her mouth.

The brittle silence that followed offered no reprieve from the discomfort, so she went back outside and left him to gather up the tins. She went behind an overblown hydrangea and quietly threw up, feeling momentarily irritated that she'd just got rid of the only nutritious food she'd eaten in days. She covered the vomit with a rock so the dog wouldn't go near it and returned to the doorway.

They worked quickly. It took less than ten minutes for them to fill the jeep. There was enough dried, preserved and tinned food to last several weeks if they were careful. She climbed back into the driver's seat and Brin leapt over her and settled down in the footwell without needing to be told. After a few minutes, Marcus got in beside her, holding the man's gun.

'You feeling better now?' he asked.

'A bit. Not much. What about you?' She turned towards him, unable to take her eyes off the gun. A total game-changer. It took away any advantage she had with the dog.

'I've seen just as bad, maybe worse, elsewhere.'

She put her hand out to turn the key in the ignition. 'So what do you think happened in there?'

'I'd say he killed her, then himself. There wasn't any sign of other people being involved. Anyway they'd have taken the food and the gun.'

'And the baby?'

'Not a mark on him that I could see. But he'd have had no chance on his own.'

She let out a long sigh, blowing out her cheeks.

'I took the gun,' he said.

'Yeah, I can see that.'

'It's a .22 bolt-action, used for hunting. There were twenty cartridges under his chair.'

'Okay,' she said, glancing at him quickly, trying to get the measure of his thinking. Something in her wanted to buck like a trapped animal. Instead she said, 'I guess it's better we have it rather than someone else.'

'It'll make all the difference in a tight spot.'

'Okay, I'm sure you're right,' she said briskly.

She started the engine and once the jeep was back on the road, she rushed to put the house behind them. Neither of them said a word for what felt like a long time. After a while, Marcus started rummaging around inside his coat.

'I have something for you… if you want it,' he said.

'Oh?'

'It belonged to the woman, so I don't know if...' He held it up so she could see. It was a white toilette bag with a long gold zip. 'It has soap in it, toothbrushes, things for women, stuff like that.' He looked embarrassed, like a teenager instead of a man who had once had a wife.

'Oh, okay. Thank you,' she said. She was disturbed by the gesture but couldn't figure out what bothered her most – the idea of using a dead woman's things, her euphoria at having 'women's things', or his thoughtfulness.

While he wiped the condensation off the inside of the windscreen, she glanced at the gold wedding ring on his other hand. It had been merely decorative to her. Her fear of him had cut her off from seeing him as another human being who had suffered great loss. Yet now she saw it as a symbol of belonging, of being someone's person, someone else's world. She suddenly felt like saying something comforting but couldn't find the right words and the feeling passed. But in that moment, the rain seemed to ease and the light to change.

By mid-morning they had returned to his cottage. When she suggested splitting the tins of food between them he didn't say anything, just carried his share into the house and left hers in the back of the jeep covered in coats. Had he changed his mind about them staying together to work as a team, she wondered. Maybe he'd grown tired of her already. Back inside the kitchen, they hung the drenched outerwear over the backs of the chairs. The room was still warm – warmer than outside – and felt like home to her, even though she'd only spent one night there. She slumped down on one of the chairs and stared at the floor while Brin nuzzled her hand, his way of checking up on her. Images from that morning's foray flashed through her mind – it was almost worse if she closed her eyes – and the smell of death had followed her back to the cottage. Marcus said nothing. He raked out the hearth and set a new fire. Soon the logs were hissing and spitting again and he hung a fresh pot of water on the crane. Then he disappeared into the bathroom, and she could hear him washing at the sink.

Something in the sound of this simple human activity roused her at last and she decided to set the table. Soothed somewhat by the ordinariness of the task, she took spoons, forks, and knives from a drawer in the old dresser and arranged them formally around two bowls and side plates. She filled mugs with ice-cold water from the tap and placed them to the right of the bowls. She rummaged around in the hot press and found some linen napkins with delicately laced edges. Folding them diagonally into perfect triangles, she set them on the side plates. She emptied two tins of tuna into a large soufflé dish and mashed it with a fork. Then she filled three separate serving bowls with cold baked beans, prunes in sweet syrup and pineapple slices, and she arranged slices of fresh apple on a dinner plate.

She sat at the table and listened carefully, wondering what he was doing now. Her mouth watered and she grew impatient, but she was reluctant to start without him, her good manners deeply ingrained. When he came in and saw her sitting there waiting, he smiled.

'Now all we're missing is wine and music,' he said in an obvious attempt to lift the mood. He pulled back his chair and sat down. 'Well, this looks lovely – a real treat.' He beamed at her.

After weeks of dog nuts and blackberries, having a choice of flavours was a gift and the shock of what they had seen only an hour or two before was temporarily put to the back of their minds. The saltiness of the tuna brought her taste buds back to life, making the rest of the food taste even more delicious. She lingered over everything – the cold beans, the plump sticky prunes, the sweet pineapple segments.

'Oh my God, these remind me of pina coladas,' she said, waving her fork around.

'Nah, too sweet for me. I always went for the whiskey sours.'

When all the bowls and plates were empty, they sat back in their chairs. Marcus burped and immediately apologised, which made her laugh. But suddenly it all came flooding back – the dead woman and her newborn baby – and for a moment she thought she was going to be sick again.

'It doesn't feel right somehow,' she said.

'What do you mean?'

'To have all this. It's come from such a terrible place.'

'Beggars can't be choosers!'

He was obviously better at moving on from things, or at least compartmentalising. Typical man, she thought.

'What was your wife like?' she asked, giving herself a little shake. 'Tell me about her… if you feel able to.'

'Mmm…'

'Only if you feel like it.' She shifted on her chair. 'If it's too much, I'm sorry.'

'No, no, it's fine.' A cloud seemed to pass across his eyes. 'She was lovely. A brilliant mum. Funny, kind. She didn't deserve…'

'Were you together long?'

'Only four years. She was my second wife.'

'Oh, I see.'

'Yeah, my first wife and I were divorced.'

'Ah, okay. So did you have children first time around?'

'Nope. Just the one. Just Harry.' His voice caught on his son's name.

'So how did you meet? Work or…?'

He looked up at her. 'You won't like this.'

'Ah now, you don't know what I like or don't like.'

'I've got a good idea of the kind of person you are.' He pursed his lips and gently tapped the table with one hand. Then he said, 'I was with her when I was still married. Not my proudest moment. My wife found out and I chose Helen. The divorce was messy but at least there were no kids involved.'

'Jesus, I bet it was.' She sat back on her chair and studied him, frowning.

'So have you ever done that?'

'Done what?'

'Been unfaithful.'

She shook her head. 'Well, in college there was a lot of temptation, but my conscience always kicked in. I have a hell of a conscience. Can't live with guilt – of any kind. It eats me up. Anyway, before all this, it was probably my greatest fear – being cheated on.'

'Surely there are worse things than that?'

'Not for me. It's so cruel. That casual disregard for someone's feelings. The damage you're inflicting but you do it anyway and somehow justify it to yourself. To be with someone who you believe loves you and they do something like that? I can't get my head round it.'

'Yeah, okay.' He shrugged. 'Well, love's complicated. You can't help who you fall for.'

'That's no excuse. Your partner deserves to know – otherwise they're just living a lie. It's massively unfair to them.'

'I can't argue with any of that.' He looked over at the fire.

She sighed. 'Sure what is love really? It's different for everyone.'

'What do you mean?' He turned back towards her.

'Well, isn't it mostly chemicals? Dopamine and oxytocin and all that. We all have different biochemistry, so we all react differently.'

'Do you really believe that?' he said, sitting back and folding his arms.

'Yep. Pretty much. Maybe real love is what survives when the chemicals are spent. When those wild feelings you have when you first fall for someone are all gone, that's the chemicals burning out. But you know it's the real thing if you *still* love them after that. And they *still* love you. You know each other inside out. It's a deeper bond, a far more solid thing.'

'You sound like you know what you're talking about,' Marcus said, a bemused smile playing about his mouth.

'It's like you know that even if you never slept with them again for the rest of your life, you'd still feel a deep and enduring connection with them.' She pressed on, getting into her stride. 'Like there's a synchronicity of being.'

'Wow! *Synchronicity of being*. Holy shit, what's that when it's at home?' He laughed suddenly.

'Well, I think that's proper love,' she said, feeling a little affronted. 'A love that's more real. More resilient. Less fickle. Love without the mess and drama of all that initial chemistry.'

'Like finding a soulmate,' he said.

'I guess so, yeah.' She smiled weakly, suddenly self-conscious about drifting into intensity about such an intimate subject.

'And do you have that with your husband?' Marcus asked. 'What's his name – James, Jack. Was he your soulmate?'

'Johnny! *Is* my soulmate, not *was*.' She frowned at him. 'Yeah. I mean there are moments. Having kids changes things, but yeah, we're soulmates. And lovers, I might add, in case there's any doubt.' She laughed and could feel herself blush. She took a sip of water.

He looked down, suddenly serious again, and brushed something off his jeans. 'I know what I've lost. I've had plenty of time alone to think about all this. There were a few days where I had a rope and a tree and I thought about throwing in the towel.'

'What stopped you?' she asked softly.

'I don't know. Maybe there's still a spark in here.' He patted his chest. Then he leaned back in the chair and smiled at her. 'I'm glad I met you though. It's been interesting. You're smart. I like that.'

She looked away, not sure what to think and wary of flattery. She was enjoying the conversation too. He was articulate, sensitive, good company. They got on well. What were the odds of finding someone on the same wavelength in the middle of all this? Suddenly the old survival instinct kicked in again. He was good company and *had a gun*, she reminded herself.

'Well, it's been good to meet you too,' she said.

She got up and took the dishes to the sink to wash them. He poked the fire and put another log on. Then she opened another tin of tuna and gave it to the dog.

'I'd better go now,' she said.

'Really? But the weather hasn't changed,' he said. 'Why not wait for it to ease up a bit.'

'I prefer it when it's raining. It's less likely that people will be out on the roads.'

'But I said I'd help you find a charger.'

She hesitated. 'Yeah, thank you, but you know what… I'll be okay. I'll find one on the way.'

He stood up and put one hand on the mantelpiece. 'Has something happened?'

'No, not at all. I just need to keep going. They'll be waiting for me at the lake house…'

It crossed her mind to ask him to come with her. But to do that would be tantamount to saying that she trusted him and she still wasn't sure. She couldn't trust anyone, even someone who had provided shelter for the night and helped her find food. All of a sudden she wondered if he would let her leave. It might bring out the worst in him and he'd reveal his true colours. Fear crept back in.

'Sure you'll be fine without me. You have the rifle now,' she said, keeping things light.

'Ha! But it's not me I'm worried about.'

'I have the dog. And I've got this far.'

'Yeah, but we've done far better together over the past day than we ever did on our own.'

'Well you never know who you'll meet down the line.' She grinned unconvincingly at him.

'For the record, you were lucky to meet me. It's wild out there.'

'Lucky, was I?' She raised one eyebrow. 'Sure we might meet again in better times,' she added, knowing full well what he meant.

He walked away from her and stared out across the front garden through the window. 'The rain's so heavy. It hasn't let up. You might get stuck in the floods.'

The dog trotted up to him and stood by his leg.

She called him back quickly. 'Thanks. Thanks for everything.'

He turned and looked at her, a strange expression on his face that she couldn't quite read. 'Yeah, it was good to meet you and your dog... Listen, I need to say this. I think you're making a big mistake. You're not going to be okay on your own. People are safer together.'

'I'm driving to the lake house,' she said firmly, reaching for her coat and keeping an eye on where he had left the gun. 'On my own.'

'But how do you know that's where your family are?' he said.

'It's our backup plan. They're already there. I know it.'

There was a flicker of frustration around his eyes. 'Okay, well just think about it for a second. What if they're somewhere south, near the city, because it was the only direction they could travel? Or because that's the direction they think you've gone? Or something else has happened. You can't know for sure. At least if you listen to your phone messages, if there are any, it will rule some options out... or in. You need to remember your fuel supply too. You can't drive aimlessly in one direction when they're still holed up at your house outside Dublin. You won't make it. And it's too unstable out there for you to survive on your own.'

She thought about what he said for a moment. She didn't like admitting it, but he did have a point. 'So you do think they might still be alive! That's not what you were saying earlier.'

'I'm simply hypothesising,' he said.

'Okay, I'll spend the next hour or so looking for a charger and take it from there. I've managed by myself so far. It won't rain forever.'

'So what way will you go?'

'Probably back to that junction we were at this morning and see what's further along the road to the left. If there are more houses, there might be cars with chargers in them.'

'Okay,' he said quietly, shaking his head. He looked away, then glanced back.

She caught his eye and smiled, then turned and slipped out the back door into the pouring rain, the dog trotting at her heels.

She was hyperalert to every sound. Would he try to prevent her from leaving? Part of her expected to feel the barrel of the gun in the small of her back. But there was nothing and while she felt relieved, there was also a tinge of disappointment. Did he not like her? *Oh for God's sake, where did that thought come from!?* She ran round to the jeep at the side of the house and jumped in the driver's side. The dog leapt across to the passenger seat, soaking the upholstery.

She started the engine and pulled out of the driveway, checking the mirrors for him behind her. Nothing.

She looked back at the house once more before edging forwards and saw his silhouette at the window. She thought about waving but didn't. He had let her go without protest, without violence. She suddenly felt guilty… and stupid. He hadn't been any threat to her at all and now she'd thrown away the best chance she had of keeping safe until she found her family. She couldn't go back, she'd be mortified to tell him she'd changed her mind. *It's just survival. Nothing personal. Just assessing the risks and staying alive.*

Johnny wouldn't have trusted him an inch. Leaving was the right thing to do. But that was Johnny...

She turned on the heater which blasted warm air up onto the windscreen, slowly drying off the condensation, while the wipers worked frantically on the outside to clear small, temporary arcs of visibility through the deluge. She couldn't ever remember rain quite like this. The devastating flash floods of the previous years had come in waves, but this felt more sustained, persistent. Maybe because she was driving in the middle of it, outside the insulated protection of a house. The roads were even more flooded than they had been earlier that day, but the jeep was still able to plough on.

She pushed Marcus to the back of her mind and tried to focus instead on finding a charger for her phone. But lurid scenes from the house with the dead baby gate crashed her thoughts – the pale blue crocheted hat lying mid-stitch, the marmalade-coloured blanket, the clean, clear water swirling endlessly down the plug hole, the bone-dry stillness.

She started humming to herself, random notes vibrating through the air. The dog cocked his head at her. Eventually she would have to sit still and confront what she had seen that morning so it could move through her. The tap was probably still running in the sink, she thought, and immediately felt annoyed with herself for being bothered by something so prosaic. It wasn't as if they were going to run out of water any time soon.

When she reached the T-junction, she turned left and drove on. She had felt far more optimistic and confident back at his house. Now that she was alone and back on the road, anxiety was beginning to creep back into her bones. Thoughts of him kept intruding. Flashes of his face, him washing cups, slowly and methodically, at the sink, filling the bath with hot water for her as though he had known her all his life, the smell of him when he had pulled her close at the dead people's house. Suddenly a snapshot popped into her head: her mother in a white wool hat driving her to the train station, her rucksack packed for the city. She'd pressed money into her hand for a taxi home. *Don't walk the streets,* she'd said, tight with worry. *Better safe than sorry.* Better safe than sorry. She said the words aloud and repeated them like a mantra.

She drove on for a while, Brin curled up in the passenger footwell, oblivious to the churning water underneath as they powered along the flooded road. They passed once-luminous, vibrant homes, now nondescript, soulless buildings. At the end of each driveway she slowed to a crawl and stood up, looking for a flash of bright colours, but none had cars – at least, none that she could see from the road. The idea of checking for chargers in abandoned vehicles brought a cold dread – she didn't want to see anything like what she'd encountered that morning ever again – but she'd do it if it meant she could have contact with her family again.

Her thoughts drifted to Lila and how much the little girl loved Brin. The feeling was mutual, judging by the way the dog protected her when they were out exploring together. Just then, she spotted a skein of migrating geese flying low under the heavy clouds in the distance. How wonderful, she thought, mesmerised by their tight formation. But as it got closer, she realised with a quickening sense of dread that this was no feat of nature. The object, with its red light underneath zigzagged through the air towards her, then hovered just above, keeping pace with her vehicle.

'Oh Jesus,' she said aloud.

A drone. That meant people. People with a power supply or generator. Organised people who hunted from the air.

She accelerated, racing through the water and up the hill, taking the bend with reckless speed. She had to lose it, outrun its flight range. It was too small to be a military drone, so its range was probably about five kilometres. She had hired one years ago to make a slick video for a charity run. This one must be waterproofed in some way to protect the electronics.

She kept going, rattling along the country road, checking her mirrors for anything coming up behind her. But right around the next corner, she was confronted by a black car with raised suspension angled across the road. Three men in drenched army fatigues and black bomber jackets leaned against the vehicle, grinning. A pack of what appeared to be Rottweilers sat obediently at their feet.

She slammed on the brakes, looking for escape routes, but the ditches were waterlogged, and the hedges thick and impenetrable. She looked at them through the windscreen, revving the engine nervously with her foot. The dog jumped up onto the seat, growling softly, his hackles raised. She would have no time to turn on the narrow road. What about offering them food in return for a free pass along the road? That would only work if they were content to leave it at that. Most men wanted more. Could Brin take down all three… and their dogs? No way. She couldn't expect that of him. She sat there, the engine idling, rain bouncing off the bonnet, watching them laughing and elbowing each other as they stared at her through the pouring rain, sharing some kind of joke. She put her hand on the dog and felt the heat of his body through his fur.

The tallest man started to walk towards her with the kind of soldier-swagger she'd seen in war movies. The other two followed close behind, one of them holding something at his side. The tall man went round to the driver's side and smiled at her through the glass, water dripping off his face and nose. A second appeared at the passenger window. The dog hurled himself at him, barking and snarling. The third man stood a few metres in front of the bonnet, his legs apart, and, after tossing away a cigarette, slowly raised a crossbow and aimed it at her. Aren't they illegal, she thought absurdly. She rolled down her window a couple of centimetres.

'Hey gorgeous!' the tall man said. 'Just you and your little dog?'

'No, my people are behind me,' she said assertively, trying to sound confident.

'*My people!*' He laughed. 'I don't see no one.' He took a step closer.

'Please, stay back, for your own sake. I'm sick,' she said. 'I have a fever. No idea what it is.'

'You don't look sick. In fact, you look *very* healthy to me.' He flicked out his tongue and licked his lips. He looked like a snake. 'What do you think?' he called across the bonnet to the one with the crossbow. 'You think she looks sick?'

His mate shook his head and grinned.

'So here's the deal,' the tall one shouted. 'You'll step out and lock your dog in the jeep. If you let him loose, we'll shoot him.'

She was now frozen with terror. All her faux bravado falling away. There would be no negotiating with this man. He was going to do whatever he wanted.

'I have food in the boot. Just take it, it's yours,' she said, her voice high-pitched, constricted.

'Well now, you're a very, *very* generous woman. So what else can you do for me?' His tongue slipped out from between his teeth again; he seemed to have trouble controlling it.

Brin was barking wildly inside the jeep and now the Rottweilers had joined in, snarling and slavering in front of them.

He pulled a cable tie and a length of green paracord from the pocket of his bomber jacket.

'Out!' he roared suddenly. 'Out, or you and the dog get it.'

Her foot hovered over the accelerator; she gripped the steering wheel, her knuckles white with fear; her mind raced, scrambling for a miracle. She turned and looked straight at him. His teeth were straight and cosmetically white; he was clean-shaven, well-fed and wearing clean clothes. Before the floods, he wouldn't have looked out of place in an estate agent's office or a bank. Now, his eyes were cold as steel, his face impassive. And that restless tongue, tasting the air, savouring her fear.

'You're not fit to be a man,' she said suddenly, her voice deep and full of anger. 'You're a wild animal.'

He raised his eyebrows in mock surprise. 'Hear that, boys?' he shouted, laughing. 'I'm a wild animal. What does that make you motherfuckers?'

They grinned and the one with the crossbow switched target from her to the dog who was now out of his mind with fury. She had never seen Brin like this before. But then she'd never been in this situation before. She momentarily thought of Marcus. There is no cavalry, no white horse, she told herself, then she stamped down hard on the accelerator.

The jeep surged forward, straight at the man with the crossbow. He fired a bolt which punched a hole in the jeep's windscreen and whizzed past her shoulder. But she kept going and rammed the front fender of the jeep into the boot of their vehicle, thrusting it forward with a juddering screech. Glancing in the rear-view mirror, she saw the men sprinting after her, their dogs hurling themselves at the wheels of the jeep. She crunched the gearstick into reverse and shot backwards, narrowly missing one of the men. Then back in first gear, she ploughed into the boot of their car again, this time powering through the narrow gap between it and the edge of the road. The jeep lurched to the right, tipping into the flooded ditch, but a quick yank on the steering wheel brought her back up onto the road again. She heard another bolt from the crossbow striking the jeep. Brin had slammed himself against the back window, barking like a wild dog, chest bared to the fight. In the mirror she saw the men piling into their car and turning it to go after her.

She put her foot to the floor, her heart bucking beneath her ribs. She felt elated that she had managed to bulldoze through the roadblock, but there was no time to dwell on it. Keeping an eye on her mirrors, she tore along the flooded road, the sheer force of the jeep heaving huge arcs of water over the hedges. She swung wildly to the right at a crossroads, not sure where she was, and pushed through more water, the wipers catching on the broken glass in the windscreen. Brin was quiet now on the seat beside her, but panting from the exertion. 'A full tin of tuna for you,' she muttered, wild-eyed with fear and adrenaline. He turned to look at her with his bright, trusting eyes.

She arrived at a T-junction onto a smaller road and veered right taking her in what she hoped was the direction of the cottage. There was still no sign of the men's car but the stress hormones coursing through her body powered her relentless flight. She realised she might be bringing the men to Marcus, interrupting the quiet life he had created for himself before she came along, but right now she didn't care. He had a weapon that could be used to protect her and the dog.

She drove for what seemed like a lifetime, ploughing through deep flood water caught between the overgrown hedges that lined the road. Eventually, she recognised the red-roofed barn and a signpost for the road on which she had first met him. She turned to the left and spotted the small white marker for the cul-de-sac where the death house was, the baby still in its crib. Then she took a right and found herself on the road leading back towards the cottage. Relief surged through her and she put her foot on the accelerator, desperate for the solace of safety. The road disappeared behind her in a spray of muddy water kicked up by the wheels and thick exhaust fumes.

Then suddenly she saw a dark shape in front of her wading shin-deep through the rain. She cried out when she saw the straps of the rucksack on his shoulders. Marcus stopped walking when he saw her approach and waited for her to reach him. She pulled up and reached over to fling open the passenger door.

'Get in,' she shouted in a voice she didn't recognise. 'Brin, stay. It's okay.' She held onto the dog's collar and pushed him down into the footwell.

Marcus climbed up onto the seat. Brin let out a long, low growl, then sniffed Marcus's legs and settled down. Marcus took the rifle out from under his coat and placed it muzzle down on the floor, the forestock leaning against his leg. Never had she felt more relieved to see a gun.

'How close behind? How many?' he asked, looking at her intensely.

'Oh God, three of them. I don't know how close they are. They have dogs – Rottweilers I think – and a bloody crossbow. They…' Her voice caught in her throat. 'There's just no good in them. I had to crash through.'

'Are they mobile?' His expression had hardened: his eyes were dark and alert, his jaw tense.

'Yes, they have a car of some kind. I think it's modified to get through the water. I hit the back of it, but it might still be functional. They were turning to chase me. That was maybe ten minutes ago.' Her chest was on fire and she felt like crying.

'Okay, back to the house and up the side. We need to hide the jeep and stay low until it's quiet. They'd probably been around before but just hadn't found the cottage.'

She drove on, gripping the wheel tightly to stop herself from shaking. 'You were right about being alone out there,' she said. 'I should have known. So stupid… Jesus, they weren't even that far away.'

He nodded and didn't say anything to placate her or try to make her feel better.

'Where were you going?' she asked.

He checked his side mirror and turned to look through the rear window. 'I was walking back to the house we were at this morning.'

'Why?'

'To try and start that car out the back. I just needed to find the keys and transfer some fuel from an old genny behind the house.'

'And then what?'

'I was going to follow you, see how far I could get. Just in case there was a roadblock or trouble.'

She turned to look at him for a second. 'It would have been too late,' she said quietly, feeling strangely flattered.

'Yes, it would.'

'You can say "I told you so" if you want.'

'I'm not like that.'

'Okay.'

Through the rain and the cracks in the windscreen she saw the familiar line of trees and thick spread of ivy that led to the cottage. Pulling to the right, she shot through the gateway and buried the jeep nose-first down the dark side of the house and cut the engine.

Marcus jumped out, taking the rifle with him, and set to work, quickly dragging the branches he'd cut earlier back over the roof of the jeep and propping them upright against the boot and sides. Her legs crumpled beneath her as soon as she stepped out of the vehicle and she grabbed hold of the doorframe to steady herself as she took long deep breaths. He stopped for a moment to look at her, his eyes intense and focused.

'They'll hunt you now along the roads,' he said, his voice steady, unsentimental.

'I know. Please tell me you know how to use that gun.'

'Yeah, a little. I spent a weekend with a park ranger friend of mine years ago.'

'Doing what?'

'Culling deer.'

'Did you kill any?'

'No.'

'Please tell me you did.'

'Okay, I got one.'

'Is that the truth?'

'It doesn't matter. I know how to use it.' He arranged the last of the branches over the front grill, slung his rucksack over his shoulder and picked up the rifle. 'Let's go,' he said.

'Wait!' She froze, the rain dripping off her face, the breath whipped out of her. She cocked her head to one side, straining to hear through the rain. She heard a thin, high-pitched whine high above their heads, then spotted the red 'eye' hovering just beneath the dark clouds.

'It's their drone!' she whispered frantically.

'They have a drone? You could have mentioned that earlier!'

'Jesus,' she said, suddenly defensive despite her fear, 'there was a lot going on!'

He lifted the rifle and pulled the bolt back hard. Squinting through the sight, he pointed the muzzle skyward and squeezed the trigger with his forefinger. There was a loud crack and seconds later, the drone tumbled out of the sky and crashed into the trees at the front of the garden.

'We need to get inside,' she said, noticing a flicker of satisfaction on his face.

'Yep, they'll know we're here now.'

She called the dog who had been sniffing around the wheels of the jeep. He bounded towards her, shaking the water off his coat.

They ran around the back and went into the house. The room was exactly as they had left it. Marcus pulled off his coat and tossed it on the floor near the fireplace. They stood in the semi-darkness, silent and still, waiting to see what would happen next.

'Will you be able to… take them…?' she asked, her voice barely above a whisper. 'If you have to?'

'Yeah.' He pushed the sleeves of his jumper up over his elbows.

'They may not find us,' she said with little conviction. 'Anything I can do?'

'Go to the drawer and get a kitchen knife.'
'What?… I don't know if I'd be able to…'
'You will if you have to.'

The low steady sound of an approaching car was almost imperceptible at first, but it grew louder and louder and then stopped abruptly. Marcus peered out the window.

'This is it,' he said under his breath, stepping back to raise the gun.

The image of her daughter's face rose in Sara's mind. Beautiful Lila, all pink-cheeked and freckled from long summer days on the beach; the feel of her little girl's arms tight around her neck at bedtime; the warm sweet smell of her first thing in the morning

The men called out to each other at the end of the driveway as though they wanted to announce themselves. Brin began to bark loudly. She shushed him sharply, tugged at his collar, and he slunk down beside her feet. Marcus knelt on the floor at the window, raised the rifle butt to his shoulder and squinted through the sights. She could hear the men's boots crunching on the overgrown gravel. Their sudden laughter and a celebratory whoop suggested that they'd found the jeep.

'Can you see them?' she whispered.
'Not anymore.'

Then there was the creak of the back door, a rush of cold air, and suddenly a man was standing in the room, a crossbow levelled at her head. Where had he come from?

Brin leapt at him, front legs up, teeth bared. The bolt caught him mid-flight, piercing his chest. He cried out like a child and hit the floor with a thud. Sounds spilled from her that she'd never heard before and she rushed to him, taking his lovely soft head in her hands. A shot rang out. She looked up and saw the man with the crossbow down on his knees, blood gushing from a bullet hole in his throat. As she watched, a second shot punched into his temple and he finally keeled over.

A woman was screaming, but she wasn't sure where it was coming from. *Is it me? Maybe it's me...* There was more shouting, another shot and the sound of splintering glass. Running footsteps on the gravel, an engine revving, a third shot; the sound of the engine faded into the distance. There was a soft whine and then it fell silent, except for the ringing in her ears.

Sara buried her face in the warm fur of Brin's neck, her fingers sticky from the wound in his chest, her keening wail tearing apart the silence.

She heard footsteps behind her, then a comforting arm was around her shoulders and a coat placed gently over Brin. After a few minutes she lay down beside him, her head on his body, and closed her eyes to the world, stroking the dog's still-warm paws with her thumb. She didn't care that a dead man lay only feet away. She didn't care much about anything. She stayed like that for a while.

'It's done,' Marcus said sometime later, as he washed his hands at the kitchen sink.

'Oh?' she whispered, faintly.

'I've a place dug for Brin.'

'And the man?'

'Down the bottom of a ditch at the back. It's a good enough grave.'

He knelt in front of her and, lifting her chin gently with his forefinger, looked her straight in the eye.

'We have to leave,' he said. 'I heard them calling for him, then shouting that they'd be back. They'll be better prepared next time now they know we've a gun.'

He stood up and offered her his hand. She gripped his wrist and allowed him to pull her to her feet. He carefully tucked the coat around the dog and lifted him off the ground, staggering a little under his weight. She trailed him out to the sodden garden where he had dug a shallow trench with a rusty spade. He set Brin on the ground beside it.

'Would you like to do it?' he asked.

She nodded. Light-headed and dizzy, she knelt and placed her hands on his body for a moment, then with her throat tight and aching, she rolled him into the grave. The coat peeled off and he landed at the bottom, legs akimbo, head back. Marcus got to work, covering him quickly with the wet, heavy soil and sealing the top with thick, square-cut sods. Then he found a plank of white painted wood and stuck it in deep to mark the spot. They stood there in silence for a few moments.

'Sorry for your loss,' he eventually said, somewhat clumsily.

She nodded.

'I'm going to put my share of the food back in the jeep,' he said. 'We move together now, okay?'

'Okay.'

'Let's go. Pack up.'

'Yeah.' She had run out of options. Trusting Marcus was no longer a choice; it was an imperative. Everything was different now.

They worked together quickly and silently, packing as much as they could into the jeep before pulling out of the driveway and leaving the cottage for the last time.

4

The next morning, she awoke inside the jeep, covered in blankets taken from the house. Marcus was in the front cab. The rain seemed to have eased, and the dark sky was slowly pinking to the east. Low, thin fog hovered like gossamer above the ground.

She had been lying awake for a while, ignoring the urge to pee, when she felt a blast of sharp, brittle air and heard him close the cab door behind him. Her eyes strained to see him through the window as he moved towards a thicket of trees that banked the low-lying floods. Absentmindedly she thought about feeding the dog, then remembered with a cold lurch that he was gone. The world felt like a smaller place and somehow more fragile.

The loss of Brin compounded her barely suppressed panic that the same fate had befallen her children. For the first time she allowed herself to consider the idea that they might not have survived, that everything was much worse than she imagined. Were the events of the last two days the new normal now? She sat up and wept, ostensibly for Brin, but also for her children, for her husband, for the state of the world, for the planet. She cried for what seemed a long, long time until her throat hurt and her eyes puffed up to fill her face.

Marcus eventually returned and started pottering about, the edges of him blurred by the condensation inside the jeep and the frost on the glass outside.

She pulled a blanket over her head to block out the daylight and take comfort in the muffled dark. She couldn't think straight. The plans that used to fill her thoughts were now jumbled and rudderless. She heard the heavy clunk of the door latch, and a belt of cold air swept in as he opened the boot and peered in at her.

She pulled the blanket off her head and looked at him. He was rubbing his hands together vigorously and was wearing his hat pulled down over his ears. He regarded her as though she were something to be wary of.

'Hey,' he said gently. 'I'm going to light a small fire. Boil some water to drink. Maybe heat up some beans in a tin.' He said 'maybe' as though he was considering it, though she knew him well enough now to know he'd already decided.

She shrugged and stared out past him into the frost-covered field. The weather had changed. He left the door of the jeep slightly ajar and walked away. Before long the faint smell of woodsmoke curled in through the gap and she heard the crackling of sticks. Sighing, she pulled on her boots. They were wet and very cold.

She clambered out and crouched down beside the fire, warming her hands.

'Thank you,' she said.

He nodded. 'Sleep, okay?'

'Nah, not really. Bad dreams. Lots of them. You?'

'It's not comfortable up there.' He nodded towards the cab of the jeep.

'Yeah, we can swap tonight. I don't care really.'

'Let's try to find another house instead.'

'Will the roads not be badly flooded up ahead? We definitely can't go back.'

He shrugged. 'I'm going to walk across some of the fields,' he said, taking out his knife and cleaning the blade with a dirty rag. 'See what I can find. There's bound to be an abandoned building of some kind out there.' He arced his arm in the general direction of the fields behind.

'Yeah, good idea,' she said flatly. 'Hey, I really need to… you know. Can you stay here for a bit?'

He glanced up and quickly understood. 'Sure thing.'

She walked to the other side of the jeep and, wriggling her jeans down below her knees, crouched down. Steam rose from the earth between her legs. She idly found herself thinking of her bathroom at home – the clean white tiles and underfloor heating, expensive fitted sinks and luxurious power shower, her cabinet filled with luxury nail polish and perfumes. She looked down at her hand which was holding her jeans out of the way – dirty, with chipped nails – and sighed. She shook her rear end rather than wipe herself with frozen leaves and pulled up her panties and jeans. She came back to the fire and hunkered down next to it, holding her palms up to the flames and rubbing her hands briskly.

'God, it's so cold,' she murmured.

'Yeah.'

'Hey, how are *you* doing?' she asked, suddenly remembering she wasn't the only one to have been through an ordeal. 'I'm sorry for bringing all that down on you yesterday.'

He shrugged.

She wondered what it felt like for him. He'd killed a man. She felt guilty, responsible, so God only knows how he felt.

'It is what it is,' he said eventually. 'Look, we need to make a proper plan. We can't just drift through the day.'

'Yeah, of course.'

'We also need to find diesel. There's only an hour or so left, even if we add the fuel can.'

'I suppose,' she said softy.

He looked at her again. 'I know you're not okay. Yesterday was…'

'Yeah, it was horrific. I know,' she said, cutting him off.

He cleaned out two empty tins, filled them with water, and placed them beside the fire. Removing the top of the can of beans with the ring pull, he set the can on the fire. A few minutes later, he put on a glove and quickly lifted the can from the fire and set it, sizzling, on dead leaves to cool. Then he took two spoons out of his coat pocket and handed one to her. They ate the beans quickly and drank the warmed water, cradling the tins in their hands afterwards for any remaining heat. It was barely enough but they needed to ration.

'So are you going to have a look around then?' she asked.

'Yeah, I think it's the best thing to do.'

'Well, I'll wait here until you come back.'

'You sure? Do you not think it would be better to stick together?'

'I want to watch the jeep. All we have is in it.'

'Fair enough.'

'If you leave me the gun, I'll be okay.'

He hesitated. 'Fine. I'll try not to be too long. Depends on what I find. I'll go through this field and then cross country.' He pointed west.

He took the rifle out of the jeep and propped it against the side near her. It was significant that he was leaving it with her and she was suddenly grateful for his trust. For a country where it was illegal to have a gun except with a hunting licence, they were lucky to have found it. It hadn't been very lucky for its previous owner.

She shivered and stood up. 'I can clear this up if you want to head off before it gets too bright.'

'You want me to talk you through it?' he said, nodding toward the gun.

'No, no, it's okay. I think I have it figured out.'

'Right, if I'm not back by midday, call the guards, eh?' He laughed.

She forced herself to smile, then watched him follow the ditch to the end of the field and disappear into a thicket of trees, the grass flattened in his wake. She stared at the fire for a while, warming her hands off the glowing embers, then stamped it out. She couldn't risk anyone spotting the wisps of smoke. She must stay low and watchful, alert to drones, even more so now that Brin was gone.

She went back into the jeep and rummaged around for the toilette bag Marcus had given her. She eventually found it behind the tinned foods, wedged against a side panel. It was filled with luxuries: a full carton of Tampax, a small bar of soap, a new toothbrush and a tube of toothpaste. She used the toothbrush outside for ten minutes, cleaning vigorously and rinsing her mouth out with fresh water from one of the bottles they'd brought. Afterwards, her mouth felt wonderful, so much so that her mood lightened. She took the small bar of soap and, using the ends of the warmed water left in her can, worked it up into a lather and washed her face. The scent of lavender was almost overpowering. She closed her eyes for a moment and thought of warm meadows and tall grasses swaying in a light summer breeze. But she couldn't hold it for long.

If Johnny was here, he'd hate Marcus for being the hero, the one who's protecting me. But if I hadn't met him on the road, I'd have gone on and those men would have eventually tracked me down. I'd probably be dead by now... or worse – held captive and gang-raped, the same fate for probably thousands of other women... Okay, come on now, stay positive. Think of flowers, sunlight dancing on water, rainbows, puppies... Oh, poor Brin. A sob caught the back of her throat. *I'm so tired of being out here, feeling scared and panicky. So tired of being in my own head with all these awful thoughts. I wonder if Lila and Conor are okay. I'll never forgive Johnny if hasn't kept them safe. Right, that's it. Stop with the negative thoughts this minute, Sara Casey.*

She rinsed the soap off her face as best she could, glad that the fragrance lingered on her skin, and busied herself tidying the inside of the jeep. She wiped down the surfaces and windows in the front cab with a small cloth, then took her time organising the clothes they had taken from the house into neat rolls and stacking them on some folded coats. Her handbag, now faintly ridiculous, sat atop a pile of blankets. She took out her phone and put it in the pocket of her jeans. It was the only connection she had left to her family, other than blind faith and luck, and it felt right to keep it close. Anyway, they might be able to find a charger.

She sat back in the driver's seat and pulled her coat around her shoulders, the gun by her side. She played with it for a while until she was comfortable loading and aiming it. The clock on the dashboard said 08:12, and it was exquisitely peaceful. She thought she heard sheep bleating far off in the distance. A chorus of birdsong moved in waves through the early morning air. Small grey clouds were gathering almost imperceptibly on the horizon. A light easterly wind picked up, fussing at the stiff, cold leaves on the unkempt copper beech hedge. The field behind it rolled down towards a flooded dip, the surface water of the impromptu lake remaining glassy and smooth despite the breeze.

She wondered for the first time how she might die in this new world. Probably from something ordinary like a urinary tract infection or sepsis from a cut. Returning to the relative civility of two years ago seemed impossible now. The tipping point had been well and truly passed and the collapse that followed had put them far beyond any point of immediate recovery.

There had been no blueprint for this environmental and civic disaster. No centralised emergency response plan had been drafted, let alone rehearsed. What seemed so clear now was that the rainstorms, maybe even weaponised cloud seeding, had been a distraction from other problems plaguing the world. Democracy had been rotting from the inside out for decades. The culture of hatred in the media had created a climate of distrust and paranoia, prompting ultra-libertarian foot soldiers to take the law into their own hands. The bad weather hadn't helped, of course. In the early months of the storms, people struggled to maintain that sense of community spirit and cooperation they needed to survive in a time of crisis, and they eventually fell into a political vacuum. Now they were reduced to their base instincts in order to survive. Whatever came next would either have to be built from the remnants of the old system, or created anew, from scratch, some kind of society where good governance and security nurtured strong leadership and the restoration of order. It was going to take a long time to bounce back from this, and even then the world would be utterly different.

She sighed and pressed her head back hard against the headrest, her mind running hot. *God, we're all so stupid, assuming someone else would sort it out. There we were, ordering stuff online we didn't need, believing we were keeping the economy running. I was as bad as everyone else. Who cares about pink champagne nail varnish or two-hour delivery times. I can't believe I bought into all that bullshit! Meanwhile, the world melted and drowned. Serves us right.*

She closed her eyes and tucked her hands between her legs to warm them, her thoughts shifting from memory to memory until sleep moved in and carried her to a still, empty place.

The sound of hailstones bouncing off the roof and windscreen woke her. A dark, heavy sky had moved in, and for a moment she thought it was nighttime. She glanced at the clock – 11:37. He had been gone for hours. She stretched and rolled down the window a bit to clear the condensation. Sleet hurled itself through the gap, landing on her face and hair before melting quickly.

She jumped out of the jeep, bringing the gun with her, and looked across the field. There was no sign of him. She listened long and hard, her breath billowing out in front of her, clouds of white into the grey. Everything was still. Half an hour passed and she grew stiff and very cold despite pacing up and down. Then bursting through the silence came the mournful, eerie moan of what sounded like a metal door scraping heavily on its hinges. It came from the direction she had seen him walk towards. Her hand tightened around the gun and she forgot to breathe as she stood rigid and alert. Silence.

It might have been him, closing the door of a farm building. Or it might be other people lurking in that direction. She decided at that point that he was late.

A pale sun moved slowly across the sky between drifting showers, casting small shafts of light before fading behind bands of skittering sleety rain. Keeping a close eye on the landscape around her, she tramped the length of the hedge to keep warm, the rifle slung low beneath her jacket. Under the cover of trees, she practised releasing the safety and peering through the crosshairs, aiming at random branches and stones near the ditches. A robin flitted around the bottom of a hedgerow and much to her dismay, she caught herself training her aim on him. She immediately swung the muzzle back towards a rock protruding from a mossy bank.

Time passed slowly, and the sleet came and went. She stayed within range of the jeep, moving around to stay warm, but was fixated on the corner of the field where she had last seen him. Her feet were wet and her legs were numb all the way up to her knees. She thought about getting the fire going again but changed her mind. Where the hell was he?

A beautiful auburn fox stood on the brow of a hillock, sniffing the cold air, then vanished as quickly as it had appeared. A murmuration of starlings whirred through the air above her, descending in a thick flurry on the powerlines along the road, chattering and whistling to each other in glorious chorus. She glanced in at the clock in the jeep – 13:05 – and stared out across the field. The light would fade fast in the afternoon and he would need to get back soon. Then she heard that sound again, the grinding abrasion of metal on metal. There was a clunk and then silence.

New bonds of attachment to him pricked her conscience and she alternated between deciding to leave him and drive on alone and worrying about what trouble he might be in. She paced, vexed and indecisive, for another hour, then locked the jeep, lifted the gun and set out in the direction he had gone.

It was at times like these, when she felt on edge and fearful, that she found herself contrasting her current situation with the abundant, easy life she had lived before. All the anxiety she'd experienced as she'd worried about what to wear for cocktails at seven, or the irritation she'd felt at having to sort through piles of laundry instead of working on a work presentation, now seemed so shallow and petty. She'd lived a life of extraordinary privilege. So to find herself here, starving and swallowing blind panic, desperate to see her children, was a living nightmare. Never had she thought she'd feel so grateful for a fire, tinned fruit and a wash in a derelict cottage.

She thought it would be hard to follow him, but he had left deep boot marks in the ground that were easy to see and the grass was still partially flattened. He had used his hatchet to work through a thin line of sally trees and he'd kicked down the wire-mesh fence that ran behind them. Once in the next field, she traced him to a gate diagonally opposite, which brought her to another long meadow. She walked fast and low, the weight of the rifle under her jacket making her arm ache.

The sky seemed to be clearing from the south; although the wind had dropped slightly, it was still cold. A lone buzzard lifted from the long grass and disappeared into the neighbouring field. The body of a cow lay half-submerged in a ditch nearby, its jutting hip bones and stripped flanks stark against the black water.

She clambered over a low mossy drystone wall to a tilled field that had been left untended. She stopped and scanned the expanse of stubble and weeds and glimpsed a small building with a slate roof through the bushes. Hugging the perimeter of the field, she walked quickly towards it, her boots sinking into the soft, wet earth as she followed old machine tracks, the remnants of a long-ago harvest.

There was something familiar about the building. She studied the ground carefully. Several sets of boot prints converged along this stretch. Other people had used this field, not just Marcus. Crouching down, she shuffled along the ditch, her heart beating fast. She had broken out in a sweat now. It was so very quiet.

A gap in the hedge at the far side allowed her to step down onto a thick branch above the water and peer through. The building turned out to be an old country schoolhouse; it had its own small car park, and the children's playground was still marked out in faded paint for hopscotch and snakes and ladders. Two burnt-out cars sat by the front wall as if someone had parked them there, and broken glass glittered on the ground. A long, steel shipping container stood at the back of the building, probably once used for equipment and storage. Straining her ears for the sound of voices or movement, she heard nothing – just the trill of blackbirds and the gentle rustle of dead leaves.

She wriggled down through the gap and sat on the branch, dangling her legs above the ditch water. Maybe it was the men's base – the men with the drone, the men who had killed Brin. She swallowed hard. They might be holding Marcus captive, torturing him to find out her whereabouts. Her imagination ran wild for a moment until she calmed down enough to notice that their souped-up car wasn't there and there was no sign of their dogs.

She could neither pluck up the courage to approach the container nor return to the jeep and leave Marcus to his fate. Sure he might have already got back using a different route, she argued with herself. In a state of suspended indecision, she waited, picking stubs of bark off the branches and fidgeting with the safety catch on the rifle. A fat rat slunk along the waterline and disappeared; a cloud of midges gathered above her head. Nothing happened. She thought about the jeep sitting back there, unguarded. Then she tried to remember, for the umpteenth time, when she had last seen the children. She had been rushing to collect the jeep and Johnny had set them to work packing up their belongings. So it hadn't been 'goodbye' – more like an 'I'll be back in a few minutes' type of conversation. Not much for her to hold onto.

What sounded like a squeaky bolt being opened or closed rang out through the stillness. She sat up, stiff and alert, watching for movement. The door of the container swung open, the noise unmistakably the same as she had heard earlier. A man emerged, followed by a woman waddling along in a voluminous dress and short blue puffer jacket that lay open, revealing her huge belly. Leaving the door to the container slightly ajar, the man helped the woman around the side of the container and they disappeared.

Sara scrambled to stand up on the branch she'd been sitting on, but she could see no more from there. She would have to get closer. Clutching the gun tightly and taking a deep breath, she leapt from the branch across the ditch and into the field next to the school. Her heart was racing. Once she'd got her balance, she released the safety catch on the gun and began to walk forwards.

Suddenly she heard the sound of children talking in soft high voices. She shook her head. Had she imagined it? Was her mind playing tricks on her. But then she heard a deeper voice, a man's voice, talking, shushing them. A second man spoke. She immediately recognised Marcus's voice.

She kept walking, all the while training the barrel of the gun on the container, clambering over a low wall that separated the field from the school and carrying on into the centre of the schoolyard. Just then, the woman re-emerged from the side of the container and, eyes bulging with fear and shock, she let out a strangled wail. The man came running up behind her and stopped dead when he saw Sara. Fear lined their faces.

'Hey, I'm just looking for someone,' Sara shouted. 'I don't care about you.'

The man stepped in front of the woman, his hands raised. The woman had started to shake uncontrollably and she clung to his back, peering over his shoulder.

'We have two children in there,' she cried out, her voice breaking.

'Don't come no further now,' the man shouted.

'Listen, I'm a mother myself,' Sara said. 'I've no interest in harming anyone. I'm just looking for a man that I'm travelling with. He's tall, fair hair, beard.' She caught movement out of the corner of her eye and swung the barrel of the gun to the container door, then back to the couple. 'You can tell whoever's in there to come out. Not the children. If you don't show yourself, I'll have to go in myself. I don't want to scare your kids, okay?'

Had she really said that? It was like she was acting in a badly directed movie. She took a step forward.

'It's my brother,' the man said. 'Tony, out ye get.'

Tony stepped out, his face worn and tired. 'Your friend's inside,' he said. 'He's told us all about you.'

'Bring him out so,' Sara said sharply.

'He's free to come and go whenever he wants,' Tony said.

The woman stepped out from behind the other man. 'I'm going inside to my children,' she said, her voice shaking. She had stopped crying but she was still shivering violently from the shock.

'Okay, fine. You two stay,' Sara said, pointing the rifle first at Tony, then at the other man.

Just then, Marcus stepped out onto the gravel, grinning at her from under his hat. 'Hey,' he said. His eyes were twinkling.

She suddenly felt ridiculous, standing there holding the gun as if she knew what she was doing. She lowered it a little.

'You okay?' she asked tightly.

'Yeah, we were just getting to know each other. Then you turned up.'

'You're bloody late!' she snapped, then instantly felt foolish and angry.

A child's head appeared at the door of the container and was swiftly pulled back out of sight.

'They thought I was one of the lads with the drone,' he said. 'I was telling them that we took it down, along with one of their crew. Then we got talking. Took a while to get things settled.'

'They've us tormented,' said the man. 'We've been hiding out here for months and my wife can't take much more of it. I'm Paul by the way.' He stepped forward, his hand outstretched. When Sara didn't move he stuffed it back in his pocket, reddening slightly.

'Okay,' she said, lowering the rifle. 'When did you see them last?'

'Maybe two weeks ago. What's your name?'

'Doesn't matter. When's she due?' Sara gestured towards the container with the gun.

'Any day now.'

'It's not her first, is it?'

'No, third.'

'Jesus.'

Paul nodded, saying nothing.

Sara glanced at Marcus; he seemed utterly unperturbed. 'Okay, time to go,' she said, staring at him hard.

'Sure. Though you might want to wait a bit.'

'Why?'

'I'm in the middle of a bit of horse-trading.'

'What do you mean?'

'They have something you were hoping to find – something to power up that phone of yours.'

'Oh!' She felt momentarily confused. She really wanted to put the gun down now but the idea of it made her feel vulnerable.

'So what do they want in return?' she asked.

'We have some food we can offer.'

'We don't have much to spare.'

'Do you want the charger or not?' Marcus said impatiently.

'Okay, okay.' She bristled at his tone. 'Can you bring the charger out and show us?' she said, hardly believing it was a possibility.

Tony disappeared back into the container, then reappeared with a white cable in his hand. 'It works. You have my word. When the two cars there were working, we ran the phone off them, but there was a fire…'

He handed the cable to Marcus who inspected it. 'Yep, looks good,' he said.

'Okay, we have some tins of fish and beans, fresh apples – your kids and their mother will need them most,' Sara said.

'How many tins can we have?' Tony asked.

'We can spare maybe ten fish, five beans.' Sara glanced at Marcus. He was watching her with renewed interest. She felt suddenly conscious that she was bargaining without his agreement on their shared resources. She'd have been furious if he'd done that to her. 'One of you will have to come back with us,' she added.

'I'll go,' Tony said. 'You stay with Siobhan and the kids, Paul, just in case she has that baby with the shock, or these folks act up and leave me dead in a ditch. You can put that away, you know.' He nodded towards the gun. 'There'll be no trouble here.'

She lowered the muzzle, but still couldn't fully relax. 'We're not far away,' she said. 'You won't be more than a couple of hours. When was the last time you used your phone?'

'Ahhhh, a good while back now. Hard to keep track of time out here.'

'So what's going on out there in the big bad world?' she asked. 'Is there any sign of things getting better?'

Tony shook his head. 'Nope. It's all gone to hell.'

'What, everywhere?'

'Yep,' Paul said, joining in. 'Well, most of Europe and ourselves. That's all we know.'

'Any talk of Dublin? The government or the Defence Forces?'

'Ha! You must be joking,' he replied. 'It's hard to tell what's old army and what's the new lot. A few video shorts of the streets. Lots of fires. The hospitals not coping, from what I can tell. Lots of burnings on the roofs of apartment buildings – cremations we reckon. But what's true and what isn't is anyone's guess…' He trailed off.

Sara's heart sank. 'Before we go, can I talk to your wife… Siobhan, is that her name?'

'Why?'

'I want to check she's okay and say sorry for frightening her- and the kids.'

Paul raised his eyebrows. 'She mightn't want that.'

'Well, can I just try. I won't be long.'

He hesitated, looking her up and down. 'Yeah, okay but get rid of *that* first.' He looked at the gun.

Sara nodded and as she handed the rifle to Marcus, their eyes met. His seemed to be glinting with merriment. Up close he looked fine – no bruises or cuts that she could see. He was obviously there of his own volition. She suddenly felt annoyed with him for making a fool out of her and for being so cavalier about it, but it was tempered by relief that he was safe, and gratitude for him finding a phone charger.

She went over to the door of the container and looked in. It was dim and stuffy but well-organised into areas for sleeping and living. Two children sat on the floor playing with plastic cups and a few stuffed toys. They were thin and pale, their eyes almost too big for their faces. Siobhan was sitting on what looked like a school-issue plastic chair, her legs splayed out in front of her, her eyes closed and her hands cupping her huge belly.

'I'm so sorry,' Sara said quietly.

Siobhan hauled herself upright and glared at her. 'You should be. I thought that was the end of me and the kids.'

'Can I come in?'

'Can I stop you?'

Sara walked into the container, her eyes adjusting to the murky light. 'I can explain,' she began softly.

'Yeah, sure you can.'

'I'm Sara. You're Siobhan, right?'

'Yeah,' Siobhan eventually replied. 'That's me, for what it's worth…'

'I'm really sorry to have put you through all that,' Sara said. 'It's just that there are men close to here, really dangerous men, and I didn't know if this was their base. My friend, he was late coming back to me. I thought he might have got caught up in something and I had to be careful. I'm worried they're tracking us… we killed one of them… self-defence.' The words tumbled out of her.

Siobhan stared at her open-mouthed. 'Tracking you?… and now you're here with us? Well, that's just great. Thanks for that.'

'Hey, I know, I'm sorry. It wasn't intentional.'

'Yeah, of course it wasn't.' Siobhan shook her head, then shrugged as though she realised that being angry was absolutely pointless. 'So what were they like?' she asked. 'What did they look like?'

'They were wearing black militia-style gear, no guns that we could see, but they had a crossbow. Oh, and dogs. Nasty ones. The main guy, the one who did all the talking, was super freaky… sleazy, reminded me of a snake.'

'Oh God, I think I know the ones you mean. They drove us out of the house. The dogs were terrifying.' Siobhan frowned. 'They took everything – even Katie, my niece.' She started to cry softly.

'Oh God!'

'Yeah, that was well over a month ago. She's barely fifteen. Never even had a boyfriend...'

There was silence for a moment. The children seemed frozen to the spot, exquisitely attuned to the tension of the conversation.

'Are you going to stay here or move on?' Sara asked gently.

'We'll stay here I suppose until... until...' She waved a thin hand down her belly and let it rest on the crown. 'Then we'll decide.' She seemed unconvinced by her own words.

Sara scrabbled to think of something to say that might make the situation seem more normal. 'So what did you do before this?' she asked, crouching down on her hunkers so the children would feel less afraid. They watched her quietly, eyes like saucers.

'What do you mean?'

'Your work... like, professionally.'

'Oh, that! God, it feels like a lifetime ago. I was partner in an accountancy firm. Now I wish I'd studied medicine, even veterinary. It would have been far more useful now.'

'Yeah, I know what you mean.' She stopped for a minute to let the silence unfold, a small gesture of awareness to the seriousness of Siobhan's circumstances. Then, she continued more softly. "Listen, in exchange for your phone charger, we're giving you some food – some tinned fish and beans. Tony's coming back with us to fetch the food. You should try to eat as much protein as possible – you and the kids.' Sara leaned forward hesitantly, lowering her voice to a whisper. 'Also, I have something that might help... a bottle of tranquillisers. I found them a few days back in a house.'

'A bottle of what now?' Siobhan stared at her.

'Benzodiazepine. I can give them to Tony with the food. Anyway, the offer's there if you want them, just in case things get bad for you. So you have options...' She knew it sounded insane, but she would have wanted the choice if she was in Siobhan's position.

Siobhan stared hard at her, then turned to look at her children. 'Yeah, sure. I guess it's better to have it and not need it than not have it and want it.'

'I'm sure you'll be all right, but if there's a problem that can't be fixed or, you know… worst case scenario…'

She remembered the births of her own children as though it were yesterday. The hospital had saved her life after Lila – a massive blood transfusion and an emergency section. It had been such a shock after Conor's delivery had been so straightforward. The thought of giving birth out here in the wild… no pain relief, no skilled midwives, the risk of complications. She shuddered.

Siobhan nodded, her eyes suddenly brimming with tears. 'I don't know whether to be really angry with you or to say thanks,' she said, sounding suddenly breathless.

'It's the least I can do after frightening you. I wish I could help more.'

'Just be grateful you can run. I'm a sitting duck.'

'When are you due?'

'Any day now.' Siobhan tried to hoist herself up out of the chair, but her enormous belly had shifted her centre of gravity and she flopped back down again, stretching her legs out again. Her ankles were swollen and undefined and varicose veins threaded their way up her puffy legs. Under normal circumstances she would probably be under medical observation. 'I don't even know where the head is,' she added. 'Anyway, I'm in God's hands now, aren't I? So where are you going next? What's the plan?'

'We've a house up north. I'm hoping my husband is already there with the kids. We got separated from each other weeks ago when I left to buy a jeep. We thought we were getting out on time, but we left it too late.'

'So who's that beardy fella out there then?'

'Just a man I met along the way. I had a dog before. He was killed yesterday by that gang. So now the dog's gone, I reckon it's better to have him around.'

'He seems decent. The kids like him, which says a lot.'

'Mmm, I suppose that's a good sign… He says he was a dad himself before…'

'And you take his word for it?'

'No choice but to trust him for now. I'm just taking it one minute at a time really.'

'So is it safe up there – at your house in the north? Safe for children?' Siobhan looked at her plaintively.

It flashed across Sara's mind that Siobhan was angling for her to take her children with her. 'It's beside a lake in the middle of nowhere.'

'Oh, you're so lucky. We're so exposed here.' Siobhan started to cry. One of the children walked over and put his hand on his mother's tummy and rubbed it gently.

'You're so lucky to have them,' Sara said. 'I don't know where mine are or even if they're alive. It's killing me. At least you have them around you.' She stood up and glanced down at the children. 'I'm sorry, I need to leave now.'

Siobhan nodded. The two women regarded each other in silence.

'You'll be okay,' Sara said eventually, trying to sound confident. 'Sure come up north once you've had the baby. You can stay with us in the house until you find your feet, and then we'll help you find somewhere safe close by.'

The woman looked at her, hope flickering briefly, one hand on her belly and the other on the head of her youngest child. 'You'd really do that for us?'

'Sure. The nearest big town is Manorhamilton, close to the border. West of there you should see signposts for an organic centre.

If you can find that centre, we're a ten-minute drive away, down by the shore of the first lake.'

'Thank you,' Siobhan whispered. 'That means so much to me… to know you'd do that for me and the children.'

They stared at each other for a moment, then Sara turned and left the container, pausing briefly at the door to lift her hand in farewell.

Marcus, Tony and Paul were talking about the weather when she joined them outside. She nodded to Paul and set off with Marcus and Tony back through the fields, the sun hanging low in the sky behind them.

Tony talked endlessly about all the things that were wrong in his life – his stomach problems, his hunger, the generator using up all the diesel, his cars being torched by the passing gang – and all the things he missed – his dead mother, his friends, the pub, Friday night drinks, the football, the odd bet. He used to dream constantly about pints, he told them, but the pints had been replaced by toilets. He was running out of places to dig fresh toilet pits close to the container. 'They all start chasing me in my sleep,' he complained, 'The toilets and even Siobhan with her swollen belly running after me.'

'I'm worried about Siobhan,' Sara said, ignoring the dark carnival of his unconscious as they crossed the last field.

'Yeah, yeah, she's in a tricky situation,' Tony said.

'It's not going to be easy for her. Does Paul know how to help?'

'He was there for the other ones being born, so maybe.'

'If she gets into difficulty…'

'Look, it is what it is,' Tony interrupted. 'They shouldn't have been at it anyway. He should have kept his trousers zipped, the fucking gobshite.' He shook his head. 'Can't do much about it now. Just have to get on with it… that is, unless you want to go back and help her. We could do with another woman around.' He winked at her.

She ignored him but caught Marcus's eye. He gave her a cheeky grin.

'What's the chances of finding more of these yokes along the way?' Tony said, pointing at the rifle. He was getting out of breath trying to keep up with them. 'Ye were fortunate.'

The two men chatted at length about guns and the lack thereof and what to use instead, like petrol bombs if there was spare fuel.

She said nothing but silently seethed at Tony's casual disregard for Siobhan's plight. He wasn't the one who had to give birth and potentially risk losing his life– and the baby's – without pain relief or help. She couldn't bring herself to think about Katie, the fifteen-year-old who had been taken by the men.

The jeep, still parked in the place where they had left it, was a welcome sight and they quickened their pace. While Marcus and Tony talked about car engines and batteries, she opened the boot and counted out the agreed number of tins and apples, which Tony quickly put into a plastic bag. He handed over the charger and she put it into her coat pocket.

'Sorry we can't give you more,' she said.

'Fair's fair, I suppose,' he said with a shrug.

Marcus reached out and shook Tony's hand. 'Good to meet you. Best of luck now.'

'Yeah, yourselves too.'

Sara couldn't stop fretting about Siobhan. 'Look before you go, there's a house... maybe an hour or so's drive from here. There's stuff in there that Siobhan would be glad of. We didn't go through every room properly because... well, there were bodies.'

'Jaysus, what a world this has come to,' he said, shaking his head. 'So what's it you think herself would want there?'

'Stacks of baby products – milk powder, blankets, nappies, clothes. Useful things like that. You could maybe walk there and back in a day.

'Right, right.'

'It's not safe and the roads are badly flooded – you'll be wading up to your knees in parts – but it's better than nothing.'

'Sure give me the directions and I'll pass them on to Paul.'

She rummaged about in her bag and pulled out a pen and a crumpled shopping receipt, on the back of which she sketched a rough map, talking him through the landmarks to watch out for.

'Oh, and wait,' she said, searching for the bottle of tranquillisers. 'I told Siobhan that I'd give her these in case she needs them. They're for the pain. Promise me you'll give them to her.'

He took the bottle and squinted at the label. 'No bother. I'll pass them on.' He stuffed them in his jacket pocket.

'That's it then,' she said, remembering about the charger and anxious to start the engine and get her phone plugged in.

'Right ye are,' Tony said, and with a nod he turned and strode off across the field.

They watched in silence as he disappeared through the gap in the ditch

'Well, you seemed happy enough over there,' she said, turning abruptly to Marcus. 'A lot of smiling and grinning coming out of you.'

'Ah, it was all right,' he said with a friendly smile. 'They were more afraid of me than I was of them. I knew quickly enough they were up to their necks in it.'

'Right. So you stayed there chatting in that container for the fun?'

'No, I was negotiating. Getting us what we needed.'

'For half a day?'

Marcus's smile became a frown. 'Time flies. What's your problem?'

'What do you mean *what's my problem*? The next time you don't come back at the agreed time, I'll leave you to it.'

'The agreed time? I'd no way of telling the time!'

'So why did you tell me you'd be back at midday?'

Marcus looked puzzled for a moment, then his face cleared. 'I was only joking, for God's sake. I thought you knew that.'

Sara scowled at him. She felt silly for taking him so literally, but she was still furious with him.

'It was good to see you there in the yard,' he said quietly by way of consolation. 'You looked... how should I put it – capable.'

'I didn't feel it.'

'Well, you put on a good show.'

'There was no way I could've used the gun.'

'Ah, you would if you'd had to.'

'Well, maybe just in the leg.'

'Sometimes I want to give you a hug,' he said, suddenly grinning.

She could feel herself blush.

'Not in that way!' he added quickly. 'You just look all wound up, like you need one.'

'Oh, for God's sake, I'm grand.'

'You're not really.'

She sighed. 'I can't stop thinking about Siobhan. Having that baby out here will kill her.'

'You never know, she might make it.'

'She wasn't well. I could see it in her face. She was an awful colour.'

'Sure didn't women used to give birth in the wild all the time?'

She shook her head and looked away. *Idiot.*

'So anyway, today kind of worked out, didn't it?' he said brightly.

'I suppose.'

'What do you mean *I suppose*? You've got a charger now.'

She rummaged in her coat pocket for the phone charger. 'Yeah, I know, I know. I'm going to start up the engine now.'

'Ah now, what's wrong? I can tell there's something else.'

'It's nothing.'

'Nope, it's never nothing. I learned that the hard way.' The flicker of a memory crossed his face.

'Okay fine, I'll say it. Why did you tell them about me? They could have come looking for me had it gone wrong for you. You ratted me out.'

'Bollocks! I knew straight away there was no harm in them.'

'But still, if they'd wanted to, they could have locked you up in there.'

'They didn't and I wasn't worried. I read the room. I'm good at that.'

She rolled her eyes.

'Jesus, you're in terrible form for someone who just got what they wanted. If I were you, I wouldn't be hanging around giving out. I'd be plugging the bloody thing in. Are you afraid to turn it on or what?' he asked, sounding more irritated now.

'I'm perfectly fine.'

She turned her back on him and opened the door of the jeep.

'Anyway, you walked into the container yourself to talk to that woman,' he called out. 'Same goes for you.'

She swung around and stared at him, her cheeks flushed with anger.

When he saw her expression, something in him shifted. 'Okay, look, let's de-escalate. We've enough going on without getting stuck into each other.'

'Do I or do I not make a fair point?' she said tightly.

'You do,' he said. 'I shouldn't have mentioned you. But honestly, those lads didn't know what they were at. They just didn't have it in them to harm me. They're regular folk trying to survive. No killer instinct. But listen, if it happens again, I won't mention you, okay?' He smiled at her, seemingly unflappable even in the middle of a disagreement.

'It won't happen again,' she said stiffly. 'This is life or death. There's no room for mistakes.' As the words fell out of her mouth, she remembered that she had endangered his life by leading the men back to his cottage earlier. He could have thrown that in her face but he hadn't. She felt herself mellow a little. 'I mean it. If there is a next time, I won't come looking for you. I'll keep going,' she said, aware that her threat lacked some of its earlier edge.

'Ha! I don't believe you.'

She turned towards the cab of the jeep again so he wouldn't see the smile she couldn't suppress and jumped into the driver's seat. 'Would you have not preferred to stay with them instead?' she said, feeling better now that she'd got that off her chest. 'You might have been better off.'

'Nope, too much hassle… and I've got used to you,' he said, grinning. 'Better the devil and all that. Anyway, go on, do your thing. I'm going to see if I can find enough wood for a fire.' He walked off towards a copse of trees. 'I'll not be far away,' he called back to her.

She turned the key in the ignition and the engine burst into life. Her hands trembled as she inserted the charger into the port, connected the other end of the cable to the phone and turned it on. Adrenalin shot through her, making her heart pound.

It took several minutes to charge the phone enough to light up the screen. She held it up to her face so it could scan her corneas. Within moments, a torrent of notifications announced the arrival of many missed calls and text messages. She went to the messaging app first and tapped it. She held her breath as she opened the first message, dated Wednesday 4th August and sent at 16:23. Johnny's familiar style of expression flashed up on the screen:

> *Hey, just found the passports. Have everything now. Just left you a voicemail. Where are you?*

Then another, Thursday 5th at 11:00:

> *Still here. Very worried about you now. Can't stay*

> here much longer, not safe anymore. We're going
> straight to Glenade so don't come back, we'll see you
> there. Going to get as far as we can in the neighbour's
> car, will try find better 4wd on the way. Low on
> battery, power gone again so will turn this off for a
> bit.
>
> Kids fine I'm fine

A second text followed on the same day:

> Btw most of village blocked off with sandbags and
> cars but think we can take back roads up through the
> midlands. Hope you ok. We def shld have gone sooner.

Then on Friday 6th, 15:00:

> Gerry finally died. Can't believe he lasted this long
> but bad timing. Mrs Ruane is not well. Going to
> stay and help her figure out what to do with his body
> so not leaving tonight. We'll go first thing in the
> morning. Told kids you're on your way to get house
> ready.

She looked out the front windscreen. It looked so calm and settled out there, everything the same as it had been moments before. Now nothing would ever be the same again. She took a deep breath and went back to the phone.

The next message was sent Saturday 7th, 11:19:

> Hey – half a bar left. Kids are ok. Waded to village
> last night. Not good. Lads packed with knives. No
> way past with car and most roads still underwater. I
> offered cash to get through the upper church road in
> the morning. One put knife to my throat

There were a dozen hysterical messages from Mrs Ruane, their neighbour, but Sara only scanned the first few words. Then two more from Johnny, one saying *'Hope to God you're ok. X'*, and the other a selfie of himself with Conor and Lila at the kitchen table, all smiling, trying to look normal. The room was dim, and the camera flash bleached their skin. They looked like ghosts. She traced the outline of their faces, zooming in to scrutinise their eyes – gauge their emotions.

There was another message, sent later that Saturday night:

> *Battery almost gone. Should have left Mrs R to sort it out on her own. Will leave first thing in morning. Decided we can't use car. We'll get close to railway then walk west, find something on way. It's higher ground. Will check phone when I find somewhere to charge it. Hope you ok.*

And that was it. No more text messages.

She tried accessing her voicemails, but there were none – probably deleted by the phone company weeks ago. She sat back, the air sucked out of her lungs, her thoughts like pinballs, zipping around and crashing, nowhere to go. A surge of panic flushed through her and she started to shake. Her instinct was to make a plan but she couldn't think straight. She brought Johnny's name up in her contacts and pressed Call. A tiny signal flickered in the top right-hand corner of the screen, then died. Nothing. She tried Conor's number. It went straight to voicemail: 'Hey, leave a message. Bye!' he said, his little voice like music to her ears. She called it again, just to hear his voice, but her phone hadn't charged enough. She felt like flinging the phone through the windscreen.

So much time had passed since the messages had been sent. Could they have made the journey on foot? A little flame of hope ignited in her heart at the thought that they could be at the lake house now, waiting for her. But then alternative scenarios flooded her mind, alternatives that were too painful to bear. Conor was barely a teenager and Lila, still a little girl. A wave of fury swelled in her – how could Johnny have been so irresponsible, so stupid not to leave sooner! But it was quickly replaced by horror – they could all be dead. She put her forehead on the steering wheel, her entire body tense and quivering, and sat like that for a long time.

Slowly, she became aware of Marcus moving around outside and the noisy rumble of the engine. Steeling herself, she got out of the jeep and stood staring at him, her hands in her pockets. He was hunkered down on the grass, spooning tinned fruit into two empty cans. He took one look at her and stood up quickly.

'Well?' he asked.

'It's not good,' she said, her voice catching. 'Not good at all.'

He said nothing.

'I'm going to charge the phone for another few minutes,' she said quietly. 'I know we need the fuel, but it'd be good to see if we can access the GeoMap. Then we'll know how close we are and it'll maybe help us find better roads.'

'Sure. Have you been online already? Any news sites up?'

'The phones not charged enough yet. I can't tell.'

'Okay, fair enough,' he said.

He handed her one of the tins of fruits but she didn't want it. Then she started to cry, barely able to get a breath as the heaving sobs wracked her body. Marcus led her to the back of jeep, spread out a blanket and sat her down on it. Eventually, when she was all cried out, she told him what she'd read in the texts and speculated on what had happened. Maybe they'd killed him and taken the kids. Or he'd got in a fight and the kids were hiding. Or perhaps he'd been able to negotiate their way through. She talked through a dozen different scenarios, each more implausible than the last. But through it all she remained stubbornly insistent that her family were at the lake house. They were there waiting for her. It was all she could hold onto.

Marcus said nothing, offering her neither solace nor hope, and focused on the practical. He cleaned the tins and put their things back into the jeep. She got back into the cab to keep warm. She watched him wandering about outside the jeep; every so often he walked down to the receding floodwater; after a while she heard him chopping wood. He must have been cold, but he never approached the jeep. She checked the phone battery. When it got to 30%, she cut the engine.

Darkness crept in slowly, a thin veil of grey drawn across the countryside. The sleety rain had long since passed, replaced by dry chilly air that penetrated the multiple layers of clothing she had on. In her mind, she obsessively ran through different versions of Johnny's final hours and the consequences for the children. Then, she would jolt upright, shocked by the vividness of her imagination. The children would believe her to be at the lake house, but without him they would be travelling blind and completely on their own.

When night fell, Marcus knocked on the door of the cab and offered her food, but she turned it down. She clambered into the back of the jeep where her makeshift bed was and hunkered down under the blankets, pulling them up over her head. She heard him climb into the front cab, close the door quietly behind him, then toss and turn for what seemed like hours before she finally fell asleep.

She woke later in the pitch blackness with a desperate urge to pee. She scrambled around for her boots and stepped out into the freezing cold air. It took her breath away and the ice-tipped grass crunched beneath her feet. When she'd finished and pulled up her jeans, she stood staring up at the night sky. To the south a fingernail of moon hung near the horizon and a canopy of stars sparkled and twinkled overhead. She remembered something she had read about atoms and the dark matter – vibrational energy – that exists in the spaces between particles; a fusion of musical notes. Then a kind of prickling static, pleasant and warm, moved up from her feet through her hips and stomach, over her ribcage to her neck and face and down her arms to her fingertips. Suddenly, it was as though she was outside herself and inside herself all at once. A strange fragile peace enveloped her and the fear she had felt all day fell away. She closed her eyes. Something deep in her belly came loose and surged up through her heart to her neck; a kind of invocation, something ancient and forgotten, rose to the surface and escaped her lips. She sank to her knees and listened to the strange hum coming from her throat while the tingling feeling washed over her. After a while, the beautiful warm sensation ebbed away.

Her reverie was interrupted by the creak of the jeep's suspension and the click of the cab door opening.

'Hey, you okay?' Marcus called out in a low voice.

She opened her eyes to see him reaching out his hand to her. She took it and allowed him to pull her up.

Opening his coat, he put his arms around her and gathered her in. They stood like that in the dark, holding each other close, until they got too cold. Then he led her back to the jeep, one arm around her waist, and she let him tuck her back in among the blankets and coats where she fell into a deep, peaceful sleep.

5

She awoke before sunrise the next day, and almost immediately, the shock of yesterday's revelations clutched at her, threatening to drag her under. But she pushed it away and quickly found that it made her all the more determined to make the journey north. Now that she was confronted by the reality of the situation, forced to face the fact that her family might not be alive, she felt more resilient, more flexible, like a willow tree that bends and moves with the wind rather than resisting it. She had one goal and one goal only: to stay alive and make it to the lake house, where her children would be waiting for her. *Of course they'll be there. I'm not so bothered about Johnny… that's a mad thing to think! What's that all about? Why am I blaming him for not leaving in good time? It was down to both of us. This is so messed up. I'm so messed up. Am I asking for trouble if I bring Marcus to the lake house? Well, I'm not leaving him behind. I couldn't have got this far without him.* She recalled how kind and compassionate he had been the night before. She wasn't used to that in a man.

Later that morning, after they had shared a tin of beans, they walked down to the end of the field to survey the floodwaters. The levels had dropped further overnight.

'Maybe the road is passable now,' she said.

Marcus nodded.

'We're going to need to grow our own food,' she said suddenly. 'At least until there's some sort of stability in the country. That could take a couple of years, so we need to be prepared.'

He looked at her, somewhat startled.

'We'll need vegetable seeds,' she continued, 'so we have something to trade. There's an organic centre near the lake house. There might be plants and seeds and tools there that we can use.'

'Well, that's good to know,' he said. 'That is, assuming the owners aren't still there or that it hasn't been destroyed or taken over by gangs.'

'Sure, but let's see what we can find. In the meantime, we'll need to find better bags – something we can carry on our backs in case we lose the jeep or run out of diesel.'

He studied her face for a moment. 'Let's pack up and check the road then,' he said eventually. 'We'll drive until we're on higher ground and clear of the water. Maybe we'll find a house further along that has things we can use.'

'Yeah.' She rubbed her hands together enthusiastically. 'I think we need to keep to the smaller back roads and use forest tracks as much as we can. There are hundreds of hectares of commercial forest close to the border that'll give us lots of cover.'

'Sure thing. You're the boss.'

All men said that, not really believing their own words. Men always saw themselves as the boss; it seemed to be hardwired in them. Marcus would probably be happy for her to set the agenda until it didn't suit his purpose, she thought. But then she remembered his arms around her the night before. She sighed loudly and started to pack up the jeep.

They set off, driving through the receding flood with little difficulty and made good progress along the narrow roads. Signposts at junctions and crossroads kept them oriented north-westerly, and crossing into the next county brought a sense of progress. They saw no one and the roads were mostly clear of debris. Two roadblocks had been dismantled, leaving enough space for them to pass through. By mid morning, the fuel tank dipped into the red and they pulled over to refill it from the jerry can. The needle barely rose above empty as they drove on.

The landscape around them had been pressed flat by the water, and small ponds in low-lying corners of the fields shimmered in the morning sun. A long-necked grey heron soared low across the road, startling them, before gliding south and disappearing behind a line of trees. A few miles further on they crawled past a line of bungalows. All of them were damaged in some way or other – graffiti, burnt doors, windows smashed – and the road itself was carpeted in glass. Scrawny cats dived into the ditches ahead of them and lone foxes turned to look at them briefly with large yellow eyes before disappearing. Wide corrugated farm buildings set back from the road housed tall grain silos beside fields of dead Friesians.

'We need to find a smaller road,' she said. 'Something well off the beaten track.'

'Yeah, I don't like this stretch.'

'Here, can you check my phone – see if you can try and access the map again?' She handed it to him as they stared up each driveway and surveyed the blackened tarmac.

'It's hard to tell how long it's been since people were last here,' she said quietly.

'I'd say before the last rains. They set a lot of fires. Maybe our friends with the Rottweilers were responsible,' he said. 'They could still be close.'

She shuddered. 'Do you think they're tracking us?'

He didn't answer.

'I'll kill them myself if I see them,' she said, her voice low and full of menace.

Marcus stared at the phone. 'Nope, nothing. It's just endlessly loading, same as before.' He nudged her phone against her arm.

She took it from him and turned it off, slipping it back into her coat pocket again.

They drove on a little more quickly and came to another junction. A signpost for the motorway sat above the routes to towns and villages: Killashandra, Ballinamore, Corlough. She turned right, away from the sun.

'God I'm hungry,' she said.

He reached into his pocket and handed her an apple.

'Ah thanks.'

She ate it quietly, wondering how many apples she could tolerate before they would start to really affect her stomach. She had had slight cramps the previous night. The last thing she wanted was to get a dose of the runs. A male pheasant appeared out of the ditch and started at the sight of them. He scuttled about in confusion before finally rising up heavily into the air with a series of raspy squawks.

'There's far more nature up here,' she said. 'All the wild animals are living so freely.'

They approached Killashandra at a slow crawl and stopped when the church spire came into view. A green vintage water pump that had once cheerily greeted visitors was now embedded amongst a clump of dead flowers and weeds.

'We should definitely check that for water,' she said, nodding towards it.

'Yeah, good idea.'

She crawled along, trying to keep the engine quiet even though they would have been easily heard by anyone in the vicinity.

'But first, I think we should do a recce of the village,' she said, 'but not up the main street.'

'There's a side road up there to the left.' He pointed. 'Just behind that hedge.'

She turned left and had to accelerate to get uphill. The hedgerows were thick with overgrown bushes and fuchsia, some of it creating a canopy above them, with alder and birch trees flush between the gaps. The road itself was potholed with loose gravel. A gate to the right opened into a large field that bordered the grounds of the church. In one corner was a walled-off graveyard. A horse stood motionless nearby, its neck bent low. It didn't seem to hear them.

They drove on for another minute or so.

'Stop here,' Marcus said suddenly.

'Why?'

'I've an idea. Turn off the engine to save what's left. We'll have to start walking soon unless we find more diesel. So I'll take the fuel can on foot – see what I can find.'

'You sure that's a good idea?'

'I've the gun. It'll be fine. If I can't refill the can, I might be able to find bags or something sturdy to carry our food and blankets.'

She nodded. The wind rustled the beech leaves in the hedgerow beside her window. A clattering of jackdaws lifted from the upper branches of a cypress grove near the graveyard. They soared and called out to each other like a badly-tuned orchestra.

'Want to come with me?' he asked.

'I don't like being on my own without Brin, but no, I'll stay here, thanks. Anyway, you'll be less noticeable on your own.' She glanced at the clock on the dashboard. 'How long do you think you'll be this time?'

He grinned at her. 'Give me until the sun moves round to there.' He pointed at the church spire.

'Will you check the water pump while you're out there?'

'Yep.' He opened the passenger door and stopped to look at her for a moment. 'It'll be fine. I'll be back soon.'

'Mind yourself, okay?'

'I will.'

He jumped down, taking the rifle with him, then retrieved the jerrycan from the boot. He patted the roof before he left, making her wince and reminding her of the old men, long dead now, from the local farming co-op who used to slap the bonnet of her father's car to send it on its way, as though it were an old dairy cow. She watched the rear-view mirror as Marcus strode boldly down the middle of the road, the rifle in one hand looking for all the world like a gamesman setting out to shoot deer and rabbits.

She waited until he vanished from sight before closing her eyes, then sat for a while listening to the ticks of the cooling engine and the noisy swirling birds. After a while she grew restless and jumped out onto the road leaving the door slightly open. She scoured the countryside around her, seeing nothing to immediately cause alarm, then climbed the gate into the field next to the jeep. She longed to have Brin with her now, the cut of grief taking its time to heal. The field sloped up to a hilltop and all the way down to the road into the village. She walked up to the ridge and looked out to the east, scanning for movement of any kind. The network of roads below was wild and overgrown; small white houses and farms with rust-red barns dotted the countryside. She kicked off her boots and sat down heavily on the exposed roots of a large sycamore. Pulling off her socks, she planted the soles of her feet firmly on the cold earth, spreading her toes out as much as she could and rooting herself to the spot. Weak sunshine occasionally broke through whipped clouds, and when it passed over her face, she closed her eyes and pretended to be sitting in her favourite rattan garden chair, the lawn freshly mowed and the scent of white roses, honeysuckle and sweet pea adrift in the air around her. Suzanne and Aishling came sashaying across the grass in their designer wedges, maxi dresses and giant sunglasses, bearing a bottle of vintage Veuve Clicquot. *I wonder what they'd think of Marcus. Would they fancy him? Aishling liked beards, so maybe she would. God, where are they now? I can't even imagine how they're coping, Suzanne without her insulin and Aishling with that arsehole husband of hers.* Johnny's face suddenly appeared in her mind's eye and she found she was crying, big fat tears rolling silently down her cheeks.

A blast of cold wind brought her back to the slope overlooking the village, the clouds returned to block out the rays of the sun and it was winter again. She put her damp socks back on and slipped her feet into the old boots. She longed to get dried out and warmed up. She couldn't remember what that felt like, to be really cosy. So she walked back across the top of the field to get some heat into her, hugging the hedgerows so she didn't feel quite so exposed. The branches above were dotted with empty bird's nests, and tunnels and holes in the ditches suggested badgers, rabbits and foxes. A sense of calm enveloped her as she noticed each small thing around her and listened to the distinctive voices of different birds.

Just then she felt a warm trickle run down the inside of her leg and she felt the familiar cramp in her belly. That was a surprise, and she wasn't sure whether to be glad or irritated. She hadn't had a regular period cycle for the last two years; the food shortages had left her underweight and malnourished and played havoc with her hormones. She'd been pretty sure that at thirty-eight she was too young to be peri-menopausal. She remembered the toilette bag in the jeep and walked back to get it. This could get awkward with Marcus around – her needing to attend to herself more than usual – but he was a big boy, she thought with a sigh; he'd lived with a woman before; he knew the score.

Back at the jeep, she took a tampon from the toilette bag and, sitting awkwardly in the boot, inserted it, then tidied up. Marcus reappeared just not long afterwards, looking very pleased with himself. It was infectious, and she jumped out to meet him, mirroring his big smile. His arms were laden with bulging plastic bags, with the gun slung over one shoulder and a large backpack strapped to his back.

'No food or fuel I'm afraid,' he said cheerfully, walking straight to the open boot.

'Wow,' she said, moving out of his way. 'I didn't expect you to come back with anything.'

'The village was pretty much ransacked, but I found a place no one else had.' He put the bags in the boot.

'Oh yeah?'

'A charity shop – you know, for cancer or something. Front room had been torched, but I went out the back into a private yard. Big steel shed bolted and locked, but I cracked through. It was full of stuff they hadn't sorted through yet.'

'Wow! So what did you find?'

'Fresh well water for a start.'

'Excellent.'

He swung the backpack onto the ground beside him. It was more like a teenager's school bag than a proper rucksack but it seemed spacious. He opened one of the plastic bags.

'This one's for you,' he said. 'Trainers your size, I think. Grey jumper – fancy wool, if I was to guess. It's soft anyway.' He was enjoying himself. 'Puffer jacket. Perfect for sleeping. I mean, they're glorified sleeping bags!'

She laughed. 'Thanks!'

'And the big reveal. Drum roll, please… one hat with a pom-pom and a sealed pack of ladies' underwear, size eight to ten. That's close, right?' He looked up at her.

She blushed and nodded. 'Sure, yep, thanks.'

'Also men's wool socks still in their plastic cover. Men's are thicker than women's anyway, so bonus.'

'Brilliant,' she said, genuinely thrilled. 'This is amazing.' She put the hat on immediately.

'So as I said, the bad news is – no diesel.' He took the empty can out of the backpack and tossed it into the jeep. 'But I made up for that by finding these.' He went back into the backpack and pulled out two bottles of red wine. 'In the locked boot of a car. Still in the paper bag with the receipt. Poor bastard who bought them never got to pull the cork.'

'Oh wow!'

'Decent bottles, judging by the prices. Party tonight?' He grinned at her.

'We can celebrate when we get to the lake,' she said, immediately feeling annoyed with herself for killing the vibe.

'Ahh now, then we'll have to carry them all the way.'

'We'll see,' she said. 'Anyway, what did you find for yourself?'

'Good boots, hardly worn but in excellent condition. And a hoodie and spare jeans. Not my style but they'll do.'

'Nice.'

'How did you get on?' he asked. 'No trouble?'

'Fine. Nice quiet time with the birds for company. Did you see anyone in the village?'

'Nope. All long gone or dead. Or hiding. I suppose I looked like someone to be avoided, marching around the place with a gun. It was completely deserted.'

'Did you fill our plastic bottles with that well water?'

'Yep, and I found a shoulder bag with straps for you. It won't be that comfortable, but I can carry a lot of the heavy stuff.'

They bundled everything into the boot, jumped in the front cab and set off again. Even though the back road had grass and moss along the middle, it was wide enough for the jeep to pass through.

They drove along in silence for a while. Marcus had his legs stretched out and he eventually dozed off, despite bouncing over potholes and stones. She watched the fuel gauge constantly, her heart sinking with the needle until it quivered into the red zone and stayed there. But as long as there was life in the engine, she kept going, her thoughts meandering with each bend in the road.

God, what was the name of that therapist I used to go to – Ellen or Eleanor? Something beginning with E. She looked like a therapist you'd see in the movies, sitting in her swanky leather chair in her swanky office off Harcourt Street. I haven't thought about her in years. She used to ask great questions, but she asked them the way someone asks when they're dying to know the gossip. I wonder what she'd have to say about me sitting beside this stranger, pretending I don't like the smell of men's sweat, or the way he pulled me into him after my meltdown last night, or the way he drifts off to sleep beside me as if he's known me all his life. 'What is the biggest challenge you're facing at the moment?' she would probably ask me right now. Mmm, well, Ellen... or Eleanor or whatever your name was... I'm flying by the seat of my pants right now. Wouldn't you agree? I'm trusting a strange man I picked up on the road while trying to escape a violent gang and find my family who may or may not be dead... oh yeah, and I saw my dog being killed and a bloke shot dead beside me. 'So how does that make you feel?' Ellen would ask. Well, numb, terrified, mostly for the kids, but I'm hopeful too... and confused. Yes, definitely confused... about Johnny and this stranger. 'Think of something else you can focus on,' Ellen would suggest. Okay, good, yes, I can do that. I'll focus on the world and the way it was before the rains. No, I'd have to go back further than that... to when I was little and there used to be a gazillion moths in the evenings and the buzzing of bees in the fuchsia would drown out everything on a summer day or I'd find a beautiful shell on the beach. Everything seemed so much simpler then and I had the time to stop and pay more attention.

Her favourite time of day had been twilight. In her parent's farm near the mountains, the purple-pink clouds would shimmer in the afterglow of the sunset and the faraway ocean, still ablaze, would throw its own light up into the blushing sky. She loved to sit on the old wall near the great barn when her mother threw summer parties. There were fairy lights draped over the bushes and everyone would be drinking home-made wheat beer and last season's elderflower wine. Then night would fall like a curtain, the lights would go out and the swallows would be the last to leave the day, swooping low along the hedges to catch the midges in their billowing swarms.

Then just as she dropped into second gear to get the jeep up a hill, the engine spluttered, a death rattle, and finally cut out altogether. She pulled on the handbrake and sat staring out the windscreen, unable to move. The silence and stillness eventually woke Marcus.

'Time to pack up,' she said, almost whispering. 'We're out.'

They sat for a little while saying nothing, then he reached over and gave her hand a little squeeze. 'It'll be okay,' he said.

She looked at their hands together, enjoying the warmth from his palm, and swallowed hard. 'Yeah, sure. I know.' She nodded emphatically. 'It'll be okay.'

He smiled and, taking his hand back, rubbed his eyes. Then his face lit up as if he'd just thought of something. 'Hey, I was going to leave this for another time,' he reached into his inside pocket, 'but I might as well give it to you now.' He pulled out a tiny box and gave it to her.

She tried to read his expression. It was almost childlike, his eyes suddenly bright and soft. Lifting the lid, she peered inside.

'Oh,' she said, tears suddenly rising.

Nestling on a pad of red velvet was a little silver dog, beautifully crafted, hanging on a fine sterling silver chain.

'You like it?'

'Oh yes, yes I do.'

'Just so you'll always have him with you, you know.' Marcus cleared his throat.

'That's so thoughtful. Thank you!'

'It was a bit of a fluke finding it. It was in amongst a box full of earrings and stuff like that. Took me ages to untangle.'

'Well, it's lovely. Probably one of the nicest presents I've ever got.' She put it on herself, pulling back the clasp at the nape of her neck and attaching it to the end link. She tipped down the rear-view mirror and admired the bright little dog sitting in the hollow of her throat. 'It's an amazing find!' she said. 'I mean, if I was in the city looking for something like that I wouldn't have found one.'

He looked delighted with himself, then seemed to catch himself on. 'Okay let's get going,' he said gruffly. 'We're losing light and we need to find somewhere to shelter from the cold and rain.'

'Could we not stay in the jeep one more night?'

'Yeah, but I really could do with a bed... any bed. I'm not sleeping very well in the cab and I need to charge up if we're going to be walking for a while. You okay with that?'

'Yeah, fair enough. I understand.'

She patted the old leather steering wheel before dismounting from the jeep for the last time.

They left very little behind in the boot, distributing the food between them, although he insisted on carrying the heavy tins. 'Sure the bag'll get lighter by the day,' he said. She put the dried food in the new shoulder bag and packed two plastic bags with blankets and spare clothes; the contents of the toilet bag went into her handbag, which she strapped over her left shoulder.

Marcus changed into the new boots he'd found that morning and they started walking, Sara looking back fondly at the jeep that had got her so far.

⥎

By dusk they found themselves standing at the front gates of what appeared to be a deserted old farm. They walked in through the gates and stood in the middle of a wide concrete yard. It was heaped with rubber tyres and the rusted metal of old machines and ploughs, and grass sprouted up between cracks in the surface.

There was no sign of activity, just outbuildings and an empty cattle byre with long aluminium feeding troughs bolted under the head rails. They walked through the yard, Marcus holding the gun at the ready. The byre was empty, as were the fields around it. Behind the buildings was a tack room filled with leather bridles and stirrups. It smelled of straw, engine oil and damp leather. At the far end of the yard was another gate that opened into a large field.

A long, fenced driveway led to the main farmhouse. A low-built stone-cut wall surrounded the garden and there was a small orchard of plum, pear and apple trees to the side. The pears and plums were long gone, and a few cooking apples on the ground had been gnawed at by some hungry creature. She pulled some shrivelled late raspberries off a bush and popped them in her mouth, delighting in the sharp, sweet tang.

They stood in front of the main door to the house. 'There could still be somebody in there,' she whispered.

'Well, there's only one way to find out. We better get a burn on. It's starting to get dark.'

He pushed the door but it was locked. They walked around to the back of the house, the withering tendrils of an old wisteria that had long outgrown its trellis folding over them like a hood. Someone had smashed a stained-glass panel in the back door and Marcus was able to put his hand through to open the door. He stepped in front of her, and they slowed their breathing, hesitating in the dimness.

'I need to find a bathroom,' she said.

'Why didn't you go outside?' he said distractedly.

'That's not the only reason I want a bathroom,' she said, staring at him as if he was meant to read her mind.

'Right,' he said, glancing back at her.

'Then maybe after we should go back to the tack shed. We could barricade the door with something and stay there for the night.'

'Mmm. Let's see what's in the house first. There might be beds.'

'God, I don't know. It's pretty creepy.'

'Come on! Where's your sense of adventure?'

Holding the gun in front of him, he stepped into what appeared to be a boot room. It was empty. They stood still for a few moments, listening intently, but there was nothing to hear. Then they released themselves from their heavy bags, setting them quietly against the wall; he brought the gun and she kept her handbag.

They walked into a roomy kitchen. A shaft of light from a side window fell on the surface of a large oak dining table. The floor was covered in broken glass and smashed crockery and chairs had been thrown around the room. All the presses and cupboards were stripped bare. Sara went to the sink and ran the cold tap. There was a clunk and gurgle, then clear water poured out in a steady stream. She let it run for a minute and lowered her head to drink thirstily. It was ice-cold and delicious. When she was finished, Marcus did the same.

The glass and delph crunched underfoot as they walked towards a door on the far side of the room. It led to a long, carpeted hallway panelled with dark wood on one side and a narrow conservatory overlooking the garden forming the other wall. Long-dead spider plants in macramé holders shivered as they walked past and a row of desiccated geraniums sat on the wood sills beneath the glass. Their long past lemony-sweet fragrance rose up, briefly, from the depths of her memory. It was almost dark outside.

'All good?' he said in a low voice.

'Just about,' she whispered. Her heart was pounding in her chest and she was barely breathing.

At the end of the hallway, another door opened into what must originally have been the good room. An expensive-looking suite of furniture – floral-patterned sofas and armchairs – was arranged around a low glass-covered coffee table, on which sat a stained mug, a small porcelain swan and a finely crocheted white doily. The room smelled faintly of stale potpourri and coal dust. There was something wonderfully dated about it – very 1980s. Another door led to another hallway and at last she found a bathroom.

'Do you mind if I…?' she stopped to ask Marcus.

'Go ahead. I'll wait out here,' he said.

She closed the door softly and squinted in the semi-darkness. She rummaged around in her handbag and urgently took out a fresh tampon. She felt so grateful to have them and she silently thanked Marcus for his thoughtfulness. She doubted she would have considered his needs in that way.

A generous pink bathtub sat beside the toilet, its elegant brass taps surrounded by an array of bottles of lotions and old bath cremes. On the cistern she found a roll of toilet paper underneath the dusty skirt of a knitted flamenco dancer, and she took her time, enjoying sitting down as much as peeing and changing her tampon. She flushed the loo when she was done, an automatic reaction, but she was totally unprepared for the racket of the refilling cistern and the clunk of the pipes, deafening in the chilly silence. She stood rigid in the dull light of the room, holding her breath, waiting for the sound to dissipate. Then she turned to the sink and washed her hands with a large bar of cracked grey soap, taking her time to clean them thoroughly.

He was standing stock-still in the hallway when she went out.

'You want to go in?' she asked.

'In a minute.'

'What's wrong?'

'Not sure.'

'Oh God, you're freaking me out.'

'It's probably nothing. Just old house creaks.'

'It's probably the plumbing. My fault. I flushed the loo.'

'Here, hold this.' He handed her the gun and went into the bathroom.

She waited right outside the door, not wanting to wander too far away without him. When he came out a few minutes later, she relaxed a little and handed him back the rifle.

They climbed the stairs to the first floor, keeping their hands on the walls to guide them. A strange sharp odour greeted them on the landing where a large Velux window let in enough light for them to see each other's faces.

There were two small bedrooms to the left, each containing a single bed covered in a heavy, embroidered bedspread. The rooms were neat and tidy, but a thin film of dust coated the windowsills and bedside tables. The smell – now like mothballs or fishy cabbage – became more noticeable as they approached the master bedroom to the right. A king-size bed occupied most of the room and cushions and pillows were scattered around the floor. Bedsheets had been tied together with giant knots, with one end of the makeshift rope wrapped around the leg of the bed, and the other end hanging out of a partially open window. They walked over and peered out. The end of the rope hung a few metres above the ground.

'Someone needed to get out in a hurry.' She looked at him worriedly.

'Yeah, looks like it.'

He opened all the wardrobe doors. They were filled with enormous coats, suits and dresses, folded linen and bath towels, rows of shoes. The door to the en suite was closed but a dark reddish-brown substance had stained the soft cream carpet by the saddle board.

'I can't do this again,' she said.

'Can't do what again?'

'Find more dead people.' She stepped back from the door.

'Well, just stay outside then.'

'You're not honestly going to open that.'

'I am.'

'Why the hell do you want to see what's in there? Haven't you seen enough already?'

'I'm curious. I want to know what happened here. Anyway, wouldn't you want to be found if it was you? Wouldn't you want to be discovered?'

'Okay, maybe. But don't tell me what you find. I don't want anything like that in my head.'

'So wait on the landing.'

She left the room and leaned against the wall beneath the dim light of the Velux. Someone had gone to great trouble and expense to wallpaper the landing with delicate blue forget-me-nots on gold filigree stems. She listened as he clicked open the door to the bathroom, then she heard him gag and retch; he closed the door again. A few moments later, he appeared on the landing wiping his mouth with the back of his hand. He looked ashen, his cheeks hollowed out.

'I'm serious, I don't want to know,' she said.

'Okay.' He fell back against the wall and inhaled deeply. 'Jesus Christ,' he muttered under his breath. 'Yeah, you were right, I shouldn't have gone in there.' He suddenly blessed himself.

'Let's get out of here. Stay in the sheds tonight.'

'No can do. We'll freeze. We can sleep in the house but in another part of it.' He closed his eyes and took a deep breath. 'Let's go,' he said almost inaudibly.

She went to the top of the stairs. 'Okay, well, those sofas in the living room looked comfy…'

They went back downstairs and, moving quietly, checked the rest of the house. Once they were sure they were alone, they brought their bags from the boot room to the living room and sat in silence on the expensive sofas eating tinned beans with spoons from the kitchen until the room became pitch black.

They took it in turns to keep watch throughout the night until dawn broke over the fields and a greyish-pink light spilled into the room around them.

6

The next day, before they set off again, Sara forced herself to go back upstairs and rummage through the drawers and closets. A warm winter scarf and a pair of white wool mittens went into her bag. She found a large Aran sweater in one of the smaller bedrooms and put it on immediately under her jacket. There was no way she was going anywhere near the master bedroom or its ensuite. But from the bathroom downstairs she took soap, toilet roll and bath creme. These things mattered. They were almost as important as food and water as far as she was concerned. This was what it had come to – stealing from other people. In another life she wouldn't have set foot on the driveway of the house, let alone spend the night in the house itself.

She found herself speculating about the scene that had greeted Marcus upstairs. Perhaps it was a suicide... a woman ending it before feral gangs swept up her driveway to take what they could from her. Or maybe it was a father who had lost his family to untamed versions of himself. The reality of what Marcus had seen could hardly be much worse than what her imagination was conjuring.

Back on the road, carrying bulging bags on their shoulders and backs, they plodded along, walking through squally showers laced with hailstones and short bursts of wintry sunshine. Maybe it was wishful thinking, but it seemed to Sara as though the dry, cold spells were becoming longer and longer. Could things be starting to settle? She did a quick calculation in her head: it would take eight days to reach the lake house if they walked for seven hours each day. Eight days.

They talked very little to each other, conserving their energy for walking with such heavy loads, often knee-deep in floodwater, and in staying alert to the houses along the way. They didn't bother investigating them anymore – they couldn't carry anything else; besides, they were probably just tombs to their previous owners – but as they moved deeper into the north midlands, they found cars parked idly in driveways, some vandalised, others untouched. They hunted for the keys in some of the houses but found none. Marcus sometimes checked the pockets of the dead while she waited outside. If they perceived movement at the windows of the homes, they moved quickly on, Marcus sliding the rifle down from his shoulder. Occasionally they heard an engine far off in the distance and they would stop and listen to try to track its direction. She kept imagining she could hear barking dogs. She couldn't shake the sense that they were being hunted by the men who had attacked them a few days ago. There was blood on Marcus's hands, a target on his back. She imagined she'd be their prize after they had finished him off.

As they trudged along, she would get utterly lost in thoughts about Johnny and the children. He'd have got them through the floods and roadblocks to safety at the lake house. What were they doing at that very moment? Which room were they in? Sara took comfort in the fact that the kitchen pantry had been well stocked with dried and tinned food, which would sustain them for weeks if they were careful. Of course, in her imagination, the lake house was exactly how she had left it, spotlessly clean and untouched by marauders, a bottle of wine left on the kitchen island for the friends who were using it next. But then she would remember everything she had seen on her journey and fear would clutch at her heart – her children were alive and well; there was no other alternative – and she forced herself to think about all the things that would need to be done when they arrived at the house. But that brought its own anxious questions: if Johnny was there, how would she explain Marcus to him? How would the two men get on?

Sara and Marcus stopped for lunch at the gate to a field, relieved to shed their bags and sit down for a while. It was only when they had finished eating that they noticed several sheep grazing in the far corner.

'Well, there's a food source,' he said.

'We can't carry more than we already have. Anyway, there are lots of them near the lake.'

'I could become a sheep farmer,' he said, leaning back on his elbows. He had taken off his hat, and his badly cut hair glinted gold in the pale October light. He closed his eyes and turned his face up to the sun.

'It's lovely,' she said. 'The sun. Kind of revives you, doesn't it? I can't believe the rain has held off the last few days. Maybe it's a sign it's ending.'

'Mmm.'

'Can I ask you something?'

'Shoot.' He opened his eyes and turned to look at her.

'You know at the cottage when that man came through the back door.'

'Yep.'

'You shot him.'

'I know.'

'How did that make you feel?'

'What do you mean *make me feel*?' He closed his eyes again.

'Well, just that I... well, if it was me, I'd be kind of... well, traumatised maybe... really shocked at the very least. I mean, it's a human life after all.'

'Well, it was either his human life or your human life.'

'I'm not criticising you or anything. I was just wondering how it made you feel. It can't be a good feeling...'

'I feel fine. I felt sadder about your dog getting killed. That was unnecessary.'

'Oh, okay.'

There was silence.

'You and I are a bit different,' he said eventually. 'I see things in terms of best or worst possible outcomes. In that scenario, it was better that he died instead of you or me.'

'Well obviously.' She picked a blade of grass and rolled it into a ball between her thumb and forefinger. 'I'm not saying I'd have done anything different. I'm just curious about how it feels having killed an actual person.'

He raised himself up on one elbow and stared at her. 'It's black and white. The guy was an animal. He belonged to a pack of animals. He made his choice and look where that got him – the bottom of a ditch in the middle of nowhere.'

She said nothing for a while. Then, 'Okay, fair enough. I still feel bad though. Like it shouldn't be up to us who lives or dies.'

He closed his eyes and lay back, linking his hands across his chest. 'Sara, we're in a different world now.'

She sighed loudly. How had they got to the place where it seemed reasonable to kill someone. 'I suppose,' she said quietly.

They walked for another few hours. Sara's feet began to ache terribly and the handles of the plastic bags were giving her blisters on the palms of her hands. She had rearranged the various loads she was carrying so that most of it was on her shoulders, but it made little difference over time. They took wild narrow roads as they moved further north. The landscape on higher ground had fewer houses, and the fields were marshy and reed filled. Large sinkholes had pulled stone cowsheds and great slices of land down into their bellies. Sometimes the road in front of them collapsed into a new riverbed and they had to take a diversion through fields before re-joining the route. Floods along lower sections of road forced them to wade for hours at a time, leaving them soaked and shivering. At one point they came across a bicycle leaning against the wall of a bungalow, and she pedalled slowly alongside him for a while after hanging some of her bags off the handlebars. But the respite was short-lived. Only moments after he took his turn, the spokes snapped and the wheels buckled. He angrily flung it into the ditch and they continued walking in silence with nothing but the squelch of their footsteps for accompaniment. Eventually she stopped and changed into the trainers he had found in the village. The relief was instantaneous, and she left her once luxurious boots behind under the hedge, a new home, perhaps, for some lucky animal.

They spent that night in a dark bungalow long emptied of people. All the rooms were freezing, and the damp carpets and curtains smelled of dirty washcloths, as though the place had been flooded at one time. The beds still had sheets and duvets on them, and hurried attempts had been made to pack travel bags. Clothes were sitting in neat piles on top of a chest of drawers, and the wardrobes, their doors lying open, were littered with wire clothes hangers. They ate some of their tinned food at a small kitchen table and Sara gave herself a quick body wash in the bathroom sink with a cloth and the soap she had found earlier.

They took it in turns to sleep, Sara going first, slipping into an uneasy slumber on a child's damp, blue-and-green dinosaur duvet, disturbed even in the dark by the bright, busy wallpaper. Later, he woke her gently to take over watch in the front room. Stumbling and feeling her way down the dark hallway, she sat for hours with the rifle, listening to him toss and turn in the bed she had just left. Sometimes he shouted out in his sleep, strange unintelligible sounds, and she wondered about the parts of him that she knew nothing about. She felt relieved when the first syrupy notes of birdsong rose from the ditches and she was able to waken him. She then got another few hours sleep until a rare shaft of early sunlight poured in through the window.

7

After a quick breakfast, they took turns in the bathroom and left the house. There was nothing in it of any value to them. Any medicines had disappeared and there were no bags with decent handles to replace the plastic carriers. Repacking her shoulder bag, she discovered the mittens at the bottom and put them on, cursing herself for forgetting about them. They made her hands hot, but they protected her hands from the plastic handles that were cutting into her.

They made steady progress north through the morning, and she gave him a running commentary about the sheep, the crows and starlings and the landscape she saw around her. He didn't respond – Brin was better company, she caught herself thinking – but he seemed deep within his own thoughts. Maybe more relaxed than usual. Perhaps it was because they were deep in the countryside, well clear of any main roads and other people. If there were people surviving in these communities, they were staying hidden and silent for now.

Suddenly a bank of dark clouds moved in from the north-east completely obscuring the sun.

'Looks like it's starting up again,' she said with a sigh, squinting at the sky.

He nodded.

When the first fat drops of rain hit the mossy, overgrown tarmac, a light wind picked up behind them. They walked on, looking for somewhere to shelter – an old barn or overhang to keep them dry. A rumble of thunder in the distance gave their search some urgency and they picked up their pace, almost jogging along the road, which narrowed into a winding lane, overgrown hedges spilling onto the gravel.

Then she stopped. 'Shh.'

They stood still, the rain beginning a steady patter around them.

'It's a motorbike,' he said, his jaw suddenly tight.

'No, I don't think so. It's different. More like a lawnmower or a hedge trimmer or something.'

He cocked his head. 'Yeah, maybe.'

They walked on more slowly, keeping close to the hedge. The road turned first to the right, then to the left. Huge potholes cratered the surface and they had to pick out a path between them. The rain was falling steadily now. The noise grew louder, then suddenly cut. Marcus walked in front with the rifle, Sara staying close behind. The motor started back up again, now unmistakably a lawn mower.

'What the hell?' she whispered.

He shook his head.

They rounded another bend and found themselves on a wider section where a bright white garden wall fronted the road.

'Let's go into the fields. We can get around that way,' she said in a low voice.

'No, wait. Look.'

She peered through the rain at a man wearing a straw beach hat and long beige cardigan who was mowing the lawn at the front of the house.

'Jesus,' he said under his breath. 'What do you want to do?'

'God, I don't know. What's he doing mowing the lawn in the rain. What a waste of petrol!'

'Well, he's not afraid, that's for sure.'

'Maybe he's lost his mind.'

'Or there's nothing else for him to be at.'

They stood watching him for a few moments

'We might scare him if we walk by,' Sara said.

'I think we should talk to him.'

'Ah no, really?'

'Yes really.'

'I think it's asking for trouble.'

'He might have medicine or antibiotics we could use later down the line. Or he might know something that could help us.'

'But what if there are other people in there?'

'Not everyone is out to kidnap and kill us,' he said, looking at her pointedly. 'We can't live through this without talking to people. We need to be... what's the word... discerning.'

'I don't know. It's just simpler with the two of us.'

'Didn't we get the charger off the last people we met? Anyway, what if he has a working car? He's got fuel for that mower. He could be useful.'

She hesitated, her gut shouting at her to turn back and cut through the fields, but her mind swayed by Marcus's argument.

'Ah come on. Sure we have this.' He lifted the rifle. 'Anyway, he looks ancient. How much trouble can he be.'

'Fine, but it's on you. Something isn't right. I can feel it.'

He ignored her and pressed on ahead, Sara following him into the middle of the road. The man didn't see them coming until he had turned the mower at the corner of the sloping lawn. Then he cut the engine and, with one hand shielding his eyes, peered at them through the rain.

'Good morning,' he shouted, raising his arm and giving them a cheery wave. 'What about all this rain? Looks like you both could do with a cup of tea. Maureen would love to meet you. Come on in and I'll put the kettle on.'

Marcus and Sara stared at each other, startled by the barrage of a welcome, and then more closely at him. After a moment's hesitation, Marcus strode forward.

'Thank you. You're very kind. I'm Marcus, this is Sara. We'd absolutely love some tea with you and your wife.' He said all this with a weird affected accent. Had she not been so uneasy at the oddness of the encounter, she would have snorted with laughter.

'Come on up. I'm Eugene. Welcome to our home,' he roared through the rain. His mouth was wide open while he spoke, revealing two rows of browning teeth. Sara cringed and put her head down. Marcus walked quickly up the driveway, reaching out a hand towards this stranger as though he was at a networking event. They shook vigorously like old friends and walked on towards the house. Sara noticed a white car parked to the side of the house and began to get an inkling of what Marcus might be up to. She followed the two men, dropping her bags reluctantly in the porch.

'Come on in,' Eugene said, wiping his hands on his cardigan. 'I don't bite.' He looked them up and down, smiling widely.

Marcus and Sara walked into a long, carpeted hallway. She detected an odour she couldn't quite identify. It reminded her of the smell of boiled ham and cabbage leaking from the nunnery kitchens in her old boarding school, but it had a strange undertone of chemicals or brine.

Eugene flung open the door of the first room on the left and ushered them in. Sara glanced around the richly furnished room with its suite of cream sofas and gold-framed prints of Renaissance cherubs.

'There she is now. Hasn't it been a long time since we've had visitors, Maureen?' Eugene said.

A thin figure sat in a wicker window seat, propped up by fat cushions embossed with squirrel and acorn-themed embroidery and angled towards the view. She was wearing a sleeveless pink and rose-patterned dress, sheer nylon tights and tan leather wedge sandals. Sara stared at the woman, then at Eugene, then at the woman again. Maureen was quite dead and had been for some time. Bile surged up Sara's throat and she forced herself to swallow it.

'She looks very well,' Marcus said, flashing Sara a side look that said *play along here, for God's sake.*

'Delighted to meet you,' Sara mumbled.

'Go on, Maureen,' Eugene chuckled. 'Don't let the side down now. Say hello to this lovely pair. Aren't they just like Fiona and George? She's not herself these days. Not since they stopped coming. But any day now they'll be back.'

'Maybe we should go, leave you two in peace,' Sara said, trying not to sound panicky. 'We don't want to disturb you.'

'No, no, no, you're not disturbing us in the slightest. Dear God, it must be a year since we've seen a soul. It's wonderful to have you here. Come on, we'll make that tea. She normally sits with me in the kitchen, but there have been too many accidents lately.' He winked at Sara and took a step closer to her.

As they followed Eugene down to the kitchen, she noticed how well the house had been kept. Other than the appalling smell, everything was tidy with only a thin layer of dust on the surfaces. It was decorated with some pleasant soft furnishings and the odd contemporary print on the wall. Poor Maureen must have been quite houseproud and paid close attention to her favourite colour schemes in the *Royal Interiors* catalogue. In the kitchen, the kettle was already hissing and spitting on top of a large, black wood-burning range and a large clock hung on the wall, its hands at half past eight. It was tremendously stuffy, making the smell even worse. She searched for open windows but there were none.

'Sit,' Eugene said, grinning from ear to ear and gesturing towards two armchairs near the range.

Close up, his teeth were more the colour of old ivory and despite his grey hair, he was much younger than she'd initially thought. He looked healthy and strong, lean but not malnourished. She watched him carefully as he put loose tea in a pot and poured in boiling water from the kettle. He lifted two mugs decorated with farm animals from a mug tree and poured some tea into them. He opened the lid of a biscuit tin.

'Just for you, my dear,' he said to Sara as he handed her a mug, trying to make eye contact with her. His hands were enormous with long nails and he had fat, stubby fingers.

She looked away and glanced at the rifle in Marcus's hand, just to remind herself that it was still there. He offered them a biscuit each and Sara nibbled at a corner not sure what to expect. It was sweet, crunchy and surprisingly fresh but the smell had pervaded her senses so thoroughly that she had to force herself to swallow. Waves of anxiety washed over her and it was all she could do to stop herself from rushing outside. She gave Marcus pointed looks which he steadfastly ignored.

'You're very kind to have us,' she said eventually, 'considering what's going on out there.'

'Well, you look grand and trustworthy to me. And a fine-looking woman, if I may say so.'

Sara forced herself to smile politely.

'So when was the last time you spoke to anyone?' Marcus asked Eugene.

'Maybe eight months now. About that.'

'And you've been alone here all this time?'

'Just me and Maureen.'

They sat for a while listening to him talk about the rain and how lucky he was to have built this house on a hill. He was delighted to encounter them both, he told them again and again, but it seemed as though he was speaking only to her, his eyes wandering over her body, making her shiver involuntarily.

As he talked, he rolled up his sleeves and rubbed his hands together. Then he stood up and paced around the kitchen seemingly busy with essential tasks. He fiddled with the presses and cabinets, taking things out and putting them back in again. He was fidgety, restless, unpredictable. It was unbearable to Sara; all the signs were there – this man was not well. She glared at Marcus again: *come on, let's go!*

'So how long have you and Maureen been married?' Marcus asked, when there was a gap in the conversation.

'Oh, we're talking maybe forty years now. Still as wonderful as the day we met. I can't say she thinks the same of me now, but I live in hope.'

'She seems lovely,' Marcus said. 'You're lucky to have her.'

Eugene turned suddenly to face him. 'What are you talking about?' he said sharply.

'I just meant you're lucky to have Maureen,' Marcus said, a little startled.

'You have your own woman. Take your eyes off mine.' Eugene narrowed his eyes at Marcus, pausing for dramatic effect, then burst into laughter. 'Haha, your face,' he roared.

Sara could feel a pulse throbbing in her neck. 'So are we really the only people you've seen in the last few months?'

Eugene's laughter faded and he stared at her for a moment, then finally sat down, spreading his legs wide. The cut grass that had been stuck to his boots flaked off and lay on the floor in fat green clumps.

'The only ones,' he said, not taking his eyes off her. He sighed loudly and she got a whiff of his rancid breath. 'There are kids that play over the road. I hear them the odd day but never see them. Beautiful children, so beautiful, but they keep themselves to themselves.'

'Oh, are there children near here?' she said.

'Yes, little ones. Didn't I take herself for a drive to have a look a few weeks back? She's much better at the small talk than me. But they'd gone into their house before we saw them. I got out and knocked on the door and there was no answer. Anyway, we didn't want to be frightening them.'

'I'm sure,' she murmured, taking a sip of tea out of politeness. Goosebumps ran up and down her spine. 'So your children – are they all grown up?'

'Oh, same age as you, I suspect,' he said, staring intensely at her. 'What are you – thirty-five? Thirty-nine?'

She gave him a watery smile and didn't answer.

'Well, anyway we've two,' he said proudly. 'Fiona, our daughter – she's married to George. And Jimmy, our son. Not married. No interest in it, I think. He has his mother's heart broken. She always wanted grandchildren. We both did.'

'And when were they last here?' Marcus asked.

Instead of answering Marcus's question, Eugene nodded at his rifle. 'I've one just like it out the back. For the rabbits. Were you out hunting today?'

'Yes, we were,' Marcus said, his expression unchanged despite learning that Eugene also had a gun. 'No luck yet though. I'm a bad shot.'

Sara was impressed by the way Marcus was holding his nerve, making small talk like a neighbour who had just popped in for a chat.

'Lots of rabbits in the back fields,' Eugene said. 'I cook them at least twice a week.'

'And would you take the car out much?' Marcus asked. 'Go further afield?'

'The odd drive. It's hard to get herself up and dressed, so I wait until it's a nice day. Old age is a terrible thing. Good sunshine helps. Then she can see the countryside.'

'Well, if you aren't using it today, would you be interested in lending it to us for an hour or so?' Marcus leaned back in the chair and stretched out his legs. 'We wouldn't be long.' He was the picture of confidence and ease.

Eugene looked at him hard. 'Now what do you mean by "lend" exactly, sir? Do you not have your own car?'

'No, we ran out of fuel a while back. Need to get to a service station. Are there any around?'

'Well, maybe twenty miles back – over towards the town – but that's been closed a while now with these fellas coming and taking things. Up near the bridge, there's a shop with a pump out the front. Can't guarantee it works – it's electric and none of that's working now.'

'Okay, good to know. Thanks.'

'You don't need a car to get there. You'd walk there no problem.' Eugene looked from Marcus to Sara. 'It's not that I don't trust you and your wife.'

Sara twitched at being referred to as Marcus's 'wife'.

'Ah sure it's no problem. I quite understand,' Marcus said amiably, his accent still holding its new form. 'So how have you kept safe from everything?'

'Never left the house only to bring Maureen out for a drive.'

'And your neighbours? How are they doing?'

'That I can't tell you. They leave us alone. Always have.'

'Are any still alive that you know of?'

'Maybe just those kids. But it's lovely and quiet now. We just keep ourselves to ourselves.'

Eugene walked over to the fridge and opened it. It was empty except for a cereal bowl filled with a brownish paste. He took it out and, having fetched a teaspoon from the drawer beneath the sink, he spread a thin layer of what she assumed was a form of pate, onto a biscuit. Then he sandwiched it with another biscuit and slid the whole thing into his mouth. He chewed loudly with his mouth open then licked his fingers and wiped his hands on the front of his cardigan. Crumbs were still stuck to his always-smiling lips.

'Can I use your bathroom?' Sara asked, standing up abruptly as her stomach churned.

'Of course, my dear,' he said gaily. 'Down the hall on the right. Don't be long now. I think you're more interesting than your husband. I have more questions for you.'

'Thanks,' she murmured. 'Be right back.'

As she walked past Marcus, still casually sprawling in his chair, she caught his eye and glared at him. She closed the kitchen door behind her and walked down the hall to the bathroom. Inside, the air was thick with chemical air freshener and bleach and it made her cough. She tried to open the small window but it was locked. At the bottom of the bath was a grimy residue of wiry grey pubic hair and soap-scum, and a yellow stain ringed the tub from years without proper cleaning. She used the toilet quickly, relieved to change her tampon, and flushed. As she washed her hands in the freezing water, the kitchen door opened and she heard voices. She stepped out of the bathroom into the stench of the hall and found Marcus standing outside waiting for her.

'Where is he?' she hissed.

'Kitchen.'

'I'm leaving. I'm not spending one more minute in this place.'

'I know, I know. Look, just let me check the car, see if it works,' he whispered.

'Seriously? He's out of his mind. I mean, his decomposing wife is in that room over there. For all we know, he killed her himself. Are you not freaked out by this?'

He held her by the arm. 'Yes, I am, but we mightn't find another car with fuel again. We have to least check it out. He has the keys on a hook by the fridge. We could cover huge ground – be at your house by tonight. Think about that.'

She hesitated but then shook herself away.

'You can't just take it, it's his. And anyway, you don't know if there's fuel in it or if it even starts. We're fine walking, even in the rain. Look, he's either mad or he's playing with us, and my guess is that he's playing with us.'

'Just calm down, will you. I have this under control. Anyway, I could take him down if it came to it.'

'Don't you tell me to calm down! I don't care about the car. It isn't safe here and I'm walking out the door now. You can come if you want.'

She pushed past him without waiting for a reply and walked into the front porch. Their bags were where they had left them. She pulled the heavy bag across her shoulder and picked up as many of the others as she could carry and marched outside. A blast of chilly air hit her face as she stepped out into the rain. She inhaled deeply, grateful for the clean fresh air.

'Hang on,' Marcus called out from behind her.

She turned for a second and saw Eugene standing beside Marcus, cup in hand, looking put out, mouth hanging open in protest. Whatever conversation they were having was drowned out by the sound of the pouring rain and her own heavy breathing as she quickened her pace down the driveway towards the road. When she passed through the gateway, she glanced back to see Marcus's bags still stacked against the door and no sign of him. *He can take care of himself. If he wants to follow, he can. I'm not staying a minute longer in that house.* Instinct took over completely. She started to walk faster, almost breaking into a run, to put as much distance between her and Eugene as she could. She would wait for Marcus further along the road. She had to take care of herself first.

After a while the adrenalin rush subsided, and she felt able to slow her pace and her breathing. She checked behind her from time to time, keeping an eye out for Eugene who, having dispatched Marcus, might be coming after her, but she saw nothing. She heard nothing either – no car engine or gunshots. She trudged on, her body becoming hot all over and her legs trembling. The rain was coming down torrentially now, hammering off her face and forcing her to blink constantly. Her head itched from wearing the sweaty hat and her mittens were soaked through. She was drained. Just when she was about to give up and sit down in the middle of the wet road, an old open-style barn came into view behind a hawthorn and bramble hedge.

Access to the barn was through a rusting wrought iron gate, tied shut with bailing twine. It was surprisingly easy to open, and she ran through to stand under the corrugated roof of the barn. She dumped the plastic bags and shoulder bag, and sat on the dry earthen ground, her back propped up against a steel upright. Her entire body ached from the stress of the last few hours and from carrying the weight of the bags. Everything around her dripped and splashed, and she thought fleetingly of the old cottage with the warm fire, sweet whiskey and her beloved Brin. She felt suddenly so very alone, an intense kind of loneliness she had never experienced before.

Then she heard a crack, loud, sharp and reverberating through the air. And then a second crack. Whether it was Marcus's rifle or Eugene's – or both – she couldn't tell. After that, silence, except for the dripping and the drumming of the rain on the roof of the barn. She waited and waited, her heart caught in her throat. Terror washed over her then subsided, replaced with fraught indecision. To move back out into the rain and put further distance between her and Eugene's house or stay where she was.

After what seemed like a long time, she heard someone running. She peeked out at the gate from the barn, not wanting to be seen if it was Eugene, and poised to sneak backwards into an adjoining field. Marcus was lumbering along the road, his rucksack on his back, drenched, red-faced and panting. She darted out to the gate.

'Come in here,' she called in a low voice. 'It's dry underneath.'

He looked relieved to see her. He ran through the gate, flung his bags on the ground and collapsed onto his knees. Then he rolled over and lay flat on his back, his eyes closed, his chest heaving beneath his coat, the rifle still clenched in his right hand. She stood watching him, waiting for him to make the first move.

'Jesus,' he said eventually.

'You okay?'

'Yeah, I guess.'

'So what happened? I heard two shots.'

'It was nothing. I'm not hurt, it's fine.'

'What about him?'

'Bit of damage there, but he'll survive.'

'I knew something would happen.'

'It was nothing.'

He rolled over on his side, then sat up. A cloud of midges gathered above them and began a stealthy assault on their sweaty faces and necks. She swatted them away with little effect and watched him intensely until he looked away.

'Come on! What happened? Tell me!' she said.

He took off his hat and ran his fingers through his hair. 'I just asked him for the car keys. Told him it was urgent. He said no. I said we could trade – food, the wine. He still wouldn't budge. Said he had everything he needed already. So I picked up the rifle.'

'You did what?

'I picked up the rifle and pointed it at him and told him to hand me the car keys.'

'Jesus.'

'He got them and I walked him to the car. Then I shot him in the foot.'

'Oh my God – you shot him?'

'Well, I shot him in both feet.'

'You did what? Jesus, Marcus! Why the hell did you do that?'

'I didn't want to kill him. I just didn't want him following us.'

'But you ran here. So where's the car?

'I didn't take it."

'Why not.'

'You don't want to know. And I don't want to talk about it. Not now.'

She said nothing for a few moments, her imagination filling the gaps. 'Okay, let me put it this way – was it worth it?'

'Was what worth it?'

'That little diversion you made us take into that man's messed-up world, despite me warning you not to. We're no better off and now a man who was minding his own business, creepy as he was, can't walk.' She shook her head and turned away from him.

'I was thinking of you, not just me. You want to get to your house and I'm trying to help you do that.'

'I'm grateful, I really am,' she said, turning back to him. 'You saved my life before and I owe you a lot. But that doesn't give you the right to make decisions that might put us in danger and hurt other people.'

'You wouldn't be quite so concerned about him if you saw what I saw,' Marcus mumbled under his breath.

'What do you mean?'

'Nothing. Forget I said anything. Let's just say he deserved what I did to him.'

'How are you the judge of that? He's probably going to die now – from an infection, if he doesn't bleed out first.'

'Oh, he deserved it all right. So do you really want to know why I shot him then? I'm warning you, you won't like it.'

She had to know now but she was damned if she going to beg him. 'This is crazy,' she said. 'You literally just said *you don't want to know*! So now you do want me to know?'

'Yeah, well, maybe it's the only way I can get you to stop looking at me like that.'

She turned her head away. 'Go on, tell me. I'm a big girl. I can take it.'

'Fine. It was those kids he was on about. I made him open the passenger door and there they were – two of them, from what

I could make out. They were naked and possibly strangled. I couldn't look for long. But their bodies had been there for a while. Months maybe.'

She gasped and covered her face with her hands. 'Oh god no.'

'Yes.' He stood up stiffly. Something in him suddenly looked cracked and broken. 'I should have put one through his head, but maybe it's better this way. A long slow death.'

She felt like throwing up. How many dark and damaged people were there in the world? 'Well, how do I know you're telling the truth? How do I know you aren't just saying that because you know I won't go back and check.'

'Why would I make something like that up?' he said, looking at her intensely. 'I don't think I could imagine something that horrific.' All the colour had left his face. 'Don't believe me if you don't want to. That's your business.'

It was as though the wind had been sucked out of him. It was the first time she had seen him like that and she wasn't sure how to respond. They sat in the barn for a while without speaking. He picked up a stone and tossed it from one hand to the other.

'I should really trust you better by this stage,' she said eventually. 'We've been through too much already. I'm sure you did the right thing.' She stood up. 'We need to get out of here. Put some miles between us and this place. No more people, okay?'

'Yeah, sure, no more people,' he said without conviction.

They redistributed the loads in their bags, Sara taking some of his tins in her shoulder bag. She was powered by a quiet fury and she set the pace, walking quickly and with renewed purpose. She was in a hurry to put miles between her and this narrow country road with all its nasty things. Marcus found it hard to keep up with her until she burned up all her excess energy, and they later fell back into rhythm, walking side by side.

They walked for what seemed like hours through the rain – long heavy deluges and light drizzle – and remained in silence for most of the afternoon. The temperature dropped, which didn't help. Her spirits lifted when they passed a signpost for Ballinamore; at least they were travelling in the right direction. She tried several times to catch Marcus's eye and start a conversation, but he seemed preoccupied, head down and thumbs tucked behind the straps of the rucksack.

'Hey, we need to stop… find somewhere for the night,' she said as the sun began to set for the day. 'We're both drenched. If we don't dry off, we'll end up sick with something.'

'Okay, you call it. Pick the house and I'll check it out.'

'I can do it this time,' she said, not sure how to interpret his tone.

'No, you're all right. I'll sort it.'

He sounded weary; that was all she could tell. If she were in his shoes, she'd still be processing what she'd seen in that car. A wave of compassion for him ran through her.

They stopped at several houses that looked promising, but each time he returned to where she was waiting with the bags and shook his head. Most were flooded, and one had a body in it. She had resolved never to sleep in a house with dead people in it again unless there were no other options. Finally, as twilight fell, he emerged from the side of a red-brick bungalow and gave her a half-hearted thumbs up.

They walked into the front room, dripping and shivering, dropped the bags and peeled off their wet clothes. He stripped down to his underwear in front of her, abandoning any sense of propriety. Good manners prompted her to turn away but not before she saw his shoulders. They were bruised purple and black from carrying the backpack and had nasty welts. Murmuring something about giving him privacy, she dragged her bag down the hallway to a poorly lit bathroom that thankfully had clean running water. She peeped into the bedrooms on the way down, taking stock of anything that might be useful to them.

163

In the bathroom, she stripped off her jeans and pulled out of her bag the nylon stockings and dress she'd brought with her from the cottage. She filled the sink with water and worked the soap into a lather in her hair. It was freezing work and she shivered violently throughout. After she rinsed it off, she quickly soaped her upper body and dried her top half. Then she washed between her legs and her feet. It felt so good to be clean and fresh again even if she was rattling from the exposure to the cold, damp air. She put on the dress and the stockings and put the Aran sweater back on. When she returned to the room, he had a different shirt on and had set a fire in the fireplace with some magazines and bits of a broken chair.

'Are you sure we should light a fire?' she said, noticing her breath in the air.

'We need to dry all this stuff somehow... and warm ourselves.'

'There are blankets on the beds down the hall. They'll be damp but they're better than nothing.'

'Good, we can wrap those around us until the room heats up.'

She laid out their drenched clothes across some dining chairs and an old fire guard. Then she went down to the bedrooms and brought back several blankets, wrapping two around her shoulders. It wasn't long before there was a roaring fire, casting welcome heat out into the room and making it feel almost jolly.

'Let's eat more than usual tonight,' she said suddenly, sitting cross-legged on the floor in front of the fireplace. Her fingers had started to thaw. 'It'll lighten the load and we could both do with the calories. We'll be able to get more food at the lake house – enough for a few weeks... unless it was raided or the kids have eaten it.'

'Okay, let's do it,' he said. 'And some wine?' He smiled and looked at her questioningly. 'It was some day. I'm sorry, I should have listened to you. You seem to have a nose for staying clear of things.'

She wrapped the blankets tighter around her shoulders. 'Not really, considering I brought some unsavoury characters back to your cottage to say the least, but yes, you could trust me more. And I say we need to lie low, away from people.'

He smiled. She couldn't tell if he was just humouring her but decided not to labour the point.

'So, drink?' he asked, looking hopeful.

'Sure.' She had little energy left to resist.

He rummaged in his rucksack and took out one of the bottles of wine, two forks, and four tins – beans, fish and fruit. He went into the kitchen and returned with plates and mugs. 'There's fresh drinking water from the tap in the kitchen,' he said with a smile.

Kneeling by the fire, he opened the tins and dished out the food. They ate ravenously despite the weird mixture of tastes. Tinned fruit and tuna had never tasted so good.

'Can you open it?' she asked, nodding at the bottle of wine.

He grinned, his eyes suddenly dancing. *'Mais oui. Voila!'* and he pulled a corkscrew out of a zip pocket on the side of his bag.

'Where did you get that?'

'The last place – the big house with the mam and her baby in the ensuite.'

'Oh, there was a baby there…' Her voice faded. She kept her eyes on the wine bottle.

'Sorry,' he said.

He deftly worked the screw down into the cork and pulled it out with a satisfying pop, then filled the mugs halfway.

'I think it's a good one,' he said, handing her a mug.

She reached out through the blankets for it and inhaled its aroma deeply. It was strong and fruity, with undertones of oak and dark chocolate. She took a sip. Delicious. Not regular garage shop wine. Soon, the warmth of the alcohol spread through her and she began to relax. Marcus sat beside her on the floor, their backs propped against one of the sofas.

'It's good to feel this cosy again,' she said, looking at the fire.

'Mm, lovely. So how are you doing now?'

'I'm okay. I could do with things being a bit the same for a while. No surprises. I don't like the world much anymore.'

'Yeah, I hear you.'

'There's just too much death out there. Awful people doing awful things. Speaking of awful things, what was the story with your cucumber sandwiches, royal garden party accent earlier?'

'Ha, indeed! Quite the impression I made? Thought I was bloody well good!'

'Rather.' She giggled and snorted at once, mocking him, and he made a funny shocked face at the noise.

'Anyway, back to what you were saying,' he said, his voice becoming more serious. 'It's like we've become desensitised to it all, to the death.'

'Have you? Even when you find... like today in the car?'

'No, not that. But everything else. It seems to take a lot to shock me now.'

'Lucky you,' she said. 'It'll take me a while to get to that stage.'

'Yeah, but you lose something with it.'

'Like what? What do you think you've lost?'

'I'm not sure.' He took a drink of wine. 'Empathy? Something like that. I just feel kind of detached from everything, like I'm watching a movie and everything in front of me is on a screen. Does that make sense?'

'Sounds like trauma to me,' she said quietly.

'Maybe. But I do care what happens to you.'

She felt herself blush and hoped he'd think it was the heat from the fire. 'Well, thanks, I guess,' she said, looking away and trying to suppress a smile. 'That makes me feel a little better.'

'Seriously,' he said, sounding even more solemn. 'I like you a lot.'

She looked down at her mug as her cheeks reddened even more. There was a long silent pause, then he raised his mug.

'Let's drink to two things.'

'Okay. What?'

'One, to your kids being alive. And two, to staying healthy and well 'cos we won't get far without that.'

She raised her mug through the gap in the blanket and clinked it against his. He caught her eye and smiled, holding her gaze for a moment until she looked away again. She sipped her wine and stared at the fire, watching the flames lick and curl at the wood.

They sat like that, talking quietly until the wet clothes hanging around them started to steam. Marcus kept the fire blazing and it cast long dancing shadows around the room. Soon they were laughing at memories of all the mistakes they had made as kids, the embarrassing situations they had found themselves in as teenagers, and it wasn't long before all the wine was drunk.

She had a vague memory of him telling some story about a construction project he'd worked on in Africa that involved a hyena and drunk German engineer, and the last thing she remembered was curling up on the floor and him putting something soft under her head as a pillow.

8

The next morning, they awoke to the familiar sound of rain falling heavily on the roof, and the already-risen sun. The wine the night before and sheer physical exhaustion had helped them to sleep longer than usual. Sara certainly had not kept watch, and by the looks of Marcus, neither had he. The room was freezing cold, the fire having burnt out during the night.

She rubbed her eyes and stretched. She was thirsty, stiff, sore and dying for a pee. When she returned from the bathroom, he was awake and sitting up, pushing his elbows out behind him and grimacing.

'Your shoulders?' she asked.

'Yes, and my back. Probably the way I slept.' He stood up slowly, easing the stiffness out of his body. 'Listen to that rain!'

'Yeah, I know. It's not great.'

'There's no point getting back out there till it stops. We'll be soaked through in minutes.'

She walked over to a window and stared out. The overgrown garden was saturated and rivulets poured down the driveway towards the road, cutting deep channels through the gravel and stones. 'God, we only got a few days off from it.'

'And this time no jeep. We've got to sit it out.'

'Really? I'll go stir-crazy sitting here waiting for it to stop.'

'No choice. We can't walk in that. Our clothes aren't even dry yet.'

'Okay,' she said eventually. 'But the minute it eases off, we go.' It could stay like this for weeks, like it had before. She reached into her bag for her phone and turned it on. There were no notifications.

'Any signal?' he asked.

She shook her head. 'Just the loading bar getting nowhere.' She went into her photo app.

'Hey, smile,' she said. He turned and looked at her.' Just to remember you by, in case in years to come I believe you were simply a construct of my traumatised mind.' He laughed, and she took the picture. His face was upturned and momentarily joyful.'

'Not too shabby,' she quipped, grinning at him and turned the phone back off.

'I'll light the fire again,' he said as if wanting to offer her some compensation for staying still. 'There are cabinets and drawers I can use as fuel. Have a look around. See if you can find a deck of cards or something. We'll keep ourselves entertained somehow.'

She gathered the blankets around her shoulders again and wandered out of the room, stopping in the kitchen to drink from the tap and refill her bottle.

It was a simple little bungalow and looked as though it had been a cherished home for someone. The farther they moved from the city, the more ordinary everything seemed. But if there was one thing she had learned over the past few weeks it was that that ordinariness was nothing but a veneer; beneath it lay damaged people and troubled lives. There would be others out there keeping their heads down, surviving quietly, hiding in fear. She felt fresh pangs of regret that they hadn't left Dublin the minute things got serious. But what could they have done? They'd people who needed them. She kept going over it and over it in her mind.

She looked through all the presses and drawers in the kitchen and then searched all the bedrooms. Not much had been left behind – a cheap dinner set, a collection of cups and mugs, a stray sock and a toy Hot Wheels car under one of the beds. The only thing of note in the bathroom was a damp roll of toilet paper covered in mould. A dried-out air freshener sat like a stone on top of the cistern. She returned to the living room empty-handed.

'Nothing,' she said.

'Let's eat then.'

He pulled some tins out of his rucksack.

'If you want, I have soap and bath creme if you fancy a wash after,' she said.

'You saying I stink?' He raised his eyebrows at her, eyes twinkling.

'Ha, maybe only a bit.'

'Yeah, I might take you up on that. In the meantime, sit down and eat – if you can handle my smell.'

She took a tin of syrupy peaches from him and sat cross-legged on the floor to eat, chewing every spoonful carefully.

'You know that man Eugene?' she said.

'Yes.'

'He's my idea of pure evil. I just somehow knew it, even before we went up his driveway.'

He cocked his head and smiled. 'Sixth sense?'

'Maybe.'

'So you can be our resident psychic,' he said, laughing. 'Keep us right.'

She didn't laugh. 'It was strange. I had such a bad feeling about the place before we even reached the garden.'

'So what's your sixth sense telling you about me then?' he asked, waving his fingers around in the air like he was casting spells.

'Very funny,' she said, punching him on the arm. 'Wait till the next time I save you.'

He looked suddenly pleased and glanced at her again the way he had the night before when they were exchanging anecdotes. Without the wine she felt shy and couldn't meet his eye. She broke the moment by asking him questions about his job and friends and listened to all the stories he must have told a thousand times before to other people because he told them so well. Then she got up to wander around the house again; he asked for the soap, which she gave him, and he disappeared into the bathroom.

She sat quietly on a dining chair in the kitchen and looked out into the back garden. The rain fell steadily and cascaded from the broken corner joins of the gutters. The rifle lay beside her on the floor, a constant companion in these strange times. She thought of Johnny and a rush of guilt swept through her. *You're clearly enjoying all this attention!* he'd say if he was watching them. He'd be angry with her, jealous… and, she realised, he had good reason to be. She forced him out of her mind. Sure he might be dead. She was shocked to catch herself thinking, *as long as the children got away; that's the main thing.*

Later, they invented a word quiz and kept score on the back of an old magazine with the stub of pencil Sara found at the back of one of the drawers. He nodded off from time to time, and she curled up under the blankets, grateful for a day or two close to a bathroom. Her period had been light and was almost done now. Night fell again and the rain seemed to lessen. This time they took turns watching the road from the front window, deciding to save the last bottle of wine for another time. They thought they heard engines revving in the distance, but the sound faded too quickly for them to be certain.

Just before dawn, they rose quietly. The rain had eased off into a drizzle. So they changed back into their now almost-dry clothes and repacked their bags, the loads thankfully lighter. Then they used the bathroom one last time and left the house through the back door. As a watery sun broke through low clouds, a fresh easterly wind cut across the fields and through the gaps in the browning hedgerows. They turned their jacket collars up and followed the road deep into the Leitrim countryside.

They settled into a brisk pace that seemed to suit them both. At one point, she accidentally brushed her hand against his and a crackle of electricity shot through her. Her heart bucked and she felt lightheaded. She said nothing – neither did he – but she quickened her pace. She found herself remembering the sheen off his back when he had pulled off his wet clothes, the muscles outlined by the half-light. Shrugging the thought off, she focused on the road ahead and kept her eye out for movement or houses along the way. He was unusually quiet, considering his bright, enthusiastic start, she sensed him glancing at her as they walked side by side.

They climbed the banks of ditches to get around the wide puddles, trying to keep their feet as dry as possible. She plucked a few sloe berries from the lower branches of a blackthorn hedge and ate them, enjoying the sweet cut of dry bitterness in her mouth. Not so long ago she would have picked them and made gin for the winter. A scattering of memories moved in, taking her back in time. She caught herself smiling and turned her head so he wouldn't see. He felt different to her now, and the subtle shift was now too hard to ignore. Oh God, she thought, what am I going to do now? *What am I going to do?*

That day they made it as far as the forests that bordered County Leitrim. They had eaten more of their food than they'd planned, but the bags were lighter and walking was easier. Sometimes Marcus talked, telling her about a stag night in Copenhagen, or sky-diving in south-east Asia, or surfing in Bali, or a trip to a mountain monastery in Borneo. She listened patiently, quietly, discovering a new talent for small talk while thinking about her children.

Then they would walk for an hour or two in easy silence, neither of them feeling the need to fill the gaps. She listened constantly for sounds of any kind, particularly engines or traces of human activity. She still worried that the men they had encountered only days earlier would be looking for them. 'We killed one of their guys,' she reminded Marcus when he tried to allay her fears, but despite him assuring her that they couldn't be tracked, she couldn't shake off the feeling. She listened to all Marcus's reasons for why the men wouldn't bother looking for them and agreed that they made sense; nonetheless, the unease wouldn't lift. It was like the feeling she'd had about Eugene.

After scoping out several houses along the way, they spent the next night in a new build that had never had occupants. It smelled of concrete, plasterboard and undercoat. The next morning, covered in white chalky dust, they packed up before first light and moved on, walking along the edge of the forests and sticking to the smaller roads, sheltering amongst the trees when showers passed overhead.

'So how much further do you think?' he asked later that day. 'Roughly.'

'My best guess is three more days. Maybe seven or eight hours walking each day.'

'We're still heading in the right direction?'

'Yep. We used to stop sometimes near these forests and have picnics with the children.'

'Okay.'

He was asking her this regularly now. It seemed to frustrate him that he had to rely on her guidance, that she was the one who called it at the junctions after checking the position of the obscured sun.

'We could probably do with a first aid kit,' he said, breaking one of their longer silences.

'There's a good one at the lake house.'

'Oh? What's in it?'

'The usual. Why? Anything the matter?'

'Yeah, but it's nothing big.'

'Nothing is never just nothing.'

'Ah seriously, it's fine – just one of my feet. All this walking.'

'Blister?'

'Something like that.'

'Want me to look at it for you?'

'Absolutely not.' He laughed. 'You really don't want to see my feet right now.'

She smiled. 'I've probably seen worse.'

'Stop.'

She laughed. 'Why? What did I say?'

'No, stop. Listen.' He cocked his head to one side.

She scanned the ditches and the fields beyond, her ears pricked. 'I can't hear anything. Not even birds. What is it?' she whispered.

'Wait.'

'Is it an engine? Voices?'

They stood in silence for a minute. Then she heard it. Barking. A dog barking. A shower of hail suddenly skittered over them, covering the road in small white stones.

'It's not getting closer,' he said.

'Okay, well let's keep going.'

They picked up their pace, almost breaking into a slow run. The barking continued for a few minutes and then stopped.

'It could be one of their Rottweilers,' she said, remembering the flickering tongue of that horrible man.

'Are you still on about that? It could be any dog.'

'I suppose so.'

'Loads of people still have dogs. Stop worrying. We can deal with it.'

He shook the rifle to remind her. She wished she had one of her own, something to carry in her own hands just in case.

'Can we slow down a bit?' he said. 'My foot's killing me.' It was the first time she noticed him limping.

They cut their pace and she kept an eye on him for a while.

'I should probably look at that for you.'

'I'll do it myself later.'

'Can't have you going lame on us.'

After an hour, they arrived at the entrance to a public woodland where they stopped and offloaded their bags around an old picnic table. The air was thick with the smell of pine, damp earth and decaying leaves. They swept the trees, looking out for strange colours or sudden movement. He sat down on the bench, undid the laces of his right boot and grimaced as he pulled it off.

'Ah now, that doesn't look great,' she said, peering over his shoulder.

Blood had soaked through his sock at the heel, and when he peeled off the sock, it revealed a wide oozing blister that had burst long ago.

'We'll need to get antiseptic on that and a big band-aid before it gets infected,' she said.

'Yeah…'

'Look, let me take the bag for a while.'

'The bag's too heavy for you.'

'I can take it for a little while,' she insisted.

'Does your husband – Jimmy or John or whatever – does he keep clothes at the house?'

'Yes, and it's Johnny.'

'I might need to borrow some when we get there.'

'I'm sure he won't mind. Anyway, if he's there you can ask him yourself.' She allowed that thought to settle in her and see how it felt, but it created nothing but a low-level anxiety.

He rummaged in his bag and pulled out a spare T-shirt. He ripped the material into strips and wrapped them around his heel and foot, covering the open sore with several layers of fabric before carefully pulling the sock back on. Then, easing his foot back into the boot, he laced it back up and tested his weight.

'That'll do for a little while,' he said.

'We'll need to keep an eye on it. It looks nasty.'

'It'll be grand. I don't get infections easily. Good immune system. Anyway, do you want to eat something?'

'No, not yet. I'd rather wait until the end of the day when we can rest and enjoy it.'

'Okay. So I've an idea.' He stood up and walked over and back, wincing at each step. 'These farms we're passing.'

'What about them?' She got up from the bench and started picking up her bags again.

'Well, we don't want to go near them in case the owners have shotguns or whatever.'

'Yes, quite sensibly. And?'

'Well, they'll have farm vehicles, right? Tractors, four-by-fours.'

'I suppose.'

'Well, I think we should look at finding one. We could watch a farm and check it out. If it looks good, we go in and hunt for keys. Even a tractor would get us to your lake house in a few hours.'

'But we could lose half a day waiting to see if a farm's clear or not.' She stood there, bags all loaded, looking at him in frustration.

'I was fine walking and hoping we'd find a car. But now I'm not.'

'I know you're in pain and walking is hard, but we need to stay below the radar. Tractors are too noisy – too high. It's too risky. So no, I'm not going for that one.'

'Fine. We'll push on so.' He looked dark, mutinous, sulky.

'I'm sorry your foot is so painful,' she said softly.

'I'm not talking about it anymore.'

'Let's try another mile or two.'

'No choice, have I?'

He walked around in a wide circle pushing down on his right foot, checking the rub of his heel against the boot leather and wincing. Then he pulled the straps of the rucksack up over his shoulders and picked up the rifle.

'Ready?' she asked.

'As I'll ever be.'

She decided to leave him alone for a while.

The narrow road beside the forest was overgrown and covered in fallen branches and wet leaves. Wild grasses and moss pushed in from the verge, their roots snaking across the asphalt. They walked on, Sara deciding to ignore his limp. They came across very few houses on this stretch of the road and then arrived at a junction. They took the road to the left, which led them down into the bogs and marshes near the lake. Then the road turned sharply to the right, revealing a row of small white cottages.

'Oh good,' she said, slowing her pace. 'I remember this place. We're close to Drumkeeran village.'

They stopped in the middle of the road.

'Do you think we should go there?' he asked.

'I'm not sure.'

'What's in it?'

'Old pubs. A credit union. That's all I remember.'

'A shop?'

'Maybe a garage. I honestly can't remember.'

'Is there a way around it?'

'Don't think so.' She chewed her lip.

'Maybe we should just chance walking through – like what we did the last time.'

'Where you go in and check it out and I wait?'

'Yeah.'

'No, let's do it together.'

He laughed but she didn't understand why. Was he poking fun at her for not wanting to be left on her own or was there something she was missing? It irritated her that she now cared what he thought of her.

He took the safety off the gun and raised it. 'We need to find some kind of vehicle,' he said. 'This walking is killing me.'

They walked on, keeping to the side of the road nearest the white cottages.

'I wonder what kind of people live here,' he said.

'Normal country people, I suppose.'

They passed a bin that was overflowing with rubbish. Crows or wild animals had been pulling at it, scavenging what they could. Plastic containers rolled around in the breeze, wet paper was pasted to the road.

'Let's check them out,' Marcus said, pointing at two cars parked towards the end of the street. The rear windscreens were smashed out.

He picked up the pace, seemingly oblivious to his sore foot. She stayed alert to the houses they passed, looking out for the twitch of a lace curtain, shadow-shapes, the click of a lock. But there was nothing. They walked on, turning every now and again to look behind them. When they got to the cars, Marcus's shoulders slumped and she soon saw why – someone had ripped out the ignition in them both. There was nothing but wires.

'Look under the seats,' she said.

'What for?'

'Sometimes there's a first aid kit.'

He reached under. 'Nope.'

'I'll try the boot.'

Both car boots were locked.

'Come on, just keep going. There are more houses up ahead.' She pushed forward, anxious not to stand still for too long.

'I'm going to the credit union,' he said. 'They might have something with an engine at the back. Jesus, even a bicycle would do at this point.'

'What if there are people in there? Come on, it's not worth the hassle. Let's keep going. There'll be more up ahead.'

He gave the front door a shove but it was locked. 'Fine. But you shouldn't be so scared all the time.'

'I'm not scared. I'm cautious.'

'You're risk-averse.'

'It's kept me alive this long. We're so close now. No point doing stupid stuff. Come on.'

He shrugged and, grumpily kicking a stone across the street, walked on. They left the village behind them and found themselves on a wider road bordered by forest and soggy farmland. Stopping for a drink near a block-built cattle shelter, they found evidence of a recently extinguished fire. The smell of burning charcoal and smoke still lingered in the air. The damp concrete floor was littered with rubbish and empty food containers. They scoured the fields around them with renewed anxiety but saw no one and heard nothing. A short while later, they reached a newly fenced stretch of road, the old line of barbed poles hanging askance over the ditch.

'Hey look,' she said.

To the left, set far back from the road, was a small yard. An ugly industrial unit, the kind often funded by local enterprise grants, stood on a bed of hardcore and weedy gravel. Parked beside it were four minivans and a mechanical digger.

'Hallelujah!' he said, throwing his arms in the air. 'What are the chances! Please let there be a full fuel tank.'

She laughed, relieved by the shift in his mood and annoyed that his mood affected her at all. He ran towards the vans and tried each door. They were all locked. He kicked one of the tyres in frustration, then breaking into a limping jog, he disappeared around the back of the building. She stood between the vans and listened to him banging and rattling, fretting about the noise. She heard breaking glass. Scuffles and a loud clatter. She scanned the boundary of the site for movement. Five minutes passed. Then she heard an engine turn over and die, turn over again and kick into life. The engine revved loudly and a minute or so later Marcus came round the side of the building in a small white trade van, elbow out the window, beaming at her.

'Jump in. Quick.'

She opened the back doors and threw their bags in on top of a load of floor tiles, tools, bags of grout and cement. Then she slammed the doors shut and ran around to the passenger seat.

'Nice one!' she said, hopping in and instinctively pulling the seatbelt across.

'Let's go,' he said, jubilantly. 'It's as if someone left it as a gift. The back office door was unlocked and the keys were on the desk. No sign of anyone.'

'Brilliant.'

'Maybe they were watching, but saw the gun and decided we weren't worth the hassle.'

'Thank God for the gun, if that's the case. How much fuel?'

'Half a tank.'

'Jesus, how lucky can you get?'

'Maybe I should have checked the other vans for fuel.'

'Better to keep going.

'Nearly there now though, right?'

'Yes, I'd say we're an hour away now, maybe less.'

Her heart soared. What if Johnny and the children were there waiting for her, keeping watch on the long driveway from the kitchen window, longing to see her coming to join them. Her joy was tempered by anxiety that it was too much to hope for, but she was filled with nervous energy.

He pulled out onto the road, carving through the gravel and kicking up stones in his enthusiasm. They tore down the country lanes and through junctions without even checking the side roads. There were more heavy showers, and he laughed gleefully at the protection the van gave them from the downpours. An old packet of apple drops sat on the dash, and they shared them, savouring the sticky sweetness.

'I'm guessing from your reaction that you're not looking forward to seeing the house again,' he said, his eyes twinkling as they drove along.

To say she was looking forward to it was an understatement. 'It's my only home now,' she said softly, ignoring his attempt at humour. 'It's all that's left. I just hope it hasn't been ransacked or burnt to the ground. And that they're all there and no one else.'

'Try and stay positive, yeah?'

'Yeah.'

'It'll be okay. It'll be a relief for us to have a base for a while.'

There he goes again. All this us-ness.

He glanced at her, upbeat and smiley. 'You're lucky to own it.'

'I'm not sure that matters anymore.'

'What do you mean?'

'Whether you own something or not, when someone else can just decide to take it for themselves.'

'It'll matter eventually. When things rebuild.'

'I wonder what that'll look like.' She tried to picture it in her head. 'Hypothetically, if you had to oversee putting it back together, what would you do?' she asked. 'Same again or different?'

'Different.'

'In what way?'

'Well, I'd want decisions to be made quicker. Less red tape.'

'How would that be better?'

'Too much time's wasted consulting with people. Decision by committee delays decisions. Costs lives. Livelihoods. Nothing gets done.'

'But that's how things are done in a democracy!' she protested.

'But it's inefficient democracy. It's too slow. I prefer the presidential model, like the United States – one man driving the agenda.'

'Or one woman.'

'Sure, yeah, of course.'

'But they still have to run everything through layers of public representatives who vote,' she said.

'Well, we can work on that.'

'Mmm. I'm not sure I like your version of society.'

'So how would you rebuild this mess? What was there before was well and truly broken.'

'It wasn't perfect, I'll give you that, but we have to take collective responsibility for having voted in all the parish-pump populists.'

'A big job's ahead for whoever's next up to the plate, starting with distribution of medication and resources for survivors. All these diseases rampant and no healthcare available or vaccination programmes for kids. And how would you begin to restart the economy? What would that even resemble? I think we need to deal with the maniacs who are feeding off the chaos and the power vacuum first. And then there's the justice system.' His jaw clenched and unclenched as his emotions rose.

'We've good templates for that.'

'But nobody's putting up their hands to do the work.' His eyes flashed with vitality as he spoke.

'You've actually thought about this, haven't you.'

'A lot.' A frown creased his forehead.

'It sounds to me like you'd prefer a mini-dictatorship.'

'Maybe so, if that's what it takes in the beginning.'

'They never end well.'

'But they get things done,' he said.

'Really? Power tends to corrupt, etcetera.' She enunciated the *etcetera* pointedly.

'Ahh, that old chestnut.'

'So do you fancy yourself as up to the task?' she asked.

'Well, I wouldn't refuse an invitation, put it that way.'

'I see.'

'Anyway, there's a long way to go yet, my dear. Everyone's out for themselves now.'

She was troubled by what he had said, not because of his views, which he was entitled to, but because what needed to get done was so overwhelming. Someone out there was probably already working on a new society, using the political vacuum to their advantage, doing what they had to win resources, legitimise status, take land and property. And what about the constitution? Would it still hold firm? What legal measures were left to hold those to account if the constitution was abandoned or sidestepped? She shuddered. How had it come to this? How were they so ill-prepared?

'Which way here?' he asked at another junction.

'Left. Then straight on for twenty minutes or so.'

'It's all forest. I've never seen so many trees.'

'Yeah, the land isn't great, so the only way they could make money was from this awful monoculture. All commercial planting. You'll see the lakes soon.'

They rarely saw a house now at all, and after a while the trees thinned out, the sky opened up and the land rolled out in front of them – hillocks and narrow flooded valleys sliced with fencing and old drystone walls. There were quite a few sheep grazing in the higher reed-filled fields, surviving off what was left of the grass, their heavy wool coats scraggy and streeling.

She sat upright in the seat. 'See that mountain ridge ahead? We go around that on the higher road. Stay on this one for the moment. Then in about fifteen minutes we'll take a right.'

'Fifteen minutes! Brilliant!'

'The organic centre is signposted down a track. Then you'll see the lake below. Another few kilometres along and we'll get to the track up to the house.'

He looked at her with a big grin on his face. 'Nearly there! Can you believe it!?'

They tore along the road, wheels rutting off the potholes and the suspension getting a good workout. She watched the countryside flash past the window, a blur of greens and browns. *They will be there; they must be there.*

He slowed down as they descended to the valley floor. Dips and troughs on the lower roads were flooded and he had to navigate them carefully to avoid the fissures and holes hidden beneath the water. The mountain loomed above them, its grey, gnarled rock formations jutting out above layers of scree and narrow limestone gorges. Small white crosses and faded plastic wreaths stuck in the verge announced a stretch of the road where families had lost loved ones to accidents over the years. They pushed on, not paying much heed, passing isolated smallholdings and the occasional bungalow.

'Why did you choose up here for a holiday house?' he asked. 'It's a bit bleak.'

'We didn't really. It was my grandmother's. It was her field up from the lake, so we bought the land from the family after she died and built on it.'

'I see. It's not Hawaii, is it?'

'It's not supposed to be.' She pushed her irritation at his lack of appreciation aside and focused on the possibility of seeing her children again. Maybe they'd be playing down by the lake. She hoped they hadn't been using the boat without someone to supervise.

The road tracked up towards the curve of the mountain and grew narrower as they crossed over the lower ridges, then down into the valleys below. Small lakes like blue-grey mirrors had laid claim to low-lying fields. The afternoon sun dipped slowly below the cloud-line, lending the water a pink and orange shimmer. When she glanced at him, his face was cast in gold.

'You're more than welcome to stay a few days,' she said suddenly, trying to sound matter-of-fact. 'You can build yourself up a bit. Rest and take care of your foot.' There was a short silence.

'Sure, sounds good. Thank you, I'd appreciate that.' He cleared his throat as though he was about to say more but he didn't.

The cab of the van had become stuffy, and the smell of their own bodies was making her nauseous. She rolled down the window and inhaled the cool, damp air.

'Oh look, there's the sign for the organic centre,' she said.

He slowed down and they peered through the narrow, overgrown entrance to the walled garden. She could just about see the thatched roof of the shop through the willow trees. There was no sign of the owners, a lean, vigorous couple in their sixties. But she suspected there were a lot more people around than the silence of the countryside suggested. Tomorrow she'd return and see what remained of the gardens, see if there was anything to scavenge or trade.

They surged over a little bridge spanning a swollen river and descended into the valley.

'There it is,' she whispered, overawed at the sight of the lake – *her* lake. 'There it is.'

The surface was glazed dark bronze, fading to black under the clouds. As they drew closer, she could see the water ripple in low light from the west.

They drove slowly up the long, tree-lined driveway to the house and Marcus cut the engine in front of the wide glass porch, a dangling windchime tinkling happily in the breeze. It was as though the world was holding its breath. Everything seemed to be exactly how she had left it.

She leapt out and flew over to the upside-down plant pot sitting behind an outdoor lantern. The keys were still underneath. Trembling, she opened the front door and went in. All was calm and quiet. Her carefully selected artisan lambswool throws were still folded neatly on the wicker chairs by the stove. The wide black-oak table was covered in a layer of dust. Two bottles of wine accompanied a dead moth and a small vase of withered wildflowers on the long rattan runner in the centre of the table. No one was here. No one had been here. It was exactly as she had left it over two years ago.

She wandered around the house. The bedrooms smelled sweet yet musty. Linen and blankets remained freshly laundered. Her children's wellingtons and rain boots were neatly lined up against the dressers. Toys and books lined the windowsills overlooking a garden that sloped down to a jetty and diving pontoon. She was drawn to the soft silk pillows in the master bedroom with its soft, teal-coloured bedspread and matching armchair. Running her hands across the spot where she and Johnny used to lie together, she remembered the lazy, summer sounds as they'd drifted off to sleep, the low murmur of water, the breeze stirring the trees. *They aren't here.*

A thump and clatter in the hallway reminded her that she was not alone. She stepped backwards, trying to find the wall to steady herself, and slid to the floor. By the time Marcus got to her, she was curled up into a ball, quivering softly and in some faraway place where he couldn't reach her.

9

Her children shot like stray bullets through her dreams that night as she spun in and out of sleep, her body lurching awake on cold, soaked sheets, her eyes wide open to the dark. Her hands flew to her mouth to muffle the strange, shrill noises leaking from her throat until the sounds lapsed into quiet sobs. Her heart raced and faltered, and she fell back onto her pillow where she lay for an hour mouthing silent prayers for miracles before sleep poured in and the whole process started again.

When morning finally broke over the east side of the lake, she jerked awake and went to the window, aching and shivering. The room overlooked the front of the house and she noticed that he had moved the van out of sight. There didn't seem to be much of a breeze and the lake surface was unruffled. A grey heron stood beneath an awning of hawthorn near the shore. She strained to see the road, searching in vain for familiar faces but saw nothing – no small figures with colourful backpacks, no sign of human life at all.

With a sigh, she turned back to the room, trying to process her meltdown the night before. *'He had some morning,' Johnny said, after the student doctor left the delivery suite. The poor man was in full-blown shock and pretending not to be. The noise of it. All the shit and water and blood, and me roaring and crying and laughing with relief when Conor came out, purple and pink and roaring and crying himself. The silence of it too: the ward with eight empty beds, and me and Conor standing in the corner by the window staring at each other, listening to the hoot and rumble of city traffic. All I've ever wanted is to mind them, to be their mother for ever and ever.*

She looked down at the bed. Marcus had put her there the night before with all her clothes on, leaving smudges of dirt and grime on the sheets. But what would have brought irritation rising to the top in the past, was now insignificant. Dirty sheets didn't matter anymore. She sat down on the armchair and listened to the silence of the house. It was only when she caught the drift of woodsmoke and heard him clank the door of the stove in the kitchen that something stirred in her and she re-awakened to the hope of their imminent arrival. She must ready the house for them, make sure there was food and warmth. She must look like their mother again, ready to nurture and love and heal.

She stood up too quickly. After a dizzy spell passed, she opened the bedroom door and padded barefoot down to the kitchen with a renewed hope and energy. When she stepped into the kitchen, she found Marcus kneeling in front of the stove. *This is my home and he is now my guest*, she found herself thinking. He was feeding a hungry blaze with dry sticks and kindling and jumped at the sight of her in the doorway.

Standing up, he wiped his hands on his coat and stepped towards her, but then he hesitated.

'You're all right!' he said, with a wary smile.

'Yes, I am. Thank you for...' She nodded towards the bedroom.

'Ah, no problem. I was worried. I thought you'd –'

'It was just exhaustion. How about you? Did you sleep okay?'

'Yes, like a baby. I'm only just up.'

'Did you find a bed?'

'Oh, no, well, yes – the sofa.' He gestured to the couch on the far side of the dining table. 'I didn't want to use your kids' beds.'

'You must have been cold.'

'No, not at all. You have nice blanket things.'

'Thanks for lighting that.' She nodded towards the stove.

'No problem. I was going to find a pot and boil water. Make some tea.'

There was an awkward silence.

'Shall I show you around?' she said, asserting herself. 'Give you a tour? There's a cupboard full of cereal and porridge oats.

They're probably stale but they'll do. There should be jars of honey, jam. Cream crackers. Probably out of date but –'

'Yeah, I found them. I had a look already.'

'Oh, okay.'

'Is it all right that I made myself at home?' he asked, raising an eyebrow.

'Sure, yes, of course… no problem.'

He stood staring at her.

'So let's eat then,' she said eventually. 'After that, we can get cleaned up and change our clothes, unpack what we have and decide what to do next.'

'Cool.'

'How's your foot?'

'It's okay. I found the first aid kit under the sink.'

'Good. Well, that's that done.' She looked around her, thinking quickly. 'I'll get the porridge on then. Can you bring in more wood? There's a lean-to full of logs around the back.'

'Will do.' He narrowed his eyes at her for a moment, assessing things, then turned and went outside.

With the kitchen to herself, she leaned over the table, pressing the palms of her hands into the polished oak wood. *They will come. Manifestation 101. Speak it into existence. Believe it enough and they will come.* She moved the two bottles of wine and the vase of dead flowers from the table to the kitchen countertop. Golden pollen, seeds and dried petals littered the floor behind her as she walked, so she took the dustpan and brush from the corner, swept them up and tapped it all into the bin.

After she made the porridge, they sat down and ate hungrily – a full bowl each. They sweetened it with a spoonful of honey, and they drank breakfast tea from blue pottery cups.

He cleaned up the breakfast things and turned the bowls and cups upside down on the draining board. She was about to ask him to dry them and put them away but stopped herself. Old parts of herself that she didn't like, like perfectionism in the kitchen, were returning too quickly. It was good of him to clean up.

Then they went out to the garden and crossed the gravel driveway to the lakeshore. He stood on the rough sand and inhaled deeply.

'It's beautiful,' he said. 'What a place to live.'

'So are you happy it's not Hawaii now?'

'Ha! Yes. Much nicer. A great second home.'

'Yeah, we plan to move here when the kids fly the nest – grow vegetables, read, grow old in peace, get involved in the community.'

'Do you think he's still alive – James or…?' He gave her a sheepish grin. 'Sorry, I keep forgetting his name.'

'Johnny, and I don't know,' she said quietly. 'If he's gone, then maybe the kids are too, and I can't face that thought. I have to keep thinking that they're on their way. You understand, don't you?'

'Yeah, 'course I do.'

'I don't know if I'm strong enough to…' She didn't know why she'd started the sentence and had no idea how to finish it.

They stared out across the water. He bent down and picked up a handful of sand, rubbing it between his thumb and forefinger. There was no sound but the gentle rustle of the reeds in the shallows and the light wash of water at the shore.

'I'll bring you out on the boat later,' she said. 'If you want. See the islands to the left of the landbank? We sometimes have picnics out there. Swim on the really hot days.'

'Sounds good.'

They stood there taking it all in for a few minutes.

Sara suddenly clapped her hands. A startled mallard lifted out of the reeds. 'Right, we should get busy. When they arrive, I want everything to be perfect.'

'Okay.' A frown flickered on his face for a second. 'Anything I can help with?'

'Yes, we'll need lots of wood for the winter. Dry wood. There's an axe in the tool shed at the back. There's a chainsaw too, but I don't think we should use it. Too noisy. Plus fuel, if there is any, is too precious to waste. You happy to do the chopping?'

'Yeah. Sure.'

'Then we need to go to the organic centre to see what's left. Fruit, vegetables, seeds, stuff like that. I'm hoping the owners are still there and won't mind us taking some stuff. They were nice people.'

'What about power? Is it all electric here?'

'Yeah, unfortunately. I wanted Johnny to install a wind generator, but he didn't like them. No gas either.'

'Right, well, we can figure something out. For now, we can use the stove for hot water and heat. You look like the kind of person who had lots of candles.'

She nodded and laughed.

The sun had moved over the mountains to the east and the light spilled down into the valley and onto the lake. They turned their faces to it almost instinctively and enjoyed its tentative warmth. Sara was suddenly acutely aware of his presence, and her body began to tingle, an energy with a mind of its own. Had she been twenty years old and here with him alone, would she behave differently? Would she take advantage of that emotional freedom that comes with wide open space and no responsibilities?

Marcus turned to say something, and for a moment she thought he had read her mind.

'Can I have a wash and change my clothes first?' he said. 'I can smell myself and it's not great.'

'Yeah, of course,' she said.

'Can I borrow one of your husband's T-shirts?'

'Sure. I'll get one for you. There are jeans too, work trousers... though they might be a bit small.' She glanced at his legs to size him up and he laughed – at what, she wasn't sure of. 'I'll leave them in the spare room. You can sleep there for the moment.'

'Thank you.' He smiled at her. 'Right, let's get to it.'

He put his arms up in the air and stretched, then rubbed his hands together. She noticed that for the first time in days, he didn't have the gun with him.

'You left it in the house?'

'What?'

'The rifle.'

'Oh, yeah. I should probably keep it with me, but it feels so secluded and safe here. You're right though, we can't let our guard down.'

They walked back to the house together and he refilled the stove with logs until it blazed even higher. The heat started to spread out into the room. She dug out some of Johnny's spare clothes, burying her nose in them to see if she could still smell him. But there was no trace. It was as though the fabric had forgotten him. Now it would warm the body of another man.

Marcus worked it out that it would take an hour to boil enough water for him to have a good wash and another hour for her to have a bath. So he insisted that she went first; he could be chopping wood while he waited. She didn't argue and accepted his gesture gratefully.

Submerging her head beneath the hot water, she closed her eyes to the world above and ran her hands along her arms and legs and belly as if to remind herself that they were there. As she soaped herself, she washed away the strange farmhouse with the sheet rope dangling from the window, the house with the marigold blankets and desiccated bodies, Siobhan and her children in the old shipping container, the leering gang leader with the flickering tongue. She found a spare razor in the cabinet above the sink and by the time she emerged from the water, pink and smooth, she felt that she had somehow cleansed herself inside and out. She dried herself with a large fluffy bath towel and pulled on a fresh T-shirt and pair of grey sweatpants she'd found in a drawer in her room.

She dried her hair with a towel and brushed it. Observing herself in the mirror, she could see she was still thin and pale, but she looked a lot better than the reflection that had greeted her in Marcus's cottage. When had that been? She'd lost all track of time. She brushed her teeth, cut her fingernails and took one last look at herself before leaving the room.

When she came into the kitchen, he was at the stove, watching a huge pot come to the boil. He turned round.

'Wow, you look different,' he said.

'Ha, yes. Maybe just clean.'

'Well, yes that too. But lighter, happier too.'

'I feel lighter. Everything will be okay. When the kids make it, everything will be okay. Normal.'

He smiled at her and said nothing. She didn't care if he thought she was delusional. She had to believe it was only a matter of time before she would hold her children again, tuck them into bed at night, listen to their chatter.

Eventually Marcus had filled the bath with enough hot water, and he went into the bathroom with the selection of fresh clothes she had left out for him and a large clean towel. She noticed that he'd set the gun by the front door and it reassured her. While he was in the bathroom, she set about scrubbing the dirty clothes they had brought with them, the ones that could be worn again.

Marcus had emptied his pockets, leaving his wallet and dead phone on the table. She'd love to see the contents of his phone, find photos of his deceased wife and child, read his text messages, see what he was really like with his mates, his family. He hadn't asked if he could charge his phone in the old jeep. She wondered why. Maybe he wasn't ready to see his past life again.

Sorting through the cupboards and presses, she made a list of all the remaining food. There was enough to survive for three weeks if they were prudent with it. In the utility room, she found a large bag of dog nuts and tins of wet food. The sight of it reawakened her grief over the loss of Brin yet she gagged at the memories of forcing herself to eat it to stay alive. She found a stash of chocolates left as thank-you gifts from friends. The use-by date had long passed, but they might still be a lovely treat. In addition to the two bottles of wine already at the house and the bottle they had brought with them, six cans of beer sat on a shelf in the larder. They had enough alcohol to throw a small party.

When he eventually emerged from the bathroom, she barely recognised him. He had trimmed his beard right back so she could see the contours of his face and jaw. He was attractive enough, she decided, in a sort of northern European way; perhaps one of his grandparents had been Danish or German. He came towards her, standing closer than he normally did, and grinned a little self-consciously.

'Well, what would you give me out of ten?'

His eyes were ever-changing with the light; blue eyes seemed to do that. Deep, dark wells of unknowingness, then sparkling like the sea. She caught herself on and took a step back.

'Um, a decent seven.'

'Only seven? Harsh.' He pouted. 'Am I a stranger again?'

'It's good to see what you really look like underneath all that...' She waved a finger around in front of his face where the beard had been.

He grinned. 'Okay, I'll take most of that as a compliment.'

She stood there feeling awkward and searched for something to say.

'Could you do something for me?' he asked. 'I'd do it myself but I wouldn't do it very well.'

'What?'

'Take a bit off my hair at the back?'
'Oh… ehh, I'm not great with hair.'
'I'm not looking for barbershop quality. Just trim it. Tidy it up.'
'Okay, sure. There's a first time for everything I guess. Now?'
'Yep. It's still wet so it's easier… I'll sit here.'

He pulled a dining chair into the middle of the kitchen and sat down on it, not giving her time to change her mind. She hesitated for a moment, then took the scissors from a drawer in the kitchen and approached him. They hadn't really touched each other much – not consciously. There was that time he almost carried her back to the jeep after she'd got all the messages on her phone. And the time he'd taken her hand in the jeep when they ran out of fuel. And there was last night, when he'd put her to bed.

She stood behind him. 'Are you sure about this? These are just old kitchen scissors.'

'Yeah, it can't get any worse than it is.'

'I don't know about that.' She laughed.

She ran her fingers through his hair with her left hand and pulled chunks up between her fingers. It was soft and curled at the ends. Her hands trembled slightly and her heart started to beat faster.

'No need for perfection, now,' he warned her. 'Just trim the long bits.'

'Okay, okay, just getting my bearings.'

'Did you never do your kids' hair?'

'Yes, of course, when they were small, but that's easier.'

'Ah sure look, who's going to see me only you?'

'Maybe others will too.'

'What others?'

'Judgemental people who'll decide you're unkempt and weird and not to be trusted.'

'Ah yes, those folks. Milling about outside in their thousands.'

She laughed. Working around the back of his neck, she trimmed the hair to all the same length as best she could, gently pushing his head down to tidy up around the nape of his neck. He smelled sweet, soapy. She put a finger under his chin to guide his head back up and trimmed the sides around his ears.

'It kind of suits you to have a longer fringe,' she said. 'You should keep it that way.'

'Okay. Whatever you think.'

'So any plans for the weekend? Holiday booked?'

He laughed. 'Nope but heading off with the lads to the Algarve next month.'

'Sounds like fun.'

'Yeah, just the boys for a few beers. No interest in the local talent though.'

'Oh really? I've heard that one before.'

'It's true. There are much nicer women at home.'

She felt herself blush. Taking a step back, she ruffled his hair, like she'd seen hairdressers do.

'Done,' she said. 'Basic, but it has some semblance of order I think.'

She brushed the cuttings off his shoulders with her hand and nearly leaned in to blow off the rest. He stood up and ran his fingers through it.

'Feels much better. Thanks.'

'You're welcome.'

She went to retrieve the brush and dustpan and when she returned to sweep the floor, he had gone back to the bathroom.

That afternoon they drove down to the organic centre and parked the van beneath a cover of trees. The air was infused with the scent of lovage and celery, tomato vines and herbs. So there was still some plant life then. Her heart lifted.

They wandered around the large gardens at the rear and found three vegetable patches recently dug and weeded. Either the owners were still alive, or someone was coming regularly to tend to the beds. The shop was locked. Sara was reluctant to break in without knowing if the owners were still around, and so she dissuaded Marcus from forcing the door. A polytunnel at the back was full of tomatoes, peppers and squashes that were well watered. Celery and kale were thriving in another. A plot had been cleared completely. Whoever had harvested the vegetables grown there had stored them somewhere else.

She gathered a handful of black seed pods from older kale plants and cut the heads off some withered sunflowers so she could deseed them at home. She also took cuttings of lovage, thyme and rosemary to pot on and nurture over the winter. She found herself alone under the hanging branches of a weeping willow and caught the faint scent of lemon balm, parsley and cut chives. A wood pigeon flapped down from a nearby poplar, startling her. Eventually she returned to the van and saw him down near a potting shed. He was standing with his head back, looking up into the trees. He was suddenly quite a different man from the one she had first met.

'I think I could live here,' he said when she caught up with him.
'Yeah, you seem more relaxed.'
'I haven't felt this good in a while now.'

They left the organic centre half an hour later with a selection of vegetables from the polytunnels. So as not to upset whoever had been tending them, she scribbled a thank-you note with a pencil and scrap of paper she'd found in the van and stuck it halfway into the letterbox beside the shop door.

In the evening they walked around the lake before it got dark so she could show him the view of the house from the far shore. It was just about visible through the trees; smoke from its chimney trailed thinly through the air. He gathered dry branches and set them in piles to collect another time. The next day they planned to dig out beds at the back of the house and ready the earth for planting in the early spring. All the time they were away from the house she turned periodically to check the driveway for movement, waiting for small, colourful figures to approach from the road. Images of her children appearing like little rainbows were seared into her mind.

When they got back to the house, he was limping slightly again but didn't complain about it. The rooms were dark, so she set a few tea-light candles into old jam jars and placed them in the middle of the dining table.

'Want to eat?' he said.

'Let's.'

They moved quietly between the kitchen and the table, setting it with plates and cutlery. He washed some tomatoes, cut them in half and sprinkled salt over them, then sliced the peppers into long, thin strips. He shredded the kale leaves and arranged them on the plates. She found an unopened bottle of olive oil and gave it to him to drizzle over his makeshift salad. Then she tipped three cans-worth of beans into a saucepan, heated them on the stove and transferred them into two bowls.

'Wine?' she asked. 'Might liven it all up a bit.'

'Thought you'd never ask!'

He took one of the bottles off the table and pulled out the cork with a novelty corkscrew he'd found, shaped like a person spreading their arms out wide to the sun. He filled two large wine glasses almost to the top and handed one to her.

'Thank you.'

'No, thank *you*,' he said.

'For what?'

'For having me here. You could have booted me out a few houses back and gone on your merry way.'

She took a sip and then a bigger mouthful. It was very pleasant. 'You're welcome, and anyway, I probably wouldn't have made it without you.'

'Same here. I was in a bad way when we met on that road.' He pointed at his head and shook it.

She sat down at the table. 'Oh, I think you'd have been fine.'

'You've no idea. It could have gone either way at one point.' He sat down opposite her and raised his glass. 'To good luck and a better future,' he said, clinking the glass against hers.

'And to finding those we love.'

'Yes. To you and your children.'

They began to eat, marvelling at the crispness of the vegetables, the seasoning, the explosion of taste in their mouths. It had been so long since they had eaten fresh food other than apples.

'So who are we now?' she said.

'Straight in with the deep stuff already.' He laughed.

'Seriously, who are we in all of this?'

'I think you already know the answer.'

'And what do you think that is?' she asked.

'Good people. We are good people.'

'What do good people like us do now?'

'Just get through each hour, each day. Make the best decisions we can. Do no harm and stay the hell alive.'

'Do you think my children are alive?'

She took a drink and watched him carefully. The flickering candlelight cast intriguing shadows across his face.

He pushed his empty plate to the side and put his elbows on the table, resting his chin on folded hands. 'I think it's better if I don't share my thoughts with you on that.'

'Why not?'

'I think you're a bit fragile right now. Understandably, of course. I would be too.'

'No, I'm good. I'm much better today.'

'And you need to stay that way... stay hopeful. Last thing you need is me being... well, me.'

'They'll come. I know it.'

'Good, I'm glad.' He sat back in his chair and smiled. 'So I've been thinking about your house.'

'Go on?' She twirled her wine glass, holding it by the stem, and watched the dark crimson liquid swirl around the sides.

'Well, I feel we're reasonably safe here, but we need to look at a few things. Sooner the better.'

'Like what?'

'More people will probably come, spreading out from the cities and across the border. It's only a matter of time before larger groups organise better and reach places like this. Folks will take land that isn't theirs out of pure necessity, and when they're installed, they'll defend it. We'd do the same. If we didn't have this place, we'd be looking for somewhere to base ourselves.'

'Yeah, I guess you're right.'

'It'll take years for this to settle, and that's not taking account of the climate. No one knows what the weather will throw at us next, especially now the Met Office is out of action.'

'But things will go back to normal eventually. It'll just be a different normal,' she said.

'It may not go back to the way you'd prefer. It could be decades of this kind of upheaval.'

'Yeah, sure. We talked about this before. Normal is whatever we're forced to adjust to.'

'I can think ahead for us… that is, if you want me to.' He caught her eye and held it for a moment, then took a drink.

'Okay, and do what exactly?'

'We might need to go a bit medieval, crazy as it sounds. We only have what we have, but at least we can have some kind of plan.'

'Like a watch system? That kind of thing. Is that what you mean?'

'Yes, at night and throughout the day. And maybe we could set things like sound traps along the driveway to alert us to people approaching. And agree a designated place for us to go outdoors if the house becomes unsafe.'

'I see.'

'Just be prepared really. It would be stupid to get too comfortable.'

She listened carefully. He had obviously been giving this some thought. He had devised several plans and strategies to deal with just about any situation, his shoulders rising and falling, his hands gesturing excitedly, as he explained. He was enjoying this new role as defender of the realm.

'You want to take all that on?' she asked, when he seemed to have run out of steam.

'Glad to.'

'Thank you! Just don't accidentally take me out when I'm gardening, okay?' She gave him a mock scolding look and raised her eyebrow, which made him laugh.

They fell silent.

'You're lovely,' he said suddenly.

She visibly started. 'Oh.'

'Sorry, that was probably a bit forward…'

'Umm, well, it's a while since anyone said that to me.' She could feel herself blush again. This was becoming a habit.

'I just feel like we've known each other for ages, so I hope you don't mind me saying it. After all this time we've spent together, I've really got to like you.'

She shifted in her seat, trying to gauge her emotions. Something was fizzing inside her but what was it? Anxiety? Attraction? Uncertainty? All of those at once, she decided as she reached for the wine bottle, trying to figure out his facial expression and control her own. 'Mmm, it's been a pretty intense experience…' She poured what was left of the wine into her glass.

'You've taken lots of risks with me.'

'Yeah, when Brin was killed by that gang, I had nothing left after that. I don't think I thanked you properly for taking care of him. For burying him.'

'Happy to be of service.'

She smiled, leaning back in her chair. 'Remember when you said something about needing to trust people, that we need community to survive?'

'Yeah, I remember.'

'Well, I agree and that means I need to trust you now.'

'And I you.'

'Ha! What do you need to trust me for?' She grinned.

'Well for one, to take care of my heart.'

'Ah now. Too much wine!'

Their eyes met for a few moments before she looked away shyly. She took another drink; it was delicious. The room was lovely and warm and she could feel her cheeks glowing.

They sat in companionable silence as they finished off their glasses. Then they cleared the table and went into the kitchen to do the dishes. There was little light around the sink and it was hard to see.

'I can bring a candle over,' she said.

'No need. Our eyes will get used to it.'

She rinsed the dishes at the sink and Marcus dried them on an old tea towel beside her. As she turned to hand him the last of the cutlery, she found him standing close to her, quiet and familiar. A warm tingling sensation spread up through her body and she took a sudden deep breath.

'I'm going to head off to bed now,' she said quickly. 'I'm pretty tired.'

'Okay.'

'Um, goodnight, and thanks for a little piece of normal. It felt like the old days.'

'Sure thing. Want to stay up and talk more?'

She could feel his breath warm on her cheek. 'Maybe tomorrow. I should sleep. So much to catch up on. Remember, you're in the guest room, okay? No more couch-surfing for you.'

'Thanks. I appreciate that.'

She touched his arm lightly as she left the room and swallowing hard, she didn't look back.

At dawn the next morning it was overcast with a light drizzle. Sara's first task, fast becoming a ritual, was to check the roads for any signs of the children or of Johnny as if her looking might somehow manifest their arrival. Marcus, too, was up early and they had porridge and honey together again. Afterwards, he went outside to take stock of their wood supplies and chop more. She watched him through the window as she tidied the breakfast things away and tended to the stove. She thought about his words the night before: *You're lovely.* She still wasn't sure how she felt about it.

The day passed quickly, filled with physical work and planning. She found some old fishing rods they could use out on the lake and decided which part of the garden would be the best place to dig a vegetable patch, setting out its border with short willow slips. Marcus said he could fence it entirely with willow weave to keep wildlife out. As they worked alongside each other, she grew more and more comfortable around him. Now that he had rested, he was chattier and funnier. She found herself laughing at his quips and she teased him back, the banter coming easily as they went about their tasks.

That night they fired up the stove again and soaked in hot baths, easing their aching limbs from the strenuous work. Marcus prepared a simple meal of tinned fruit, tuna and cream crackers dipped in honey. The stove blazed away, making them drowsy and relaxed in each other's company. When it became pitch black outside, Sara pulled down the window blinds. Then she found a half bottle of whiskey at the back of the games cupboard and made hot toddies using cloves and cinnamon from the spice rack. After they cleared the table, she washed the plates in the sink and he made two fresh whiskeys.

'It's a bit strong,' he said, placing the glasses on the counter and drawing close. 'I lash in the measures.'

'That's okay. Thanks.' There was silence, the only sound in the room coming from the stove.

'Sara,' he said abruptly, clearing his throat.

'Yep?' She looked at him quizzically as she reached across him for her whisky.

'I'm... in a bit of bother really...'

'Oh? What, is it your foot? Is it not healing?'

No, no, that's grand. It's hard to...' He looked away and inhaled deeply.

'What?' She stared at him, sensing something was coming which was about to change everything.

'Ok, I'll just say it. I'm just finding it hard to... when I'm around you.'

'Oh, I see.' She looked up at him, her pulse quickening, yet not moving away.

He stepped toward her and without waiting for her to say anything, lifted his hand to her face, gently rubbing his thumb across her cheek. She held her breath, hardly daring to move. Then he pushed his fingers back through her hair and looked into eyes, holding her gaze for what felt like an eternity. They stood like that, her heart beating furiously in her chest until she could hardly stand, yet he didn't move or say a word. Then, pulling her towards him, he leaned in and slowly kissed her, his lips soft and warm, his mouth slightly open. Her legs almost went beneath her as he pushed forward, his other hand finding its way to her hips and back. Something in her began to burn and tremble. Something that was more powerful than her rational, practical mind.

They never spoke and she didn't resist, not even when he picked her up and carried her down to her bedroom, kissing her as he walked and lowering her gently onto the bed. She pulled him to her as they tugged at each other's clothes, finding him with her fingers in the dark, running her hands over his back and shoulders. The sheets were cool beneath their bodies, and when he moved into her she surrendered completely to him, allowing him to take and explore her breasts with his mouth.

She pulled herself up onto him and cupped his face with her hands, feeling the contours of his jaw, tracing the outline of his mouth with her thumbs. They stayed like that for a moment, holding each other, time suspended, until deep inside her he could wait no more, and he pulled her beneath him. Then, with his mouth pressed hard against hers, he whispered something that she couldn't quite make out and surged forward one last time before sinking down onto her.

They lay like that for a while, breathing heavily in unison, their hearts keeping pace.

'Thank you,' he whispered.

She kissed his cheek and said nothing, all words and thoughts caught in her throat.

Afterwards, they lay tangled together in the dark, whispering and laughing. Then they fell asleep for a few hours and woke next to each other, delighted and surprised to find each other there.

He kissed her face and shoulders. 'Are you awake?' he whispered.

'Mmm.'

'Can you believe this?'

'I really can't. I wasn't expecting this at all. I'd no idea you felt that way.'

'And I'd no idea you did either.'

'I didn't know myself. The alcohol must have...'

'Ah maybe. You're very beautiful, you know.'

'Oh, go on. I am not.' She laughed.

'I think you are.'

'Flattery gets you nowhere.'

'Does it not?' He grinned. 'What if I've already got what I wanted? Then this flattery must be the truth.'

She tried to make out his face in the darkness. 'When did *you* know you wanted this?'

'Long before you, I suspect.'

She giggled. 'When?'

'Umm, probably when you sat by my fire drinking my whiskey in that old lady dress and cardigan.'

'Ha! You're so weird.' She giggled. 'Old lady clothes. Now I see what you're all about.'

He leaned forward and kissed her hard. She pushed all unpleasant thoughts of her infidelity to Johnny out of her head.

They laughed and held each other as he drifted off to sleep again. In those hours before dawn, she curled up close to his chest, his arm lying heavy across her hips and belly, and she listened to the still, calm world outside, the silence only broken by the intermittent tinkling of the windchimes in the porch and the sound of his deep, even breathing.

10

When she woke again later, he had gone to the kitchen in his boxers and made them cups of instant coffee, which he placed on the bedside table. Still naked beneath the sheets, she pulled them up below her neck, suddenly shy of her body in the full light of day.

'That was fun,' he said, sitting on the edge of the bed and smiling at her. 'How's the head?'

'It's fine, amazingly. Thanks for the coffee.'

She sat up, still clutching the sheet with one hand, picked up her cup with the other hand and took a sip. Then she put the cup down and coaxed him back under the sheets. This time she was able to watch his face as he followed the curves of her body with his hands. Soft, fair hair ran along his arms, across his chest and down his thighs. She had expected to see a bad tattoo inked onto his body from his student days, but there was none. They spent the morning in bed, kissing, laughing and sleeping. Sometimes she awoke with him moving inside her from behind and she would arch her back, turning her face to find his mouth.

When they eventually got up, it was midday and they were hungry. She washed in the bathroom and put on fresh clothes before joining him in the kitchen. The fire in the stove had been rekindled and a fresh pot of water was boiling on the hot plate. Walking to the porch at the front, she stood and looked down the driveway, still searching for movement on the road, though now the appearance of Johnny would bring unthinkable complications. She tried to push images of him out of her mind, increasingly guilty and uncomfortable. A thin drizzle veiled the view and visibility across the swollen lake was poor. He called her to the table where he'd set out a small plate of crackers and a pot of hot coffee.

He sat back in his chair and regarded her thoughtfully. 'So how are you doing?'

'Good. You?'

'Really good.' He smiled. 'Happy, for the first time in a very long time.' He reached over and took her hand, stroking it softly with his thumb. 'This must feel... um... difficult for you.'

'Yeah... yes it is. I don't know if I can think too hard about it right now.'

'I get that. But no regrets though, right?'

'No, definitely no regrets.' She smiled at him.

But thoughts of Johnny persistently crept in around the edges. She couldn't process the guilt, the betrayal, whether he was alive or dead. It wasn't so long ago that she had judged Marcus for having an affair; she was a hypocrite. The speech she had given him on fidelity turned out to be nothing but a hollow, self-aggrandising spiel.

'So one day at a time?' he said, watching her carefully.

'Yes, one day at a time.'

'Or one night at a time.' He winked.

'You're bold.' She laughed and slapped his arm. 'We can work more on the vegetable garden today. Dig out some large beds, gather more wood.'

'Are there fish in that lake?'

'Yes, I think so. Coarse fish like pike or dace. I'll take you out in the boat if you like.'

'Great! Let's do that. There might be trout. I'll figure out how to make bait or flies.'

He got up and stretched, ready to get to work. As he walked about the room, she regarded his body in an entirely new way, almost as though it now belonged to her. Something in her had shifted, diluting guilt. It was all about survival and instinct now. Everything had changed. Johnny would have done the same thing in her shoes, she decided.

By late afternoon, they had dug out three vegetable beds and pulled the weeds and stones out of the clumpy wet earth. It was poor-quality soil and they would need to get nutrients into it; there would be something at the organic centre. It was twilight by the time they finished and so they left the boat trip for the next day. They ate mostly in silence, catching each other's glances and smiling. Then they moved to the bedroom, leaving the dishes unwashed by the sink. He moved gently into her again and she held him close, surrendering to his rhythm. Afterwards, they whispered and kissed and laughed, but exhaustion overpowered them, Marcus falling asleep with his head on her breast. She rolled him onto his side, wrapped her arm around his waist and pulled herself close to his back. Neither of them stirred until dawn, completely forgetting their plans to keep watch.

The next day, revived, they made a list of activities that included another trip to the organic centre to see if the note they'd left had been read and to find some compost. Marcus pottered outside in the garden for an hour or two, mostly clearing foliage and reeds to make space for a walled garden. Sara thought it would be essential to build one to provide shelter for fruit trees and delicate plants. After lunch the weather brightened, and she finally brought him out on the boat. They rowed across to the island where they sat on the rough, blackened bedrock near the waterline and looked out over the lake.

'This is known as Jealous Valley,' she said, waving her hand from left to right.

'Oh yeah? Why?'

'Well, legend has it that after the Great Flood, the first man and woman to reach Ireland arrived here. They had a fight over whether it was beautiful or not. One of them thought it was beautiful, and the other absolutely hated it.'

'Then what happened?'

'That's all I know. Maybe the man was jealous of the love she had for the valley, believing it was greater than her love for him.'

'Or the other way around.'

'Yeah, I suppose so. Oh, and there's a myth as well. Apparently a half-dog, half-otter lives at a great depth in the lake.'

He snorted with laughter.

'Back in the seventeen hundreds, it killed a woman washing clothes at the lake. The story goes that her husband found her body and vowed to kill the otter in revenge. Then he and his brother eventually caught and killed some kind of creature. A stone carving of it is in a graveyard near the tomb of the dead woman.' She smiled, amused at his incredulous expression.

'You do know it was probably the husband or the brother that murdered her and blamed the poor imaginary lake monster,' he said, laughing. 'Hey, maybe it's called Jealous Valley because there was a love triangle going on between the dead wife and the brothers!'

She shrugged. 'People believed anything back then.'

'Maybe not so different now.'

He watched for signs of fish rippling the waters and thought he saw wild trout make their splashy rise for low midges. They talked about the fish dishes they could make in the spring with herbs and fresh salad.

Later, on the way back to the house, he stopped rowing in the middle of the lake and trailed his hand across the surface before lifting it out and flicking water all over her face. She went to lunge at him in jest, standing across the wooden seat and causing the boat to sway and pitch.

'Easy now,' he said, laughing. 'No dancing in small boats.'

'I wasn't dancing,' she protested, wiping her face with the back of her hand.

'You're dancing on the inside,' he said. 'I can see it.'

She sat back and smiled at him. 'Maybe I am.'

She watched him as he pulled on the oars, taking them back to the shore, and wondered what her children would make of him. They'd like him, she decided. In time they might even grow to see him as more than their mother's 'friend'. What was he to her anyway? Was there a word for that feeling that set fire to her heart when she watched him working, lost in his own thoughts, or when his mouth was on her body? It couldn't be love. Probably just simple chemistry. But Johnny would know immediately what was going on. She wouldn't deny it, she decided. It was a new world, a new reality.

They pulled up to the jetty and she jumped out and tied the line to the wooden post. He handed her up the oars, which she set on the jetty, and they walked up to the house together. They hung their coats up in the porch and kicked off their shoes, but as soon as they went into the main room, they knew something was wrong. The stove was blazing, despite the fact that they had been gone for so long, and there was a heavy, sour smell that made her gag.

The source of the stench was immediately apparent. Dumped on the long oak dining table was the rotting, filthy body of a dead dog, its legs jutting out stiff and black. Brin. Sara screamed, her pounding heart trying to leap out of her mouth. Then they heard a sharp click and a man stepped out from the kitchen, a rifle – their rifle – pointed straight at them. He was grinning at them, his tongue flicking in and out over his perfect teeth, his hungry predator eyes shifting from Marcus's face to Sara's and down her body. She recognised the intruder instantly and let out a small, peculiar sound. She reached out blindly behind her seeking Marcus's hand but she couldn't find it.

'Get down on your knees,' the man barked.

He moved the rifle backwards and forwards, from one to the other. Sara lowered herself to the floor, barely able to breathe. How could they have been so stupid as to leave the gun behind! Where was their plan now? They had no plan for this. She sensed Marcus kneeling behind her, taut, tense, terrified.

'Nice place you got here,' the man said, his lips curling. 'I put more logs on the fire for you, in case you needed something to warm you up later. I hope you don't mind if I move in with you.'

Sara's mind was racing, playing out all the possible scenarios and what she could do to stop him, stop him doing what she feared he wanted from her all along.

'Warm fire, food, clean beds,' he went on, waving the gun around as though it was an extension of his arms. 'You got this lovely little farm life going. Maybe I want that for me too. But you really are something, you pair. I went looking for my brother after you killed him and found a little grave. So I thought maybe these guys aren't so bad after all. At least they did the good Christian thing. But it was your mangey dog you buried. You left my brother in a ditch. Now that's a sick, sick thing to do, don't ya think?'

He leaned forward and stroked her face with the muzzle of the gun, running it down her throat and tracing the curves under her breasts. She jerked back from it, then he pushed it under her chin, lifting her face.

'Sick,' he roared.

She closed her eyes for a few seconds. 'Back off. Get away from me.' Her voice was shrill and unfamiliar. The artery on the side of his neck pulsed violently above a fading line of inked calligraphy: *Flood the Zone with Shit.*

'Easy now, missus. No need to upset yourself. To be honest I thought you'd be more grateful. I've come a long way to bring back your dog, do the decent thing.'

'How did you find us?' she asked, trying to sound confident, firm.

'I met a man on the road near where you killed my brother. He was carrying a bag full of baby stuff, bless him. So he kindly introduced me to this pregnant woman and her husband. I told her I'd spare her kids if she told us where you were headed. But oops, my knife slipped. I reckon I did her a favour. Having that baby would have killed her anyway.' He laughed. 'Didn't take long to check all the places around here and find you. It's not exactly the metropolis, is it?'

Sara hung her head as she recalled the invitation she had given to Siobhan. She'd needed hope, the promise of a safe place if she survived the delivery of the child. Sara felt foolish, dizzy. Her compassion would be the death of her.

'Take the house,' she said. 'Just take it and let us go. We just want to be left alone.'

'I don't want your house. I have two houses already and they're not stuck in a wet swamp like this shithole.'

'Then take our food. Whatever you want, it's yours. There's no need for any of this.'

'What I want first is to know which one of you killed my brother,' the man said. 'Was it your boyfriend here?' He turned to Marcus. 'It was you, wasn't it? You aren't afraid to pull a trigger.'

Sara turned around and saw a face she didn't recognise. Marcus was alight with rage and frustration.

'Your brother was going to kill us both,' Marcus growled. 'I had no choice.'

'Oh, but you did have a choice. You could have given him what he wanted. I'd asked him to fetch back *this* woman' – the man waved the muzzle at Sara again – 'I found her. She's mine. But look what you did to him for my following orders. That's not right!'

'She's not your woman.' Marcus's voice was like cold steel.

'Oh, she is. She certainly is now. There aren't many lookers like her around these days. And she has a bit of go in her. I like that.'

Marcus leapt up and lunged forward, fists up, like a drunk rushing to a bar fight. 'Don't you dare touch her,' he said, snarling.

A shot rang out, cracking the air between them. Sara clapped her hands to her ears and fell backwards to the floor. As she fell, she saw Marcus jerk sideways, clutching his left arm. He roared in rage and pain and straightened himself up again. Blood oozed through the sleeve of his sweater and started to drip onto the floor.

Her heart thumped wildly in terror but she forced herself to stand up.

'Stop, please stop.' Her ears were ringing, and her voice sounded distorted and muffled. 'We can negotiate. Anything at all. What do you want?'

'I want you,' the man said casually. 'And whatever else I decide to do with your boyfriend.' He smiled at her, stripping her naked with his eyes.

The smell of the dog on the table filled every corner of the room now, accelerated by the heat pumping out from the stove. Sara turned around to look at Marcus again and was terrified to see so much blood dribbling down the inside of his arm. It needed to be bound and bandaged to stem the flow. Marcus looked up at her, his eyes angry, defiant. He staggered to his feet and took an unsteady step forward, one arm out shielding Sara.

'You can't take someone because you feel like it,' Marcus shouted. 'People aren't possessions.'

'Who's going to stop me? Little old you?' The man laughed again and pointed the muzzle at Marcus's chest. 'Head or heart? Which way do you want to go?'

'Stop,' she whispered. 'I'll do whatever you want. Just name it.' She was crying now and shaking violently.

'Sorry, I didn't quite catch that. Could you say it a bit louder... pleeeease?' The man was grinning at her. He waited.

'I'll do whatever you want,' Sara repeated, her voice low but clear.

'Oh baby, there's no need to cry,' he cooed at her. 'You're going to have such a good time.' He sighed and watched her for a moment. 'I think we need to put this mutt down first.' He jerked his thumb at Marcus. 'That's what you would do, right? Put the pet out of its misery?'

'NO, no, don't,' she shrieked.

'Okay, here's what we're going to do next.'

Before Sara had any time to object, the man yanked Marcus forward by the arm and kicked him hard in the stomach. Marcus doubled over onto his knees. Then he bound Sara's wrists behind her back with a cable tie and shoved her onto the floor. Her chin smashed off the wooden floorboards and blood dripped from her lip where she had bitten it. She lay there, curled up, frozen, helpless. She closed her eyes when the man began kicking Marcus in the head and ribs, and sobbed quietly after a boot in the arm made him yell out in agony. Marcus surged forward, roaring, enraged, but the man kicked him hard in the groin and caught him on the back of the head as he fell.

'Up,' the man yelled at Marcus. 'Get up.' He poked him with the muzzle.

Marcus staggered back to his feet and fell onto a dining chair that had been pulled out from the table. Sara watched as his arms were pulled back and bound together at the wrists behind the chair. He looked up once to catch her eye. It was a look of the purest sorrow. Then he seemed to almost pass out.

She rolled over and looked frantically around for anything she could use to defend herself. The broom stood idly in the corner; the kitchen knives were tucked safely in the drawer at the far end of the counter.

'Front row seat for him,' he said, turning to her and licking his lips. 'Stand up.'

'I can't.'

He reached out and kicked her on the shin. 'Up,' he said, almost spitting at her.

She heaved herself up onto her knees. Her wrists were burning now from the cut of the plastic tie. Still holding the rifle in one hand, he yanked her up with his other hand and shoved her against the wall. It was then she saw the crossbow on the table behind the body of the dog. He took her throat with one hand and squeezed it tightly, pinning her to the wall.

'Do you like this kind of play, woman?' he asked softly. He pressed himself against her, moaning and grunting.

She felt the hard bulge of an erection against her thigh. She closed her eyes and tried to breathe, her legs beginning to fold beneath her.

'Not so fast,' he said, laughing. 'I want you awake for this.'

He loosened his grip on her throat and she took huge gulps of air despite the sour staleness of his breath. Then she became aware of a distant roaring in the room and thought it strange. There was banging and scraping and more roaring. It was Marcus trying to save her from the pawing, clawing fingers. She felt the man's hand move up her hip to her waist and underneath her T-shirt. He pinched her nipples and mauled her breasts, completely lost in what he was doing. She started to cry again as he leaned into her neck and licked her face from chin to forehead with a long, wet tongue.

'You taste so good,' he said, ignoring the shouting and fury coming from the chair behind him. 'So clean.'

He set the rifle down, leaning it against the wall beside her, and pushed that hand down the front of her jeans, trying to navigate her pants, pulling her closer. Then a fresh pulse of outrage moved up through her, fuelled by the fury of generations of women.

'I know what you want,' she whispered into his ear. 'I know exactly what you want.'

He cocked his head and looked at her, eyes glassy with arousal.

She looked at him coyly from under her eyelashes. He groaned and moved his hand down further. She made herself open her legs a little. Then with a lightning-fast crack, she headbutted him, hitting him full force on the bridge of his nose. He staggered backwards, lost his balance and stumbled to the floor, banging his head off the side of the oak table. She rushed forward and caught him on the chin with her boot, sending his head flying backwards. He made a grab for her ankle, but she kicked him hard on the temple and again on the underside of his nose. Blood streamed from both nostrils.

'Oh, you're one stupid bitch,' he roared. 'You're fucking dead.'

He tried once more to get up, but she rained furious kicks on his neck and skull as though it were nothing but a sack of rotting potatoes. She kicked harder and harder, aiming for his nose, teeth and throat. She was beyond stopping now. Kicks to his windpipe, eye socket and the base of his skull left him stunned, bloody and prone. She took advantage of his vulnerability and released a series of blows on his now soft male organ. He could only lie there and groan.

'What's wrong with you?' she yelled at him. 'I thought you liked a woman with a bit of go.'

She stamped on his throat and gave him one final kick in the kidneys. He had fallen silent and she stepped back, panting and exhausted, rigid with fury, tears rolling down her cheeks.

'You made me do it,' she screamed at him. 'You left me no choice.' She was crying now, and her right foot and forehead throbbed violently.

A weak raspy voice coming from the chair behind her penetrated the riot inside her head. 'You've done it,' it was saying. 'Now quick, finish him off.'

Spinning around, she saw Marcus, pale and swollen, listing in the chair, blood pooling beneath it. He could barely keep his eyes open

'Oh my God, I need to get you off that chair,' she said.

She looked down at the man lying on the floor. He was still breathing. She gave him another few kicks for good measure, then raced to the cutlery drawer and, with her back to it, fumbled for a knife. She pressed it against the plastic tie at her wrists and started to saw at it, sliding her hands up and down against the blade. She kept an eye on the motionless body on the floor as she worked, watching out for any twitch or flicker of life. Eventually, the tie snapped and she pulled a long carving knife out of the drawer. She sprinted back to the man and stood over him.

'Open your eyes,' she growled. She slapped his face. 'Open your fucking eyes.'

He moaned and moved his head from side to side.

Looking up at Marcus sinking and listing in his chair, Sara knew what she had to do. With trembling hands, she penetrated his skin with the point of the knife and cut a deep fissure along the side of his neck with the mid-section of the blade. Blood pulsed out, spreading onto the floor around his head. He twitched and jerked. Then holding the knife with both hands over his abdomen, she thrust the knife deep into his belly. She closed her eyes and roared as she did it, tears streaming down her face. She watched his rib cage rise and fall for the last time and listened as a death rattle bubbled up from the depths of his throat. Stepping back from him, she sat on the floor and wept.

The silence in the room was deafening. All she could hear was the low crackle of the stove and the settling of slow-burning logs. She stumbled over to the front door and locked it, then ran to the sink and vomited until her stomach was empty. Wiping her face with her bloodied sleeve, she ran to Marcus and cut the ties behind his back. He slumped forward and she eased him off the chair and onto his back. She cut his T-shirt off with the kitchen scissors and looked at the bullet wound. It was deep and had taken a chunk of muscle from his inner arm.

'Did you lock the door,' he whispered.

'Yes. But I need to tend to you now, and fast. You've lost a lot of blood. How are you feeling? Are you sleepy, cold?'

He didn't answer. His eyes were closed and he was very pale.

'I'm going to have to make some kind of…' she said tenderly.

'Just do it. Follow that instinct... of yours,' he whispered, attempting a weak smile.

'I will, just try and steady your breath.'

'Have you looked outside? There might be... others...'

'Shh, it's okay. I have the gun here beside me.'

He tried to lift his head to see where it was. 'Please use it if you...'

'Stop talking. Save your energy. I've got this.'

She made a tourniquet out of his T-shirt and bound his arm tightly above the wound. Grabbing the antiseptic from the first aid kit, she sprayed it liberally over the deep gash. Then she applied pressure using a tea towel as a makeshift compress and when it became saturated, she placed another tea towel over it and kept the pressure up. After a while, the flow slowed down and stopped. Keeping one hand on the wound, she pulled a pack of bandages from the first aid kit, opening the seal with her teeth and bandaged his arm tightly with a compress in place. Marcus was shivering violently now, so she pulled a blanket off the couch and eased it under him to stop his body from losing heat to the cold floor, covered him with a soft throw and put a cushion under his head.

'I don't want to move you yet. The wound needs to clot, okay.'

'Okay.' His voice was barely above a whisper.

'You're going to be fine,' she said. 'I'll clean everything up. Just rest here and stay nice and easy, nice and calm. The bastard's gone, he's really gone. You don't have to worry. It's done.' She leaned over his face and kissed him, her hands still trembling as she stroked his hair.

'Thank you,' he said almost inaudibly. 'You were... amazing. I don't know how you did that.' He opened his eyes a little and looked at her, trying to focus on her face.

'It was luck, just pure luck. I think he hit his head off the table when he fell, half knocked himself out, so I just finished the job.' She started to shiver herself, despite the heat in the room.

'I can't believe you headbutted him.'

'Neither can I.'

He smiled weakly. 'I've gone and fallen for a hooligan haven't I?'

'Ha. There's lots you don't know about me.' She wiped tears from her eyes with the back of her wrist.

He squinted up at her. 'Oh God, your face. There's a massive lump on your…' He closed his eyes again, his breathing more rapid and shallow.

'Try not to talk,' she said. 'Just rest. It'll all be fine.'

She went to the door with the gun and peered out through the glass. It was silent and ordinary; there was no sign of anyone outside. She went back to the sink and washed her hands and arms. Splashing her face with water, she thought about what she needed to do for him. In a hospital, there would be surgery, a drip, morphine, antibiotics, stitches. There was none of that here. All she could do was stop the bleeding and make sure he got plenty of rest and good food to support his immune system; red meat to replenish his iron. The main thing would be to prevent an infection.

She had enough antiseptic spray for a few days and lots of cleaning bleach. There were also painkillers. Fever medication for the kids, though out of date, could be double-dosed with paracetamol. She ran her hands through her hair, sticky with blood, and took a deep breath as she surveyed the room. It was a theatre of macabre props – a dead man lying in a pool of blood on the floor, a knife protruding from his stomach; a rotting dog lying on the dining table; a badly injured man prone on a blanket; spurts of blood decorating the walls.

Kneeling beside Marcus, she felt for his pulse; it was weak but steady. She checked the bandages and saw that the blood had seeped through to the outer layers but was no longer soaking wet. She threw another blanket over him, went to the front door and unlocked it. The driveway was empty. The man must have parked his vehicle near the road to avoid being heard. But how had he carried the dog and crossbow up? He must have done two runs after scouting out the house, she decided, and knew he had time to make himself at home.

She started with Brin, wrapping him in large refuse sacks. As she carried him outside to the garden, the rifle slung over her shoulder, it was all she could do not to vomit at the smell. She set him down under an old willow tree, stopping to look around for any signs of movement. Then she went back into the house to deal with the dead body. She pulled the knife out of his stomach, wincing at the squelching noise it made and gagging at ooze of blood. Then she grabbed him by the wrists and dragged him across the floorboards. He was heavy and it was hard work pulling him across the mossy gravel where she left him. Even in death she didn't want him anywhere near her beloved dog. She covered him with old boat tarpaulin, weighing it down with some heavy logs. Burying them was for later.

Surely if there were others they would have made themselves known by now. The garden and the driveway were silent. She could hear no vehicles in the distance either and she found herself relaxing somewhat.

Now to tend to the living. She stopped for a moment at the door and looked out over the lake. The water was calm and glassy, the ridges of the mountains mirrored on the surface. A light wind moved like silk across her skin and ruffled her hair. A cluster of yellow leaves scattering across the stones trapped themselves among some earthenware plant pots. She turned towards the house as the thin, silvery pipes of the windchime tinkled merrily away.

⸺

It was late by the time she had scrubbed the floor and dragged one of the single mattresses out for Marcus to sleep on beside the stove. The room smelled of bleach and the antiseptic she had applied under the fresh bandages. She wasn't sure if she should undo the initial dressing, but her terror of him developing an infection prompted her to further disinfect the oozing wound. She was reluctant to move him, too, but decided it was better to get him onto a mattress where he would be more comfortable.

He slept deeply for hours on end and to her relief responded to her gentle attempts to check he had not slipped into death. Raising his head from the pillow, she regularly forced him to drink large glasses of tepid, barely salted water. Then there was the matter of changing his bedclothes and underwear and boiling them along with the used bandages. He was too weak to protest.

When he fell asleep again, she went back outside into the failing light and dug a grave for the dog under the tree, the rifle always within reach. It took her over an hour to get to a good depth, and by the time he was buried, a low mound marking the spot, it was dark.

She decided that the man's body had no place on her land. He'd have to be burnt or taken far away to be buried. But that was something for another day. She placed more logs around the tarpaulin to deter wild animals and went back to the house.

Once inside, she locked the doors and checked them and the windows obsessively, before finally pulling a chair up beside Marcus's bed and sitting down. There she stayed throughout the night, eyes wide against the dark, hands resting on the fore stock of the rifle. If she slept at all she wasn't aware of it, for her waking thoughts and kaleidoscopic dreams were indistinguishable from each other.

    When he stirred at dawn, asking for water, she allowed herself to feel some relief. But she knew the road ahead was uncertain, and she had to rise to meet it like never before.

11

She stayed close by the house for three days, tending to Marcus, ensuring he ate, and changing his dressings. In that time, she only left the house twice. The first time was to dispose of the man's body. It was too heavy to load into the back of the van. Anyway, she didn't want to leave the house unprotected. Too exhausted to do anything else, she dragged the body, still wrapped in the tarpaulin, across the garden and deposited it close to the lake on a bed of stones, searching his pockets for any possessions.

She needed to remove all trace of him in case anyone came looking for him. So she built a bonfire over his body using old newspapers and wooden wine boxes she found in the shed, covered with fallen branches and driftwood. Then she doused the bonfire with what was left of the petrol in the chainsaw. The familiar mist that hung low over the lake in the mornings conspired with her to obscure the smoke. She tossed a match into the pile and stepped back from the whoosh of the first flames.

Before long, a crackling blaze leapt up to the heavens and she watched as the fire collapsed around him, devouring his clothes and blackening his skin. She searched for more wood and other combustibles on the shores of the lake to keep the fire burning until he was nothing but ash.

She turned her back to the pyre and, holding the rifle tightly against her body, stared out across the lake, determined to deny him the decency of rites or respect. But after a while, the newly hardened part of her relented and she uttered a silent prayer of her own making for the charring remains. The prayer was more for his mother who could never have known, when holding him lovingly at birth, the man her child would become.

The second time she left the house was to find the dead man's car, which had been pulled into a hedge near the house. Leaving Marcus alone was a risk, but if anyone came looking for the man, the car was a potential giveaway. She drove it to the far side of the lake and hid it in an abandoned cattle shed, covering it in strips of willow and fir. It might be useful in the months ahead, as might the diesel in its tank.

While she was out she cleared the site of the fire, removing any unburnt flesh and bones from the ashes and stuffing them into the stove. She raked the soil at the site to a fine crumble and prepared it for planting. Willow trees grew fast and thick so she stripped a dozen strong branches, cut an angle at one end and thrust them into the earth. Then she transplanted sods of grass and daffodil bulbs; if they survived the winter temperatures, all evidence of the fire would be gone by the spring.

On the fourth day Marcus had still not developed a fever or infected wound and she took that as a sign that he was improving. He was still very weak and needed her to support him while he drank or swallowed the watery porridge she had rationed out for them both. But the absence of any worsening symptoms brought hope.

Her work was never done. She spent hours outside every day hacking through trees with a short axe and splitting the wet stumps. She piled the wood into different sections, separating it based on its dryness and suitability for burning. The stove needed to be on all day for heat, hot water and cooking. Their clothes, bed linen and towels had to be boiled along with the bandages and dressings. It was painstaking and tedious work, and she missed her washing machine and tumble dryer and the extraordinary convenience they represented. She'd never take them for granted again. When she finished the household tasks, the vegetable beds had to be finished and readied for the spring. She slept very little at night, her mind racing with plans, and when she wasn't dozing fitfully, she was listening for the sound of engines or voices in the distance. The rifle never left her side.

'Thank you,' he said quietly one evening, as she changed his bandages for the umpteenth time. Parts of the wound were slowly knitting together leaving soft, pink edges.

She smiled at him. 'You're getting better. That's official.'

'I hope so. I still feel rough.'

'You're just a little weak. It'll take time to build you back up.'

'I might try sitting up.'

'Tomorrow. I'll just raise your head a bit higher.' She took another cushion from the sofa and propped it behind his head. 'How does that feel?'

'Okay. I'm a bit lightheaded but it's bearable.'

'You need protein and iron. I'm going to have to find you some meat.'

'How?'

'A sheep. I think that's the easiest.'

'A sheep?'

'Yeah, I know. There might be a few grazing in the fields under the mountain. Not far away.'

'Can you manage that?'

'I've done worse.' She smiled at him again, this time a little sadly. 'Technically, I'm a vegetarian. Funny how that all goes out the window.'

He closed his eyes as though even this short conversation was too much.

'Mutton stew for you,' she said, patting his leg. 'We'll have you up and about for Christmas.'

She stood at the front window for a while, listening to his breathing as he fell asleep. She was glad her children had not witnessed the violence, relieved they were not there to see what their mother had become to survive. But now she hungered for the sight of them again, the pain of grief pulling at her heart.

Christmas, she told herself. They will be here by Christmas.

She got the sheep into the back of the van without too much of a struggle. It was a young ram, probably born last spring, and part of a small rangy flock that had sidled down from the hills to drink from the river. All it took was one bullet, sending the rest of the flock sprinting in fright across the marshy fields. After skinning him on the gravel behind the house, she stuffed the fleece into a refuse sack to dry out later. Then she cut the carcass up by the shoreline. It was messy, horrible work, and she had no idea if she was doing it right.

She packed the meat into a black bin bag and brought it back to the house to cook and divide it into separate meals. First, she chopped half the meat into cubes and browned it in some oil. Then she brought a large pot of water to the boil with salt, herbs and oil and added the browned mutton. She let it simmer and reduce, adding a ration of vegetables towards the end. When the stew was finished, she let it cool and began frying the remaining meat. She found a roll of aluminium foil and filled it with pieces of loin and rump. She rubbed it with more salt, oil and rosemary, and tucked bay leaves from the garden into the middle before putting it into the stove to roast. With luck they would get several days of nourishment from these meals before she would have to go out again. The strange pride she felt at having taken down an animal with one shot was enhanced by watching Marcus sit up in the bed and eat a bowl of hot, nourishing stew.

'It's good,' he said. 'But the chef has dried blood in her hair.'

'Oh, goodness,' she said, fingering her hair absentmindedly. 'It was a terrible job.'

'I'm sure. You're great to do it, and this stew tastes wonderful.'

'Really? I've nothing to compare it to, but thanks.'

'I suggest adding some red wine and garlic the next time.' He smiled.

'Ha, the wine's not going into the cooking. Far too precious.

'Hmmm. We'll see. So what do you miss most? Foodwise, I mean.'

'Probably fresh sourdough, good olive oil...'

'Oh yes, good choice.'

'You?'

'Brownies. Chocolate brownies with caramel sauce.'

'That's like something my kids would say.' She laughed. 'Here was I thinking it would be a fat steak or a triple-decker burger.'

'Nope. Just brownies. I'm a simple man with simple pleasures.'

'If I believe that, I'll believe anything.'

She leaned forward and kissed him. His face was gaunt and his skin yellowish and dull. It would be a long road for him, but he'd get there.

She spent the rest of the day in the garden, even though it started to rain again. She began by digging a shallow pit at the back where she buried the sheep carcass with its innards so it wouldn't attract flies and rats. Afterwards, she went out in the boat for a while and sat close to the shore, the gun by her side, keeping watch on the house. A slight breeze riffled her hair and carried her slowly away from the jetty. But the rain got heavier as the day went on, each drop sending a multitude of ripples across the surface of the lake. Everything was still and she felt as though the boat, cradling her in the water, was the safest place to be. Nothing could reach her there, only the rain and the thoughts that tumbled around her head. *I've spent the last two years dancing in small boats,* she thought, remembering the old proverb Marcus had quoted only days before. *How amazing that I haven't capsized... yet.*

As the days went by, the afternoons were shortened by darkness, and showers of sleet and snow became more frequent, sticking fast to the ridges of the mountains. The freezing bog pools and waterfalls on higher slopes, reflecting dazzling light in those rare moments when the sun appeared, spoke of deep midwinter. She went out on the boat less and less as the bitter wind that cut through the valley flayed her skin red. All her attempts to catch fish failed and she resigned herself to hunting the mountain sheep. So she pulled the boat ashore and turned it upside down until the spring. Whenever she left the house to hunt for sheep, she made Marcus promise to keep the crossbow beside him and pointed at the door.

She made weekly trips to the organic centre to gather fresh vegetables from the polytunnels. There was never anyone there but the notes she left were always gone when she returned. Once she found a box of potatoes, six eggs and parsnips left out with her previous message sitting on top. There was nothing written in reply, but she took heart from the generosity. If they wanted to be seen, they would have shown themselves. She returned on foot when the snow was too deep to drive through and left a few tins and a Tupperware container of mutton casserole with mashed potatoes. This anonymous barter of food continued, and she was glad of it.

A few weeks later, Marcus was able to stand up and make his own way to the bathroom, so she remade the bed in the spare room and settled him there with extra blankets from the other beds. Sometimes she caught him staring at her with love as she moved around the house, performing the little daily tasks required to keep them cosy, always watchful of the snow-laden driveway and the distant road.

The violent storms lessened in frequency as the calendar shifted into December and a cold front moved in. The sky became clear and bright, the sun shining low during the day, and the stars putting on a show at night. As Marcus's strength returned, he eventually moved back into her room and they lay together in the dark, keeping each other warm and talking for hours about their previous lives, all the things they needed to do the next day and what they wanted to do in the year ahead.

When she was alone, she felt for her children, trying to sense them, so that they were alive in every moment that she waited. *It was only a matter of time,* she said over and over to herself. It was only a matter of time.

Early one morning, a rising wave of nausea woke her from a deep sleep. She sat quietly on the edge of the bed as her eyes got used to the dark. Her mouth tasted of metal and her head suddenly ached. Leaving Marcus warm and asleep in the bed, she felt her way to the bathroom and vomited into the toilet bowl. She stayed there for a long time, waiting for the nausea to subside. Then as the light grew outside the window, she made her way down to the kitchen to rekindle the stove and boil water for their breakfast. She paced up and down, pulling her cardigan around her to stave off the sharp chill in the air. When the water eventually came to the boil, she made nettle tea and set out some of the oat biscuits he'd made during the week and called to him. She heard him grunt and go into the bathroom where he peed for the longest time. Then he made his way to the table, kissing the top of her head before he sat down to eat.

'Are you okay? Did I hear you being sick?'

'Yeah, I think I ate something off yesterday.'

'Feeling better now?'

'Sort of, just kind of nauseous. I'd say the meat wasn't cooked through. How about you?'

'Well, I ate the same as you and I'm okay.'

'Maybe it's just that I'm not used to eating meat.'

'Yeah, maybe. So what do we need to do today? Anything I can do?'

She smiled at him. 'Sorry, it's another day of food prep for you – nothing too strenuous. I'll go and check the wood supply, chop some more. We can never have too much chopped wood. You're not ready yet for the heavy work.'

He frowned and sighed, his shoulders slumping. 'I feel like a spare…'

'None of that self-pity stuff now. You're nearly there. Patience, yeah?'

'Yeah.'

He poured himself more tea and refilled her cup. 'Maybe I could go to the organic centre? Bring them some of these biscuits and cooked meat. See if they've left anything out for us?'

He had been so proud of his biscuits, made with ground oats and seasoned only with salt and dried herbs.

She sat back in her chair and pushed her plate away. 'Let's wait till next week and we'll see. It'll have to thaw a bit to take the van and it's too big a walk for you just yet.'

'Ahh fine. You're the boss.' He pouted.

She laughed and tousled his hair, then got up to go to the bathroom. Staring at her pale, drawn complexion in the mirror she sighed. Hopefully she wasn't coming down with something or hadn't got food poisoning. She took off her T-shirt, then reaching for her bra, she hooked it behind her back. Had it shrunk? It barely fit. Her boobs were spilling out of it. She stared at herself in the glass, eyes wide and unblinking. She took the bra off and felt her breasts; they were tender and seemed heavier, bigger. A lump formed in her throat. She swallowed hard. *No, no, no, no, no, no, no, no.* She held onto the edge of the sink and started to sweat. *It's just hormones. I've been eating better, so maybe my periods are becoming more regular.* Her rational brain scrabbled for something to hold on to, some fact that would land and make perfect sense. *When was my last period? Oh God, I haven't had one since we started sleeping together. But I might just be late.* But there was nothing except her body whispering things to her that her heart understood. *It's that same creeping sick feeling I had with Lila, that warm, swollen feeling in my belly. Oh Jesus, how the hell am I going to do this?*

If she was pregnant, there was no way she could do it without help. She suddenly thought about Siobhan in the container at the school. She took a deep breath, pulled on the rest of her clothes, splashed her face and went back out to the kitchen.

Marcus had finished cleaning up and was leafing through a recipe book.

'There you are,' he said cheerily without looking up. 'What about white wine mushroom risotto this evening? Or maybe chicken and chorizo jambalaya with Spanish sausage and sweet peppers with plum and brandy clafoutis with cream for dessert. God, I miss restaurants.' He continued thumbing through the pages, smiling at the memory.

'Not feeling so hot for any of it, though I'm sure they're lovely,' she said. 'They sound as if they come from a different planet.'

He looked up at her. 'What's up? Still feeling sick?'

'Kind of.'

'Can I do anything?' He put the book down on the counter and walked over to her, pulling her gently into him. 'You look all... I dunno, sort of helpless or something. I don't like seeing you like this. I like brave, sheep-hunting Sara, the one with the gun.' He grinned.

She allowed herself to be held for a moment, closing her eyes and inhaling the smell of his T-shirt. 'I think we've a problem.'

'What kind of problem?' He kissed her forehead, then stepped back to get a better look at her face.

'Well, I don't know if it's an actual problem yet...'

'Don't leave me hanging here. What's wrong?' He looked concerned as he scanned her face, trying to get a read on her expression.

'There's a chance that... well, I haven't had a period since before we got here.'

He stared at her, frowning. 'What are you getting at?'

'I mean it's been eight, maybe nine weeks since I had a period, and now I'm suddenly sick and I'm having all these weird symptoms. They could be nothing but I know my own body and I don't know what to do or think and I'm kind of freaking out here.' She burst into tears.

Marcus's eyes were wide and blue and startled. 'No way!'

She was sobbing so much she couldn't speak.

'Okay, okay. Don't worry, we'll deal with it.' He pulled her in close and let her cry on his shoulder for a while.

'So what do we do next?' he asked, when her tears turned to sniffles.

'We wait, I guess. I either am or I'm not. My cycle had all but stopped for the last few years… it could be just that… Only time will tell. No tests out here.'

'But you think you are?'

'It's a possibility.'

'Okay.'

'If I am, it could literally kill me.'

'Oh! Were your others… dangerous?'

'Conor, the first, was okay. But Lila, yeah, I wouldn't have made it. She wouldn't have either. I had to have an emergency C-section.'

'Okay, I can see why you'd be worried.' He hugged her again.

She pushed him away. 'If I am pregnant, how could we have been so stupid. Who wants to bring a child into this freaking broken country?' She swept the angry tears off her cheeks with the palm of her hand.

He sighed and pulled her tight. 'It'll be okay,' he said.

They stood like that for a while, arms wrapped around each other as if they were slow dancing.

They spent the day quiet and watchful of each other, only talking about practical day-to-day things. She felt sick all the time and just about got through her daily chores. After she brought in the wood and kindling to dry, stacking it in the alcove near the stove, she lay on the couch and covered herself with a blanket. Marcus had a way of setting his face to solemn whenever there were knotty problems to work out. She imagined he was playing out at least ten different scenarios and trying to future-proof them all. If she died, what would he do with the baby? If they both died, how would he feel, being left alone all over again? If they both survived, he would be their sole support and protector until she was back on her feet again. Then there was a matter of food and protection. They would need more of everything.

Late in the afternoon he pulled on his coat and hat and went out into the snow. She could see him from the sofa as he paced backwards and forwards along the shore of the lake near the jetty. She wondered what was going through his mind. She sighed and pulled the blanket up under her chin, closing her eyes against everything. Now that she'd had a day to think about it, she was more aware than ever of the new sensations in her body, the pulse of new life that was flickering and growing inside her. She had come to terms with it in both heart and mind, and she hoped he would too.

As the days passed and it became clearer that she was indeed pregnant, she grieved her children's presence even more acutely. She evoked them in her mind as she worked, holding them, smelling them, connecting her heart with theirs. The unconditionality of her love for them sometimes left her breathless. And when she rested, she tumbled into memories of when they were babies, the sunlight as it fell on their hair, their small hands sticky with fruit, their hunger for her care, her approval, her safety. She was the centre of their universe, allowing them the freedom to explore the world with open-eyed curiosity and joy.

It was in deep midwinter, in the days that they guessed followed Christmas, that a tentative calm settled over their lives. The world outside the lake house stayed the same, the water perfectly silver beyond the reeds, the rocky fields reaching up the sides of the valley to the grey shoulders of the mountains; it was perpetually silent. The light took its time to appear on the shortened days, often pulling great shadows of snow clouds across the peaks. Indoors, when the yellow glow of the stove faded each night, an icy whiteness spilled in from the outside and spread itself over everything.

For Sara, the simple repetition of her daily tasks became a sort of healing meditation. What she once would have perceived as the banality of domestic work now felt like purpose in and of itself. When she and Marcus spoke to one another, it was softer, more focused on her needs, her well-being. He overruled her attempts to make him take it easy and started the day chopping wood and doing other manual chores before collapsing on the sofa for a nap in the afternoons. He built a lean-to at the back of the house, using the tools and cement that had been left in the van, to store fresh wood and help it to season more quickly.

He accompanied her to the organic centre, carrying portions of meals they had cooked. They left notes introducing themselves properly and offering their help and time if it was needed. Eventually they received a reply, a short message inside a large bag of potatoes, garlic, and parsnips: 'Thanks. Will talk soon.' Every so often they saw slow-moving lights far down the road passing the entrance of their long, snow-covered driveway, but they never saw anyone and nobody disturbed them. Once when hunting sheep and Sitka deer in the forest on the far side of the lake, they spotted movement at the back of a small, darkened bungalow. Nothing ever came of it.

Late one afternoon, she was standing by the jetty, watching him methodically chop through a basket of kindling, then carry it into the house. A flurry of large, fat snowflakes drifted silently through the air and settled on the sand by the shore. It was bitterly cold. She turned to the lake as the snow thickened and watched the flakes dissolve on the surface of the black water. Suddenly the small hairs lifted on the back of her neck. She listened carefully but heard nothing in the muffled silence around her. She went to the woodpile to carry in more logs for the night, and as she crouched down to pick them up, she felt something move behind her. Then she caught the scent of something familiar, although she couldn't quite place it. Before she had time to stand up, a cold, thin blade pressed hard against the side of her neck. She went to scream, but a hand clapped itself over her mouth. Yanked upright, she struggled in blind panic, trying to kick behind her.

'Don't bother, you bitch.'

She recognised the voice instantly and froze, terrified to move her head with the sharp end of the blade pushed against her skin.

'Did you forget about me? Huh?' His voice was low, cold, furious.

She mumbled loudly under his cupped hand. A death-like iciness crept through her body, hardening and cracking as it pushed into her followed by a flush of white-hot heat as adrenalin shot through her.

'So I see light in *our* house and wait to see if it's squatters, or you, against all the odds. I'm so fucking happy that it might be you. Then I see you, my *wife*, screwing some asshole she's picked up along the way, playing house in our house, our bed, not looking like she's too bothered about where the fuck I am... or our kids. Yeah, remember them?'

She felt faint, delirious with fear, filled with hope. Were the children close by?

'Were you thinking about them when you were getting all cosy with him?' he went on, his voice rising an octave. The tip of the blade broke the skin on her neck. 'Yeah, I've been watching you. He's no casual help. Does he fuck like a champion?' His voice cracked. He swung her round and gripped her throat with his other hand. 'Shh, shh, shh,' he said. 'Make any noise and I swear

I'll...' He took his hand away from her mouth and released his grip on her throat. He was unrecognisable – grey, gaunt, like an old man. Her Johnny utterly changed.

She took a deep lungful of air. 'Jesus, Johnny!' she said, tears streaming down her face. 'What are you playing at? Let me explain.'

'Don't bother. There's no coming back from this. Quite the little romance you've got going on here.'

'I've been waiting for you for months,' she said through her tears. 'I was nearly killed and raped, for God's sake. So much has happened. I swear I thought you were dead.'

'You gave up on me. You weren't waiting.' He gripped her jaw and squeezed before sliding his hand down to her throat and pushing up her chin. His eyes were boring into her. There was nothing there; he was a cold, empty shell. In that moment he was devoid of love for anyone or anything. She had seen him like that before, usually when he was drunk, jealous, full of blind fury.

'Where are the children?' She looked wildly around, trying to catch sight of them.

He lowered the knife and pressed it against her side just under her ribs. 'You care about them now, do you? Tell me this – why does he keep touching your belly? Why do *you* keep touching it?'

She was finding it hard to breathe and crying wasn't making that any easier.

'You know what, don't bother telling me. I already know the answer.' He started to shake her by the throat. 'Why the fuck am I even here? I'm done. I'm well broken. The kids are gone, Sara. They're gone. Months ago.'

'No, no don't say that. Stop talking.' Like a spent bellows, her voice failed her and her legs buckled. Her heart shattered into a million pieces.

He was holding her up by the throat now, her legs unable to support her.

'You've no idea,' he said, his voice thick with emotion. 'I had to watch them go, one after the other. Lila first, then Conor. They got sick. Something in the water. I got sick too but survived it somehow. I wish I hadn't. All I had was you. You were all that kept me going. But look at what you've been doing behind my back.' He squeezed tighter, his thumb pressing hard on the soft notch at the base of her throat.

All the hope she'd carried with her across the country evaporated. She closed her eyes against him and was just letting herself drift into unconsciousness when there was a sharp crack, her throat suddenly opened and she collapsed to the ground. Johnny was on his knees in front of her; over his head, she saw Marcus standing there, the gun still pointing in their direction. She reached for Johnny, arms outstretched, his mouth opening and closing soundlessly. But Marcus stepped between them and pulled her away.

'It's Johnny,' she whispered, her voice hoarse and unrecognisable. 'It's only Johnny.'

Marcus stared at her. 'What?'

'It's my Johnny. What have you done?'

He looked down at the man slumped before him on the ground. Marcus stared at her, incredulous at the revelation, then walked over and nudged him with his foot. Johnny listed to the side and a strange sound bubbled up from his throat. Then it fell quiet again, save for the lapping of the water against the lake shore.

A peculiar numbness enveloped her and her bones turned to ice. Now she knew her children were gone and her husband was lying dead at her feet, she wished she could go back to not knowing. The uncertainty was infinitely better than *this*. She would never see Lila and Conor's little faces again or hear their laughter as they played in the garden on a warm summer's day. She'd never know how their last days unfolded and if Johnny had been able to calm their fears.

Marcus tucked one arm under hers to steady her. 'Let's get you inside. It's too much.'

'It's all too much,' she echoed.

Then a high-pitched sound swelled in her ears, her face flushed and her legs buckled beneath her. The outer edges of her vision got fuzzy and unconsciousness pulled at her, a dark tangle of chaotic images. Closing her eyes, she surrendered to it.

12

They walked through the snowdrifts to the old stone church. It was quiet and peaceful in there. It smelled of oak wood, candle wax, dust. The dull gold chains of an old thurible hung off the side of the wide, marble altar, where someone had left a jam jar full of heather. A large marble statue of the crucified Christ, his head looking up towards his God, full of love and hope, stood in the sacristy.

They sat at the back in silence. Marcus placed his hand in Sara's lap, under her growing belly, and reached for her fingers.

'Do you like the name Genevieve?' she whispered.

'Yeah, sure. It's grand.'

'Okay.'

They sat there until they got very cold, then walked out to the small cemetery at the back. The graves were haphazard and disorganised, running down a hill towards a large tangle of undergrowth and thick forest. Holly and juniper trees provide shelter from the prevailing winds. Marcus put his arm around her as they walked down to Johnny's grave at the end near the wall. She searched for any signs of spring flowers around the handmade cross.

They stood holding hands and he kissed her cheek.

'I love you, you know,' he said. 'It's going to be okay.'

'Yes, of course.'

'I really do love you,' he said again emphatically, as though he was suddenly afraid.

She turned to him, as still and calm as the cold air around them, her heart beating for herself and their unborn child.

'I know,' she said. 'I know.'

Authors Bio

Oonagh Charleton was born in Dublin and grew up in County Sligo, Ireland. After four years studying Sociology and the Social Sciences in University College Dublin, she spent time working as a reporter for the *Sligo Weekender* and freelance writer for *The Irish Times* newspaper. She lectured in Communications in the ITB Blanchardstown and now works as a Consultant in Stress Management and Wellbeing and delivers training within the Construction Sector. She has recently completed a Certificate in Counselling and Psychotherapeutic Studies. She loves to paint and spend time in nature. This is her second novel.

Dedications

This book is dedicated to my family, Alec, Ben, Joshua and Eva. They have shown me the way, protected me and made this book possible. Without them, I would not have experienced the transformative nature of love, the dignity in humility, the rewards of patience and the joys of shared moments. They bring so much laughter and kindness to the world.

I owe this journey and a joy-filled life, to them.

Acknowledgements

This book was written at home in Ireland. I owe particular thanks to my husband Alec Hayden, whose love has been a gift. He has unwaveringly supported my writing journey through thick and thin, and for this I am incredibly grateful. To Averill Buchanan for her editorial magic and patient work over the last number of years.

To my dearest friends, who without their steadfast companionship, encouragement and love, I would be lost. Lewize Crothers, Sorcha Cahillane, Dearbhla O'Brien, your courage, resilience determination and fun inspires me every day. Annmarie Bowles and Caroline Lee, your kind and patient friendship has been so steady and generous over the last eighteen years. I am so grateful for you both. Antoinette Thompson, Claire Tuttlebee and Jackie Corrigan for your support and encouragement in our Writing Group days. Without you all, this book would not exist. Aoife Rooney and Fiona Finnegan and Clodagh O'Brien, you keep me connected to all that endures. To Sabrina Sheehan, Jennifer Maguire, Deirdre McGovern, Maeve Sullivan and Anna Wall and Sorcha Cahillane – you have all been the absolute best. I am so lucky to have met you all back in UCD 1996 and still have you in my life.

To Andrea Purdie, your exceptional work on the cover design and typesetting brings this book to life. To Mary Trant who nudged me along the road with much needed advice and guidance. To the late and most beloved Gerard McCarthy whose book of essays, *Old Istanbul & Other Essays*, has inspired me to travel to new territories of the creative mind. Billy Gannon, your talents know no bounds, thank you. Nora McGillan, your love of words and language have been a lifelong inspiration. Professor Tom Inglis, you taught me the ferocious power of curiosity and enquiry, discipline in writing and the enduring qualities of friendship and love. Thank you.

To my three children, Ben, Joshua and Eva Hayden who have given me meaning and life purpose. This book is for you.

Finally, it is to my parents Manus Charleton and Barbara Monks-Charleton and my two sisters Medb and Muireann Charleton, that I owe an enormous debt of gratitude. Their unconditional love for me has never wavered. Their love, support and encouragement has never faltered, reading to me as a child, encouraging my insatiable curiosity and my deep love of learning.

Thank you for teaching me about the enduring power of stories and how the simple arrangements of words on a page have the power to change us all.